THE WINGMAN

A JACK SHARPE POLITICAL THRILLER

David Pepper

St. Helena Press

This book is a work of fiction. The names, characters and events in this book are the products of the author's imagination or are used fictitiously. Any similarity to real persons living or dead is coincidental and not intended by the author.

Published by St. Helena Press

ISBN (hardcover): 9781619849051
ISBN (paperback): 9781619848719
eISBN: 9781619848726

Printed in the United States of America

For Reader Discussion Guide,
go to www.davidpepper.com

PRAISE FOR THE NOVELS OF DAVID PEPPER

Early Praise for *The Wingman*

"A labyrinthine political thriller that details a plot to steal the American presidency….[E]nergetically paced…. A cinematic and dramatic story full of delightful twists."

—*Kirkus Reviews*

"Another tour de force…Like *The People's House*, I loved this book. Pepper is a phenomenal writer, with great dialogue, intricate plot, subplots, and characters. And with his unique perch, Pepper deftly wraps the real issues and frustrations of modern-day politics into captivating story lines. I can hardly wait for the next one."

—*Jennifer Granholm, former Governor, Michigan*

"Pepper does it again! Believable and entertaining—just like the real news these days. What's fake and what's real?"

—*Jack Markell, former Governor, Delaware*

"David Pepper has once again managed to grab the reader in the first few pages. Not only does he intimately understand the world of politics but he has also managed to capture the inner workings of journalism and the military. With these worlds colliding, he has delivered another powerful thriller that keeps you guessing until the end."

—*Andrea Canning, Dateline, NBC*

"*The Wingman* by David Pepper takes readers on a rollicking ride… There are the kinds of surprises readers long for and characters they will remember long after the last page is turned."

"Well-researched and beautifully crafted, *The Wingman* is a thrilling read, a story that brilliantly depicts the political atmosphere leading up to the primaries….The characters are superbly conceived and developed to appear like people in real life….David Pepper is a master storyteller…."

"*The Wingman* by David Pepper is an exceptional political thriller… The book is well-written, interesting and, above all, suspenseful, and is therefore recommended to any reader, not just fans of political thrillers."

—*Readers' Favorites, Reviews*

Praise for *The People's House*

"[L]ively, thought-provoking…Pepper [] writes with flair and insider knowledge of everything from gerrymandering to arrogant D.C. press aides. With speed and savvy, "The People's House" emerges as a sleeper candidate for political thriller of the year."

—*Wall Street Journal*

"[A] heart-pounding must-read. I almost missed a flight connection because I just could not put it down…an irresistible page turner that combines mystery and thrill, politics and power. When you get your copy, clear your schedule: You won't be able to do anything else!"

—*Jennifer Granholm, former Governor, Michigan*

"A great political mystery written with a clairvoyant understanding of how money, power, political corruption, technology and sex can have a corrosive effect on our democracy. Although written prior to the 2016 Presidential election, recent historical events, especially Russia's interference in that election, give this book an almost prescient mystique. Read it - you won't be disappointed."

—*Ted Strickland, former Governor, Ohio*

"A wonderful intriguing story...and then you realize he wrote this before all the Russian news broke. How did he know? Scary!"

—*Jerry Springer*

"a smart, gritty, and astute story that will appeal to political junkies....An engaging tale that looks at the grimy underbelly of American political power."

—*Kirkus Reviews*

"'House of Cards' meets John Le Carré. [A] true-to-our-times political thriller. Could America's elections be stolen and its political system manipulated without anyone noticing? The answer that Pepper offers here is that it's easier than you think…[A] story that's both impossible to put down and important."

—*Matthew Kaminski, Executive Editor, POLITICO*

"Much like author John Grisham did for law firms, Pepper pulls back the curtain on how local political races really work. The result: A can't-put-it-down novel that's part thriller and part reason to pay attention to the election process -- no matter where you live."

—*Cincinnati Enquirer*

"I love this book! Only a political insider could have written this. And only a great novelist could spin out such a page turner."

—Jack Markell, former Governor, Delaware

"I loved The People's House. Loved. It. How's that for a review?...This book is a revelation of state and national politics and will have readers on the edge of their seats throughout."

—Chris Fischer, Readers' Favorite

"[A] lively and entertaining thriller which manages to engage disturbing political issues without losing its vigorous energy or falling prey to unthinking partisanship....[A] carefully-crafted thriller, a cat and mouse game between a determined, gutsy hero and a clever, manipulative villain."

—IndieReader

"[G]rabs you from the first page and keeps you guessing until the very end. A sleepy election in rural Ohio quickly explodes into a national scandal with global consequences. It provides a window into the real world of politics and leaves you wondering: could this really happen?"

—Andrea Canning, Correspondent, Dateline NBC

"[T]his fast-paced, delicious political murder mystery...horrifies, edifies, and above all, entertains....[T]he perfect complement to this November's impending circus."

—Daphne Uviller, author of ***Super in the City*** *and* ***Wife of the Day***

CONTENTS

PART 1

Chapter 1 3
Chapter 2 9
Chapter 3 15
Chapter 4 23
Chapter 5 29
Chapter 6 41
Chapter 7 53
Chapter 8 61

PART 2

Chapter 9 73
Chapter 10 79
Chapter 11 91
Chapter 12 101
Chapter 13 107
Chapter 14 115
Chapter 15 121
Chapter 16 129
Chapter 17 135
Chapter 18 139
Chapter 19 143

PART 3

Chapter 20 151
Chapter 21 159
Chapter 22 167
Chapter 23 175

Chapter 24 185
Chapter 25 195
Chapter 26 207
Chapter 27 217
Chapter 28 227

PART 4

Chapter 29 237
Chapter 30 247
Chapter 31 249
Chapter 32 259
Chapter 33 263
Chapter 34 265
Chapter 35 269
Chapter 36 271
EPILOGUE 275

PART 1

CHAPTER 1

HANOVER, NEW HAMPSHIRE

We had been in Dartmouth's red-bricked Baker Hall for 40 minutes, 300 audience members and an entire nation watching. The four Democratic candidates for the presidential nomination had jousted back and forth with predictable attacks and tired rhetoric, making no news whatsoever. As the debate's only moderator, seated behind a small black desk that faced the stage, I was solely responsible for shifting the discussion into a higher gear. Having prepped for my big moment for weeks, I was now guiding a dull and dreary conversation, and—even worse—a ratings killer.

"Move on, Jack," my producer warned through my earpiece. "People are tuning out." A few minutes remained, leaving me time for only one or two more questions. A bead of sweat snaked down my cheek. If I blew this, my debate moderating career would be over after only one try. I jumped to national defense.

"Senator, what should we do about the Jordan uprising?" I asked Michigan Senator Wendell Stevens, the most revered African-American politician on the national stage.

"We must stand with our friends," Senator Stevens said in his deep baritone, reaching forward with a clenched fist, thumb on top, Clinton-style. "King Hassan has been a great ally. Advising him is not supporting him. We have to do more."

Good rhetoric, but a dodge. "Would you send in ground troops?" I asked, pressing.

"If that's what it takes. But we should start with targeted air strikes on the insurg—"

"Typical of those who've never served," said a voice from the far left of the stage. The interruption had come from upstart Congressman Anthony Bravo, who'd barely said a word all night, let alone lobbed any bombs like this one. I was taken aback. Stevens looked as though he felt the same.

"What do you mean, Congressman?" I asked, desperately hoping to amp things up.

"Politicians who've never been on the battlefield commit troops like it's some bloodless board game," Bravo said soberly. "Doing so here would be a big mistake. I saw friends lose limbs, and others their lives, from those mistakes. I held one in my arms. Why would we send troops into another civil war?"

"Because," said Stevens, regaining his composure, "if we don't, and Jordan falls, so will its neighbors. It will only get worse."

I ignored him and turned back to the congressman. A unique opportunity had just presented itself. Bravo's best political asset was his war record. The Army had honored him for valor, and his campaign plastered photos of his time in Afghanistan and Iraq all over his literature. But Bravo had never talked about that record in detail, even when pushed. He usually made broad reference to it and then moved on.

"Tell us more about that story, Congressman."

"What story?" he asked, visibly in retreat.

"Saving that soldier." Clearly a softball, but this was my chance to save the debate. Add some drama. Maybe even a little humanity.

"That's the point," Bravo said quietly. "I couldn't save him. He died in my arms." He gently lifted both arms as he said it, palms out, as if still holding his fallen comrade.

Gasps arose from the audience, raw emotion that had been elusive all night. Still, my journalist's instincts kicked in and I said nothing, gambling that the silence would invite even more from Bravo. He obliged.

"We were in Baghdad, a section called Rusafa, during the surge," he said. "Our brigade was going door to door, and we knocked on the wrong door. A sergeant, a close friend, took a spray of bullets to the gut through a screen door. He fired back, but it was too late. I heard the gunfire, saw him fall, and dragged him to a doorstep we'd already cleared. I sat down behind him. We prayed together, cried together, and I held him until he took his final breath."

Bravo paused, grimacing, reliving his comrade's final moment before the entire country. He looked down at his hands, then back up, directly at the camera. "I think about that moment every time I hear a politician casually propose more boots on the ground. If all our politicians served, and saw what I saw, Senator, they'd make better decisions."

Having been so thoroughly called out, Senator Stevens turned from the audience and glared across the stage toward Bravo. But he said nothing.

After a few moments of stunned silence, a handful of folks ignored my pre-debate instructions and began clapping. Like a wave, the quiet applause grew into a rowdy roar until every one of the 300 well-heeled political junkies jammed into Baker Hall rose to their feet.

"Holy shit, Jack," my producer said in my ear amid the din. "You saved it."

Bravo's three opponents, even Stevens, ultimately turned Bravo's way and applauded, essentially conceding the debate. They undoubtedly realized that not cheering would have been worse—as unpatriotic as reciting the nation's pledge with your hands at your side. The small monitor in front of me showed that our cameras now panned out, capturing the war hero being honored by his more seasoned stage-mates, two men and a woman, all considered far more prepared to be president. It was an iconic image. A powerful passing of the torch. A game-changing moment.

Bravo knew it. He nodded his head, acknowledging the praise. But he also pursed his lips. Clenched his jaw. Any sense of celebration would kill the moment. He had struck a deeper chord, way beyond politics. And he carried himself accordingly. For 30 full seconds, the cheers continued.

That's when I noticed. With the cameras still pulled back to the wider shot, and the studio audience sitting well behind me, my guess was that I was the only one seeing it.

Bravo's eyes. His dark brown eyes.

They widened, then darted ever so slightly.

Left.

Right.

Then he looked at me. Directly. Impatiently. In a way no one else could have seen.

He was eager to move on. Desperate to move on.

His words may have been moving, his delivery powerful. But those eyes told the real story—they always did. As my high school coach had drilled into me as a young quarterback, "It's all about your eyes, Jack. The best players are watching your eyes, and if you're not careful, they'll betray you every time." I'd long ago learned that Coach's lesson applied way beyond football. A man could mouth whatever words he wanted, lie or tell the truth. He could smile or frown, gesture wildly or sit perfectly still. But his eyes told the real story. If he wasn't careful, and if you paid attention, the eyes told all.

Now, Bravo's eyes signaled that something was off. Discomfort, at a time when discomfort made no sense. Maybe it was a painful memory. Or maybe something about the story was not quite right. Or maybe there was more to it. Whatever it was, Bravo wanted to change topics.

And since he had saved my debut, I returned the favor, moving onto the final question of the night. But because of those eyes, I also jotted down a simple reminder on the notepad in front of me: "Check out Bravo war story."

* * *

"Jack, that was incredible television," Bridget Turner said when she called me immediately after the debate. "You drew that story out of him perfectly."

Good. Positive feedback from my network's star anchor meant as much to my success as strong ratings.

"Thanks," I said, collapsing into my dressing room chair and eyeing a small mirror. "How'd he look when he answered it?"

"Like an absolute hero. Amazing."

"Anything seem off to you?" I asked, mopping the remnants of blush from my face with a damp cloth.

"Off? Not at all. It's as if his entire life was made for that moment. We've never seen a focus group react so strongly."

She hadn't noticed Bravo's look, so I left it at that. I handed the cloth back to the young woman who'd been hovering near me all evening. A handler, I think she was called. I still wasn't used to having them around. "Thank you," I whispered. I nodded in a way that I hoped would signal that she was free to scram. She didn't get the message.

"We should dig deeper and do a story on the incident," I said to Bridget. "On his war record. Now that it's front and center."

"We absolutely must. Hell, we could do a whole special on it."

I rolled my eyes. A special. This was my daily reminder that I had joined the dark side. After watching for years as television reporters mangled story after story or simply regurgitated the scoops we print reporters had uncovered first, I'd always looked down on TV news. Now here I was, less than a year after my Abacus election-rigging story had turned Washington upside down, doing TV—debates, live shots, interviews, handlers, and now specials. After the Abacus scoop had made me famous, Bridget Turner and Republic News had made an offer I couldn't refuse. Executive producer of a new investigations bureau, with a staff of reporters and researchers to systematically dig up scoops and scandals just like Abacus. And I would have the leeway to serve as a roving reporter and commentator on political matters of my choosing. To top it all off, they'd offered me a salary five times what the *Youngstown Vindicator* had offered to keep me. That combination had overwhelmed my resistance to new media.

Outside of occasional Beltway claustrophobia, I wasn't complaining. Covering politics from a safe and high-profile pedestal had its benefits. I could still land the big scoop, but without risking my own hide, or that of my son, his wife, or my new grandson. It was a welcome change from the daily, white-knuckle fear I'd endured only a year ago. And with each month that passed, this new life buried my deepest secret that much deeper. I looked forward to the day that the compromise I'd made no longer weighed on me.

It hadn't arrived yet, but it was coming.

* * *

An hour after the debate, I scooted into the first window seat available on the Washington-bound 737, ten rows back. Moments later, longtime FOX anchor Rob Stone sat in the aisle seat of my row, with only one empty seat separating us. I nodded in acknowledgement but didn't hide my annoyance.

As the political reporter at the biggest paper in Youngstown, I'd always had the terrain all to myself. But covering national politics for a media behemoth like Republic News was the opposite—fiercely competitive, everyone trying to drag scoops out of the same sources. You jumped on even the smallest tips, and you angled for the slightest hint of what your competitors were digging into. Even in the most casual conversations, you were on guard. And whether on a bus, a plane, at the movies, whatever—you sat in different rows. But Stone had boarded too late to sit anywhere else, and he looked about as happy about it as I was. Even with a seat between us, we leaned in opposite directions.

"Decent work tonight, Sharpe," he said.

"Thanks. I know I'm a rookie, but I enjoyed it," I said, gazing out the window, matching his insincerity. The green de-icing liquid oozed off the back of the wing as we taxied through the blowing snow.

"Yeah, with the exception of that war story, it was a little dull. But I guess they're all saying the same things now anyway."

Nice zing. Subtle. As a newbie with one of the best deals in the industry, I received my fair share of hazing. But I turned to him with a smile. "Might really shake things up in the race."

"True. I think Bravo just became a national sensation. That story gave me goose bumps. I used to embed a lot back in the day. Covered those boys on the ground. Terrible stuff."

"Terrible," I muttered, turning back to the window. It hadn't taken Stone long to turn the conversation to himself. I almost admired his dexterity.

Thankfully, the cabin lights dimmed and we stopped talking as the 737 powered down the runway and took off into the wintry night. Stone was out cold by the time the pilot announced we had reached cruising altitude, but despite my long day I remained wide awake, and not because of Stone's loud, wet snores.

Our brief exchange had confirmed that Stone had missed Bravo's eyes. Bridget Turner had clearly missed them. Keen observers, both. If they hadn't noticed, chances were no one had—no one but me.

And in this industry that I now called my own, being the sole person to notice pretty much anything presented one hell of an opportunity.

CHAPTER 2

WASHINGTON, D.C.

At 10:30 the next morning, I sat at the head of our glass-topped conference room table, braced for battle. The large flat-screen monitor on the wall had just played back Congressman Bravo's breakthrough moment from the night before. Knowing my team would be skeptical about diving into a purely political story, I was doing my best to motivate them.

"Everyone will be talking about that moment, but I doubt anyone will dig into it," I said.

As usual, Cassie Knowles, sitting to my right, spoke out first. A small white opal stud gleamed from the left side of her nose, and the V-neck of her casual black shirt dropped low enough to display the large, half-moon-shaped tattoo on her upper chest. Must've been a non-camera day. When she was on air, she made sure to look as preppy as the rest of the industry.

"Jack, I don't get it," she said, frowning. "What do you want us to find out?"

The phrasing was pure Cassie. *Finding out* was her specialty, along with questioning authority. I had plucked her from the Washington bureau of the *Boston Globe* only months after she had moved to D.C. She'd won a Pulitzer for tracing a toxic water outbreak to unscrupulous contractors who were also major donors to the Massachusetts governor. The man had walked right into a trap when he'd granted her interview request, but I knew why he'd messed up. Cassie could fool you. Her bangs and wide hazel eyes made her look younger than 30. The governor had probably assumed she was harmless. But the lies she'd recorded over that hour ultimately had cost the governor his job. And now here she was, pressing *me*, her boss, wanting to find out what *I* knew.

It was too early to mention my theory about Bravo's eyes. Better to keep that shaky detail—the only source for my hunch—to myself.

"Everything," I said. "I want you to find out everything. More on Bravo's service. Who was the soldier he was talking about? What other soldiers were there that day? And while we're at it, track down his family. See what they have to say."

"Bravo's family?" Cassie asked.

"No," I said, "the family of the dead soldier. What do they think of Bravo? His story?"

"Sounds like a fluff piece," I heard mumbled at me from my left. "Isn't that better left to someone else?" Now George Vassos was piling on.

Vassos had spent years as a public records lawyer for major newspapers. When motivated, he was a master at getting documents out of government, a skill that anchored any investigation of public entities. We had enticed him to join our team by matching his lawyers' salary and pairing it with a far more exciting role, minus the billable hours. But I already worried he was coasting toward retirement. Bearded, bespectacled, and slightly overweight, he certainly didn't look the part of a crack Republic News reporter. And for the most part he was our resident naysayer, jumping in to meetings just when the rest of the team was getting excited about something, telling us the reasons our plans wouldn't work, generally playing the part of a wet blanket. He was the best at what he did, but I worried about his attitude and its effect on the rest of the operation. And now here he was, calling my idea a fluff piece.

"At the very least, we need a full accounting of what happened," I said. "Given how important this has now become, see if there's more to the story."

"Come on, Jack, you think he was lying about it?"

This came across the table from Alex Fischer. Her skepticism confirmed that I had exactly zero allies when it came to this Bravo story. Great. And out of all of my reporters, Alex was the one I most needed at my back. Alex Fischer was the celebrity of our little unit. When we'd stolen her from NBC, the television world could tell we were serious. But she'd covered the Pentagon for years, embedding in Iraq numerous times, so I wasn't surprised she was suspicious of my idea.

"It wouldn't be the first time someone lied about his war record," I said, feeling defensive. "See if you can use your old Pentagon sources to get more on the story."

"I'll see what I can dredge up," she said flatly.

"Dredge?" I said. "What's the deal, Alex?" My mind was telling me to cool it, but Alex had gotten under my skin.

"Jack, he described a friend dying in his arms. Of course he wanted to move on. I've covered these guys for years. This is not something any of them want to talk about. It seems like we're getting a little carried away. And my port security investigation is really starting to pop."

"Don't drop anything else for this," I said, looking around at all three. "We're just doing our due diligence. If there's nothing there, we'll move on."

"I'm holding you to that," Alex said.

For a moment, I doubted my instincts.

* * *

New Hampshire was just a day away. While both parties' nominations were up for grabs, the Democratic primary was the exciting one: a barn burner among four political stars.

The clear frontrunner was Colorado Governor Janet Moore, who'd blown me away when I'd interviewed her in Iowa. From suburban Denver, the tall, polished, and charismatic Moore had spent her early career getting dangerous criminals off the streets. She'd served as assistant prosecutor, then prosecutor, then attorney general of the state. Once elected governor, she had broadened her profile, championing issues that balanced her tough-on-crime profile with more progressive credentials.

The second-place finisher in the Iowa caucuses, Pennsylvania Governor Peter Nicholas, was Moore's polar opposite. Born and raised in Erie, Nicholas had earned a Purple Heart in the first Iraq war in his late twenties, entered the Pennsylvania statehouse as a fiery, if gruff, economic populist in his thirties, and had never strayed from that style as he soared to national prominence. He still sported a Marine-style crewcut, although it was now a rusty gray instead of the sandy blonde of his younger years. I wasn't sure I'd ever seen him smile in my presence.

Then there was Congressman Bravo, who was fast emerging as the rock star of the primary. He was a decorated veteran of both Iraq and Afghanistan. After returning to his native San Jose, he'd been elected congressman at 31, and was now in his fourth term. Bravo stunned the political world with his third-place Iowa finish, which had vaulted him up 15 points over the final week of that campaign. A moving speaker, he'd arrived in New Hampshire with pep in his step and a fired-up brigade of young volunteers. His chic young wife, Isabella, and two adorably photogenic kids only added to the talk that he was the Hispanic John Kennedy.

Bravo's Iowa finish had already forced Governor Bill Lopez of New Mexico to exit the race. Lopez had once been the Democratic frontrunner, on a path to becoming the country's first Hispanic president. But Bravo's surge had eclipsed him.

Finally, there was Wendell Stevens and his compelling life story. Stevens had grown up in Linwood, the toughest part of Detroit, born to a single mom in her teens. He spent most of his teenage years in one of two places: the gym, where he was a star boxer, and juvenile detention, where those boxing skills came in handy. A few drug-dealing convictions at 19 got him time as an adult. But a counselor had seen that Wendell Stevens was a natural leader and pushed him to do better. Stevens earned a bachelor's and law degree from prison. When he got out at 28, he'd never looked back. State representative, state senator, mayor of Detroit, then three-term senator of Michigan. Stevens's story of redemption, along with his powerful oratory, inspired the nation. Politics aside, the senator struck me as a truly decent man.

Four strong candidates. Four authentic stories.

And the stakes of their primary were higher than usual. The Republican side was a mess due to the Abacus scandal, which meant that the winner of the Democratic primary would be the overwhelming favorite to be America's next president.

* * *

"So the guy was a real achiever," Cassie said from across my desk. We'd reconvened to review her findings just before I was due on air.

"Who? Bravo?" I asked.

"No," she said. "Thomas Kroon, the one who died in his arms. Class president. Graduated from Virginia Military Institute. Then joined the 82nd Airborne. Three tours in Afghanistan and Iraq. A staff sergeant when he died."

"Learn anything about his family?" I asked.

"Military through and through. Four generations went to VMI. His dad was a Ranger in Vietnam. One grandfather fought in the Pacific in World War II, badly injured but survived."

A good Southern family, I thought. Like many I knew back in Ohio, service ran in their blood. As did sacrifice. "Do you know where they are now?"

"The mother and father still live near Virginia Beach. Fully retired."

"Any other details?"

"They have two other sons, both Marines. But I haven't been able to track them down."

She spread copies of three articles on my desk, one on the news of Kroon's death, a longer profile on Kroon the next day, and a third on the memorial parade that had followed a week later. A large color photo showed large crowds and flags lining a major highway as a flag-draped hearse drove by.

"Thomas's death was a major event in his hometown," she said. "Front page news."

"I'll say. A hero's welcome, and a well-earned one. Anything about Bravo in the articles?"

"Nothing. But that's not a surprise. It would've been too soon to know those details."

"You find the Bravo account anywhere else?"

"Yeah. It's how I found the name to begin with. Lieutenant Bravo received a Silver Star for his actions."

"Impressive," I said. "They don't give those out unless you really put your neck on the line."

Cassie nodded, gazing at the clipping between us.

"Well," I said. "I'll head down to Virginia Beach in the morning."

Cassie looked at me. She had clearly assumed that this case was closed. "I don't get it, Jack. What's the story?"

"For now, think of it as a human interest story. But I'll see if I can find anything else while I'm down there."

She looked glum, and I understood where she was coming from. She hadn't joined Republic to do human interest, and neither had I. The difference between us was that I had seen that look in Bravo's eyes.

CHAPTER 3

VIRGINIA BEACH, VIRGINIA

I STARED UP THE front steps of the modest ranch home, rehearsing my pitch. Asking Gold Star parents to relive the worst moment of their lives was not an enticing assignment.

After three knocks, a woman in a dark blue robe and silver hair in a prim bun cracked the door a few inches. Towering more than a foot above her, I unleashed the broad smile I'd spent years perfecting for cold calls like this.

"Mrs. Kroon?"

"Yes."

"My name is Jack Sharpe. I'm a reporter from Republic News."

She winced as if my introduction caused her physical pain. "Reporter? What kind of reporter?"

"A television reporter. Republic News."

Her eyes narrowed. The door didn't budge. "We don't like television reporters," she said. "What do you want?"

"Ma'am, we would love to do a story about your son. You must've seen the debate the other night when his name came up."

"We heard about it, but didn't see it. We're not very political."

This was a stretch. Cassie had found that both Earl and Francine Kroon had voted in every election, including every Republican primary, for decades. And Earl Kroon had been active in local Republican activities.

"Well, we wanted to know more," I said. "It sounds like your son was an amazing young man. We want to tell his story, and how Congressman Bravo was with him until the end."

"Tell him to go away!" someone bellowed from behind Mrs. Kroon. "The last thing we need is Tom's death becoming political!" From the tone of the voice and the worried look on Mrs. Kroon's face, whoever was snarling, presumably Mr. Kroon, would be the decision-maker on this visit.

I spoke louder. “Sir, we would not make it political.”

Now the grizzled face and short white hair of Earl Kroon loomed behind his wife in the doorway. “Bullshit,” he said. “This was part of a presidential debate. We're not fools. It's all political or you wouldn't be here. Time to leave.”

Mrs. Kroon wrinkled her face, embarrassed, as her husband stormed back into the depths of the house. She quietly opened the door wider and looked at me warily, as if to say, “Well, now what?”

I scrawled my cell number onto my business card, along with the words “Call me if you want to talk,” and handed it to her. She studied it for a moment and carefully placed it in the breast pocket of her robe.

Progress. Maybe.

* * *

ARLINGTON, VIRGINIA

“To what do I owe the pleasure?” asked Colonel Jim Shirey, deputy chief of public affairs of the Army.

No was the usual response from Pentagon sources in covering defense matters, but people had a much tougher time denying Alex Fischer to her face than over the phone. So here she sat in Shirey's well-appointed D-ring office. The salt-and-pepper-haired colonel faced Alex from behind a large mahogany desk as orderly as Jack Sharpe's was messy.

“I just love spending time with you big shots in your fancy uniforms,” she said, laughing. “Did you see the debate the other night?”

“The presidential one?” Shirey asked. He shrugged. “Didn't see it.”

“So disappointing, Colonel. We hosted it, you know. Congressman Bravo talked about his time in the service. And we wanted to get all the details we could.”

“Details about what?”

“His service record. When he started. When he left. Where he served. And more specifically, he told a gut-wrenching story about a fellow soldier who died in his arms. Apparently he won a medal for his actions that day. We want to get more about the incident, whatever records there are. And see if there's a list of who he served—”

“Slow down, Alex,” Shirey interrupted, holding his hand up. “Why are you here in person? You know how to request this stuff through our formal process.”

"Because I need it right away," Alex said, smiling. "If we wait months to get it, the election will be over."

"And?"

"And whatever we find will no longer be relevant." This was when the in-person strategy paid off, when she needed to convey something without putting it in writing or even saying it over the phone. "Jim, don't be difficult. I've done you enough favors, you can do me this one."

Alex exaggerated her smile, her glare piercing right through Shirey as she leaned in over his desk. He knew exactly what she was referring to: in the past year, he had begged her to spike several stories, including one on lavish spending and one on a tawdry affair at the top of the Pentagon food chain. They weren't priority stories, so she had obliged, knowing he would owe her later.

And later was now.

"I'll see what I can do," he said grudgingly. "I'll call you first thing tomorrow morning with what I have."

Alex leaned back. "I just knew you'd come through for me, Jim," she said sweetly. "Thank you." Jack's hunch had better pan out, or she'd just traded a major chip for a dog of a story.

* * *

VIRGINIA BEACH, VIRGINIA

As I waited at a McDonald's, sipping my fourth Diet Coke, I relived the previous day's conversation with Alex. Maybe she was right. Of course Bravo had been uncomfortable talking about Iraq—real heroes don't brag. Badgering the Kroons about their dead son had not felt good, even if Francine hadn't turned away my business card. And now nothing, for an hour. I was about to get up, assuming she'd only taken my card to get me to leave her alone, when the phone rang.

"Mr. Sharpe?" But here she was. I said hello. "This is Francine Kroon," she said. "I'm so sorry about my husband earlier. He despises the media. When Tommy passed, some real vultures hounded us for months."

"It can get ugly like that," I said, declining to mention that I'd been that vulture many times.

"I'm not sure how I can help you but I wanted to at least call you back. I only have a couple minutes." She sounded like she was breathing heavily, panting slightly. Running? I didn't ask. I didn't acknowledge her willingness to engage at all. Better to cut to the chase before she had second thoughts.

"Like I said, the whole nation is talking about your son's story, and we want to bring it to life."

"Well, neither I nor my husband is going to talk on camera about it."

"I assumed that, ma'am. But can you tell me any more about what happened? The basics?"

"Not much more than what was reported at the time." A few seconds passed, with only her breathing breaking the silence. Awkward silences have a way of inviting people to talk, so I said nothing. "Tom was a great soldier," she said at last. "And a wonderful son."

She paused, but again I let the silence stretch.

"All through his childhood, I dreaded him going into the service. But I knew he would. After 9/11, we knew he'd end up in something serious." Her voice quivered here. "And then the bottom fell out when Bush announced the surge. Tommy had already done two tours, and got called back. Within weeks, he was right in the middle of it. They were supposed to live among the Iraqis, buy them off. But one false step and you died. Tommy and Tony—Congressman Bravo—were in a close-knit group, and they went through hell together. Several members of their unit died in the month before Tommy's death. We were getting increasingly worried. And then we got the horrible news."

"Did they tell you exactly what happened?"

"At first it was just that he was shot during the surge, going door-to-door in Baghdad. But later we heard more details, including the part about Tony being with him till the end. That he died on a doorstep."

She kept calling him Tony. "So you knew Congressman Bravo before the incident?" I asked.

"On one tour home, a group of them visited us here in Virginia Beach, so we got to know them then, including Tony. It broke our hearts when some of the very boys who had been at our house were badly injured within months."

"Have you kept up with Congressman Bravo?"

"No, we haven't. My family just shut down. We never reconnected with those boys. We only heard his name later, once he became a congressman. And then were amazed when he started running for president. I'm glad someone from that platoon has been able to lead a good life."

"The others haven't?"

"Not at all," she said distantly. "Those who made it home haven't done well. One's in jail for killing his wife. Some have passed. Tony coming home early might've been the only thing that saved him from their fate."

Home early? I squinted at the soda cup in front of me. *Who gets to go home early?* I tried to sound casual. "What do you mean he returned early?"

"He—he must've been injured or something, because I remember that he came home earlier than the others."

I had to keep her talking. "I know that your other sons also served. Were they over in Iraq?"

"No. Afghanistan. But after the worst died down. Thank goodness they each made it back in one piece. They're both good boys leading good lives."

"Do you think they'd be willing to talk about their brother?"

"They looked up to him so much. They were devastated when he died. But they might be willing to talk."

"Where are they now? How can I reach them?"

"Will's in Washington, and Logan lives not too far from here."

She recited their phone numbers. I scribbled them down wordlessly, in case she wanted to say more. But—

"I'm home now," she said. "I'm sorry for how my husband talked to you. We've never recovered from Tommy's death. I feel that we've been going through the motions of life for a decade."

"No apologies," I said, meaning it. "I totally understand."

Although I knew my response had sounded insincere, at her mention of going through the motions, my sister Meredith's image flashed in my mind. Dad had never been the same either. Neither had I.

* * *

Five teller windows lined one side of the Ameribank branch. The customers in line watched me as I walked through the bank's revolving glass door, and their stares followed as I waded behind them. I scanned the four offices on the opposite side of the counters. The third office displayed the nameplate I was looking for: Logan Kroon. The door was slightly ajar, so I approached it, knocked softly, and pushed. A broad-shouldered man sat at a desk typing on his desktop keyboard. Blonde crew cut. Dark tan. Square jaw and a hawk nose. Looked more like a wrestler than a banker.

I waited a beat for him to speak first, but he looked at me, silent, frowning.

"Mr. Kroon," I said. "Can I talk to you for a moment?"

"Sorry, it's getting close to my lunch break," he said. "No time to open any new accounts."

"Oh, I'm not here for a new account," I said. "I'm a reporter and we're doing a story on your brother and Congressman Bravo."

He glowered. "So you're the one," he said loudly. "My mom told me about you. Why can't you guys just leave us alone? Knocking on my parents' door out of the blue? Show some class."

"I know it's a pain," I said, opening the door wider, insinuating myself into the office. "But your brother's story just became a national story, and we want to understand what happened."

Kroon didn't invite me in further, forcing me to stand in the doorway awkwardly. The bank customers only feet away looked even more suspicious of me now thanks to Kroon's audible dressing down.

"Sure you do. I still can't believe that asshole brought up my brother just to score political points."

"So you saw the debate?"

"I got a few calls that the congressman had talked about Tom, so I watched the rerun later that night. It made me sick."

I thought of Mr. Kroon, hollering from behind his wife. His son was a chip off the old block. "Did you know the congressman?" I asked.

"I met him once when they came back to Virginia Beach for a few days. Never liked the—"

A firm hand gripped my right shoulder. I spun around, finding myself only inches from a gray-haired, wiry man in a blue security uniform. He looked past me toward the desk.

"You okay, Mr. Kroon?" the guard asked in a deep southern Virginia twang. "This fella bothering you?"

"I'm fine, Gene. Just a slimy reporter digging into my brother's grave. Again."

The guard looked right at me, shaking his head and exaggerating a frown. "A real shame," he said. "Lemme know if you need me."

"Oh, I will," Logan said, laughing.

Still stuck in the doorway, I turned back toward Logan, seething at the insult but willing my way back to civility. Kill him with kindness. "Sounds like the congressman and your brother were close."

"They had to be. When you're posted in hell, you learn to get along. He seemed like a phony. And seems like one now too."

"How old were you when they came through?"

"Just eighteen. I was about to join the service myself."

"Did anything stick out while they were here?"

"No. Just a bunch of traumatized paratroopers trying to escape for a few days—beaches and bars, women, touch football. They lived it up. I didn't get it then, but they knew the hell they were going back to."

Kroon looked down at his watch, but I rolled right into my next question. "Do you remember the others who were with them?"

"I really don't. I think there were six in total."

He looked at his watch again, then back my way. "Um, I really gotta go, buddy. Can we wrap this up?"

"Sure. I just have a final few questions," I said, clawing for another minute or two. "What do you remember from your brother's death?"

Kroon paused to confront the painful topic. I guessed that his family tended to sidestep the words "death" and "dead," as many did. "My mom called me one afternoon, bawling," he said. "She told me the bad news. Killed trying to make friends with the Iraqis. Stupidest assignment I've ever heard of. Tom was my hero, so I was devastated. The parade and funeral were a blur. Then I was off to Afghanistan myself. I tried to put it all behind me, and mostly have."

I drew a deep breath. "You ever hear about Bravo's actions that day?"

"The basics. I'm glad he was with Tom when he died. But I would've been more impressed if he had kept him out of that mess in the first place." Kroon leaned forward in his chair and began to stand.

Only way to keep a guy like this talking was to throw him a zinger he couldn't ignore. "You don't blame Bravo for Tommy's death, do you?"

Kroon now stood fully, four inches shorter than me, then took a step in my direction. "Of course not," he said firmly. "The surge killed him and a whole lot of other good men. But I'm not sure why he's a hero for doing what any good soldier would do. That's just me."

Now came the final push. "Did something happen when Bravo visited here?"

"What do you mean?" Kroon asked.

"You just seem really pissed at the guy. It sounds like he was good to your brother in his final moments. Why the hostility?"

"First off, the guy's a Democrat. I'm not, okay? Second, he's using my brother to score political points. So no, I don't like him."

"So you weren't mad at him *before* he brought the story up in the debate?"

Logan Kroon stared back.

I raised my eyebrows, letting the question float between us.

"No," he said quietly.

Bullshit, I thought. This guy's anger burned from deep down, and it felt neither political nor recent. But this interview was over. Logan leaned around me and pulled open his office door, showing me the way out—in case I wasn't sure of it.

CHAPTER 4

WASHINGTON, D.C.

"JACK, THEY'RE STARTING to count the votes. We have a tight race between Governor Moore and Congressman Bravo."

Bridget Turner and I were live in her studio as the New Hampshire polls closed. I'd slipped back into D.C. from Virginia Beach late in the afternoon. All day long, we'd aired the results from Dixville Notch, a forgotten mountain village that always kicked off the nation's first primary by voting at midnight. Congressman Bravo had prevailed over Governor Moore by a vote of seven to four, with Nicholas grabbing one vote. It had made for good filler all day, but now we were eager to move onto the real, statewide results.

My heart was pounding. Even more than writing on deadline, delivering live coverage of a big election night brought back the rush of taking the field as a starting quarterback. Lots of moving parts, unpredictable events, and the whole world watching to see if you'd screw up.

"We sure do," I said to Bridget. "Huge turnout, and the exit polls show Bravo doing well with young voters. Moore earns strong support from women of all ages."

With 20% of the vote in, Moore started to pull slightly ahead. At 50%, the numbers solidified: Moore stood at 37%; Bravo was at 31%; Nicholas took 20%, and Stevens trailed at 12%. At 8:20, with Republic's musical fanfare in the background, Bridget interrupted one of our reporters. "Republic News has a projection to make: Colorado Governor Janet Moore is the winner of the New Hampshire primary. Congressman Anthony Bravo will finish second."

Within the hour, Moore and Bravo gave strong victory speeches. And then I explained what it all meant.

"Moore can claim victory because she finished first," I said at the tail end of the broadcast. "But Bravo has momentum, posting a strong second in a state whose demographics were not good for him."

* * *

"So how was the big night?" Alex asked as I snagged a shiny green apple from the office kitchen just after 10:00 a.m.

"Crushed by this job. Again," I said. She was not referring to my coverage of the New Hampshire primary, and we both knew it. She was asking about the date I was supposed to have gone on after Bridget and I went off the air, the date that had not in fact happened because our coverage had run late. Just as I'd rushed into my dressing room to mop off my makeup, my cell had chirped with a text: *Jack, I can't wait any longer. Call me when your life allows you to respect a woman's time. No sooner.* I told Alex the whole story.

"Priorities, Jack!" she said gleefully, smugly. I was a decade older, but we were both enduring the rootless lives of overworked divorced parents instead of the familial bliss of our colleagues. This led to an early natural bond and ongoing friendly banter. We shared a lot of our personal ups and downs along the way, but it had never gone beyond that.

"I'll get mine straight when you do," I said, biting into the apple. "So what did you find on Bravo?"

"Pretty straightforward stuff. He served in the 82nd Airborne, Second Brigade, rising to first lieutenant. He did two tours in Afghanistan, two in Iraq. On the fourth, his battalion deployed to Baghdad, took part in the surge, and returned to the states in October 2007. It was a bloodbath all the way through. The surge might've played well politically back home, but it was a meat grinder for the troops who carried it out."

"You learn any more about Bravo's actions? Your BFF Shirey give you anything juicier?" At the risk of appearing jealous, I enjoyed giving her grief for all the military guys she dated.

Alex rolled her eyes. "Just as he said, he held Thomas Kroon until he died and then carried him back to their Humvee. He then rescued two other badly injured men. The Army gave him a Silver Star for his actions."

So that's where the Silver Star came from. Bravo had acted even more heroically than he'd described at the debate. Most politicians would've poured it on thick, but he'd done the opposite. Interesting. "You get their names?"

"Sure did. I've requested more details on them."

"And did you find anything on when he left Baghdad?"

"Records show he left when the entire battalion brigade went home in October 2007. And that's when he left the service entirely. Honorable discharge."

"No injuries?"

"None reported."

"Well, for some reason, Kroon's mother thinks Bravo left early."

"That's weird," Alex said, her voice trailing off. "The official record is clear it was October."

"A mourning mother's clear memory versus a seemingly airtight paper trail," I said, thinking out loud.

Alex met my eyes and cocked her head knowingly. "Moms over bureaucracies every time."

I gave her a nod. "Let's get to the bottom of it."

* * *

"There's a brutal set of ads running against Moore out there," I said to Cassie as we both sat down.

Nevada was the next big state on the primary calendar, the Saturday after New Hampshire. By late morning Wednesday, I had started getting phone calls from press contacts in Vegas and Reno. By early afternoon, Cassie and I were back in the conference room, huddled around her laptop, reviewing ads that an affiliate station had shared with us.

"Janet Moore let us down, let Joey down," a grieving Colorado mother said to the camera, describing her son's death by a drunk driver when Moore was attorney general. Cassie turned away as the ad displayed a photo of a badly mangled Ford convertible.

"Janet Moore failed our state, cost us jobs," testified a former head of a small business that had been shuttered by regulations Moore had enacted as governor.

"We can't trust her," said the disembodied voiceover of a third ad, highlighting lives lost amid the state's heroin crisis.

Each ad ended with the same disclaimer: "Paid for by Americans for a Brighter Future."

"For people seeking a brighter future, they sure are negative," Cassie said. "Just brutal."

"They really are," I said. "But also well done, and running all over TV and the internet. There's real money behind that quality of production, and it's precisely targeted. Given Bravo's momentum, this could really make a difference. See if you can figure out who's behind them."

"Don't they have to disclose something if they're attacking a candidate this directly?" Cassie asked.

"Not anymore. The Supreme Court took care of that." Thanks to *Citizens United* and lax campaign finance regulation, and as the people of Nevada were now witnessing, the greatest political firepower now rested with outside groups that dropped millions of dollars against their targets through vicious ads. And they could do it in the dark so long as they followed some straightforward rules.

"All they have to do is create a nonprofit corporation that claims to advance social welfare. If they dump half the money into activities deemed non-partisan—things like public education and research—the other half can be spent on direct campaign activity without any disclosure whatsoever."

Cassie shook her head. "That's one hell of a loophole."

"Yeah, so big it's swallowed everything else."

* * *

"*The* Jack Sharpe! What an honor!"

I was looking up at a stealth fighter, one of the numerous photos of war weaponry hanging on the walls around me, when I heard the warm welcome. I spun around to see Will Kroon, the youngest of the three Kroon brothers. Tall and fit, he reached out and gripped my hand with vigor.

I had walked the six blocks to the Defense Policy Institute, a national security think tank. According to DPI's website, Will worked here as an analyst.

"I don't know about that," I said as we sat down. "Thanks for letting me drop in out of the blue." I had come quickly, hoping neither his brother nor his mom had tipped him off yet.

"No problem. I assume you're here to talk about Tom. Mom said a reporter had come by asking about him."

Too late. Which meant he was ready. "Yep," I said. "Hope that's okay."

"Of course. I'm proud of his service and sacrifice. I'm sorry my dad and brother were hard on you."

"No problem. You get used to that in this business, especially in these circumstances."

"I bet. What do you want to know?"

We walked through the grim details of his brother's death. From interviewing crime victim's families, I'd long ago learned that the key to getting through tough conversations like this is simply to listen.

"The surge churned through a lot of good people, Tom and a lot of his buddies among them. It was just so easy for insurgents to take our guys out. I'm not surprised Congressman Bravo doesn't talk about it much. Most vets never really recover from what they went through."

I nodded, recalling Youngstown family friends whose kids had returned from multiple tours overseas. If their service came up, most would go silent or quickly change the subject.

"Did you get to know Congressman Bravo at all?" I asked.

"No. I was sixteen when they came through Virginia Beach, too young to be part of the fun. But it was obvious how close he and Tom were—laughing and talking into the early morning, downing more beers than they should have. It always comforted me to know Tony was with him 'til the end. No soldier should die alone."

"Your brother doesn't seem to be as fond of him."

"You noticed? Yeah, Logan always had a problem with him, so as a family we've never talked about Bravo. For Logan and my parents, the debate the other night was like picking at an old scab."

"You have any idea why?"

Will shook his head. "It doesn't help that he's a hard-core Republican. But it's deeper than that. My brothers were best friends growing up. They did everything together. So I think it was just jealousy that Tom and Tony were close. And Tom's death hit Logan so hard. It probably just cemented the grudge."

I stayed quiet.

Will bit his lower lip, clearly still emotional about the loss. "I think Logan thinks he should've been there that day."

"I can't imagine," I said. A lie. I knew plenty about survivor's guilt. "You ever hear from the congressman after his time in the service?"

"No. I never did. But a few months after Tom died, after the burial and all the fanfare, I know he stopped through to pay his respects."

Just like Francine Kroon had said. "Were you there?" I asked, trying to sound nonchalant.

"No, just my parents met with him. I'm sure they didn't want us kids reliving it all. I had football practice anyway, but they told me to wait until late afternoon before coming home. I saw him leaving as I got back. To tell you the truth, I always wished I'd gotten to talk to him—round out my memory of Tommy."

"Did you ask them about it?"

"Yep, and they said it was Tony paying his respects."

"And that's the last time you ever saw him?"

"Yep. I'm glad for him he's done so well, though. As he said the other day, we need more combat veterans in office. Too many politicians making commitments that other people's sons and daughters have to keep."

"That definitely was the strongest moment of the debate."

"Sure was. I applauded in my living room. I've spent my career trying to find ways to avoid the kind of combat that took out Tom and so many others."

That squared with the bio I'd scanned. After two tours in Afghanistan, Will Kroon had returned stateside and earned a master's in security studies. Specializing in modern warfare and technology, he'd published numerous articles since.

I circled back to the most important revelation of our discussion, prying for any final details. "So you think he visited in the fall the year Tom died? Football season?"

"Actually, more like late summer. Preseason—we were still doing two-a-days. So July, early August at the latest. It must've been some type of leave. Standard stuff, I'd think."

"Two-a-days? Ugh. I remember those well."

"You played?"

"Quarterback, both high school and at Youngstown State. You?"

"Believe it or not, I was a cornerback back then. Used to watch guys like you like a hawk."

Damn. He'd probably seen right through me. Still, I'd gotten what I needed. Bravo had met with the Kroons in July or August, confirming his mom's account that he'd come back early—and conflicting with the official records.

I said goodbye to Will Kroon and walked back to the office quickly. Years of covering politics had taught me a lot. Go with your gut. Everything's about reading people. And, most relevant now, never dismiss small discrepancies. Dig into them, and you usually discover something far bigger.

CHAPTER 5

LAS VEGAS, NEVADA

"BELLAGIO, PLEASE," CASSIE said to the cab driver.

After enduring a cross-country flight and the long taxi line of drunk college kids, she was eager to rest up before a day she was dreading. Research on the new SuperPAC Jack wanted her to dig into would have been much easier from her cubicle back in D.C., but, these days, if you were doing a story about ads airing in Nevada, you had to stand and broadcast *from Nevada* while you did it. So dumb. Such nonsense made Cassie miss her days at the good old *Boston Globe*.

And now Jack had given her a second chore—get close enough to ask Bravo about when he'd left the Army, and capture his answer on tape. Bravo seemed authentic, as close to the real deal as politicians get these days. Pestering him felt so petty.

As the cab pulled out, she dialed George Vassos. She'd asked him to track down as much as he could on the SuperPAC, and he'd promised to stay awake for the call so he could fill her in.

"Jesus, Knowles," he said when he answered. "I didn't think you meant this late."

Ugh, Cassie thought. She and George had started out on cordial terms when they'd met and become colleagues at Republic. She knew he was an impressive old hand at what he did, and a valuable resource when it came to legal legwork, but his grousing was getting tiresome. Now their relationship was chilly, but he didn't seem to care. "What did you find on the ad buy?"

"It's a biggie. Seven million on TV, which is a ton for Nevada. And in every media market."

"Any info on Americans for a Brighter Future?"

"Yeah. It's technically not a SuperPAC. It's a dark money group. A nonprofit."

"So they don't have to disclose anything?" she asked, remembering what Jack had told her.

"Right. There's nothing on record but their IRS tax exemption form. I'm about to email it to you. They raised $290 million last year and gave away a boatload to different charitable causes so they could qualify as a nonprofit. But they look to have over $140 million left to spend in the campaign."

"Wow. That'll leave a mark."

"A whole lot of them."

"Any other details on the group?"

"Not really. They hardly have to disclose anything these days. There was nothing on the treasurer, and they have a one-person board, meaning it's a front group for sure."

"Okay. At least that's a start. Thanks, George." As usual, he hung up without saying goodbye.

She phoned Rachel as the cab turned onto the Strip. It was a gamble to try her this late, but their crazy schedules meant Cassie hadn't heard her wife's voice all day. Miraculously, after several rings, Rachel picked up. Cassie heard rustling followed by Rachel's groggy voice. "Baby, I told you not to call after 1:00. It's 2:00."

"I'm sorry," Cassie said soothingly. "I just hated not talking the whole day."

"You know I do too, but I've got to be at the hospital in five hours."

Cassie took a deep breath and exhaled. Time to change tacks. "Rach, I'm remembering the last time we were here," she said, a broad smile spreading across her face. "That fur rug and the jacuzzi."

Rachel sighed, resigned. "Now that was fun," she said.

Cassie leaned back into the cab's frayed leather seat. "I wish you could have come."

"Me too. But sitting in the hotel while you're out chasing stories is plain miserable. Plus, I've got work to do."

"I get it, I get it. Sleep tight, love. Call you in the morning."

"Love you."

Cassie smiled again as they hung up. She and Rachel had been best friends for years until it had crossed over into more in a cheesy Harrah's hotel room. Cassie had dumped her longtime boyfriend as soon as she'd returned to Boston, she and Rachel had lived together for the next two years, and had now been married over a year. Outside of her travel schedule, and Rachel's long hours as a nurse, things were perfect. It was the most comfortable she'd been since she was fourteen years old.

Even if it was just the two of them, Cassie had a family again.

* * *

PRINCE GEORGES COUNTY, MARYLAND

A screen door separated us, but the old woman's sneer came through clearly. A small dog yapped manically from behind her, leaping into the air every few barks.

"What do you want?" the woman asked.

"Are you Mrs. Jackson?" I asked.

"I am. Who are you?"

"My name is Jack Sharpe." I had to yell to be heard over the dog's shrill barks. "This is Alex Fischer. We're reporters from Republic News."

The woman's eyes narrowed further. The dog stopped barking long enough to unleash a long, low growl.

"I can't stand Republic News. That Bridget Turner is awful."

"Well, Bridget's more of a commentator," I said. "I don't always agree with her either. We're reporters. We just report the facts."

"Facts? Right. I don't believe any of you anymore."

The puny dog's high-pitched yaps resumed. It reminded me of Igor, our first and only dog, a mixed terrier my son Scott and I had quickly regretted saving from the pound.

"We wanted to ask you about your grandson Dontavius," I said. "I understand he grew up with you."

Alex had researched Staff Sergeant Dontavius Jackson and relayed her findings to me on the drive to his grandmother's house. Only a block away from Kroon's fatal skirmish, a flurry of bullets had torn through Jackson less than an hour after Kroon had been shot. He'd lost his left arm and suffered some internal injuries, but thanks to Anthony Bravo's heroics, he'd survived. After eight months recovering in Walter Reed, Jackson had moved back to Maryland. That was the end of the trail.

"You want to know about my Dontavius?" Mrs. Jackson still looked fierce, but her voice was tender as she said her grandson's name.

"Yes," Alex interjected from behind me. "Dontavius Jackson, the war hero."

"You mean the war victim," she muttered, barely audible over the dog.

"That too," I said.

"One minute." She turned around. "Bandit! DOWN!" The dog flung himself to the ground, chin flat against the floor, big eyes looking up at Mrs. Jackson as if its life depended on her next words. Bandit was way out of Igor's league.

Two minutes later, Alex and I were sitting on a couch in the small living room. Mrs. Jackson faced us from a leather chair, stroking Bandit as he lay panting in her lap. On an end table, two framed pictures captured Dontavius Jackson's life. One, a picture of a teenage boy: skinny, toothy smile, Redskins T-shirt, a half-inch of black curly hair on top of his head that faded to skin above his ears. Next to it was a photo of a grown man, no hair at all, face rounded out, chest filled out. Clad in the camouflage uniform of the 82nd Airborne. No smile, all business. A warrior.

Mrs. Jackson gestured at the photos as she spoke.

"We raised him after his mom died. Dontavius was a good boy, and such a positive force. But the war took all that potential and destroyed him. It turned him into a troubled man."

We'd decided on the drive over that I'd get us in the door, and Alex would lead once we got inside.

"I've seen a lot of that," Alex said. "Ma'am, we'd love to talk to him."

"Well, you can't do that." Her firm tone prompted a growl from Bandit.

"I'd only ask him—"

"You can't ask him anything. We lost Dontavius two years ago."

Alex jolted upright. "Lost?" she said. "He passed away?"

Mrs. Jackson cocked her head, looking at Alex out of the side of her hooded eyes. Then she turned my way. "I thought you said you were news reporters."

"We are," I replied, embarrassed, "but we found nothing indicating he had died."

"Well, when you die on the streets, and not on the battlefield, it's not news, now is it?"

"I am so sorry to hear it," Alex said. "Can you tell us what happened?"

A long pause, as if she'd prepared this answer for years. "Dontavius fell apart after coming home—too many problems, too much addiction. He started to steal from us so we kicked him out. Then he was in and out of shelters, jail and veteran's homes. He died on the streets of Baltimore. An overdose, but it was never clear if it was an accident or a suicide. Either way, it was the war that killed him."

Mrs. Jackson stared straight ahead as she spoke. Her eyes were hollow, and appeared older than the rest of her face, as if she'd shed so many tears telling this story that none were left.

"I've seen their struggles far too often," Alex said. "Again, I am so sorry."

The old woman ran right over the sympathy. "I've heard a lot of sorries, just not from anyone in a uniform. And for all their talk, no politician once said *they're* sorry. I tried to get the news to mention his military service, but they didn't care at all."

We sat quietly. Not intentionally, but because no fitting response came to mind. She was right. Our vets were treated terribly. Forgotten.

"So why do you care now?" Mrs. Jackson asked, folding her arms. Bandit stirred.

"Did you see the debate the other night?" Alex asked.

"No. But I heard about it. That congressman told the story about his unit. Dontavius's unit."

"Yes, he did. Had you heard the story before?"

"Oh, yes," Mrs. Jackson said, perking up. "When Congressman Bravo first got elected, Dontavius was so proud that someone from the unit had succeeded. Bragged about him. He even saw him once in Washington a couple years after he was elected."

"Did you ever meet the congressman?"

"No. I never did."

"Did Dontavius ever talk about any others from his unit?"

"Yes. There was a group of six of them who were very close. The congressman and Dontavius, the boy who died, another injured boy, and two others."

"The other one injured?" Alex asked. "Was that Lieutenant Cull?"

"Yes. Big guy. They called him 'Bus.' But Jimmy was his real name. I can't remember the other two."

"You know anything about them?"

"I really don't. Dontavius and Bus went through rehab together at Walter Reed. Bus lost his leg below his knee. He also struggled. I think he moved back to Texas. I have no idea what happened to the other two. One was Asian, the other was a farm boy from Indiana."

"Did he ever say anything about the group?"

The old woman smiled, rocking forward in her chair. "Just that he had never been in a more tight-knit circle of friends. They were proud of their unit and had each other's back. They thought they were invincible. Until that day. The Kroon boy dying tore them all up, especially Bravo, is what Dontavius said."

She'd warmed up, so I couldn't help but jump in. "Ma'am, I only have one question: Do you know if Bravo returned from Iraq early? Before the rest of the unit?"

"I don't know when the rest of the unit came back. But I know he paid Dontavius and Bus a visit in the summer, the year they were injured. Dontavius never forgot it."

Alex leaned forward on the couch, excited by this new nugget. But then Mrs. Jackson changed topics, looking hard at Alex. "Can I ask you something?"

"Yes."

"Are you trying to hurt Congressman Bravo?"

"Of course not," Alex said. "Why would we do that?"

The side look and folded arms returned. "You're the media. You don't ask questions like this to do nice stories. I know that for sure."

I sat up straight, eager to defend our profession. But then stopped. She was right, and would see right through any defense I mounted. Hell, Bandit would probably start barking again.

"I hope you don't hurt him," she went on. "He must be a strong man to be where he is today. He went through the same hell that buried my grandson and destroyed so many others. And now look where he is. Good for him. He's got my vote."

Alex nodded and smiled, turning her gaze at me. Mrs. Jackson had just summed up why she hated this story.

* * *

WASHINGTON, D.C.

George Vassos dragged himself into the office at ten in the morning, still annoyed that Cassie had kept him up so late. However talented, these whippersnappers needed to figure out that good research is a marathon, not a sprint. When you rush, you make mistakes, and you miss the key details.

Once at his desk, he pulled the IRS tax exemption form for Americans for a Brighter Future from his top drawer and marveled again at how little it revealed. Only one board member. Few details on what they were doing with all that money except that half was for "public education." The letters "n/a" followed most of the questions, the address was a PO Box in Delaware, and no website was listed.

Only two names appeared anywhere on the document, the sole board member and the treasurer, with nothing more on either. A phone number appeared under the treasurer's name—the same phone number as the Delaware law firm that filed the IRS form. He dialed the number and a receptionist transferred the call.

"Patricia Murphy here," the woman who picked up said. "How can I help you?" This was who George had hoped to reach. Patricia Murphy, of Murphy & Murphy, had signed the cover letter that accompanied the IRS filing.

"Patricia, I'm calling about Americans for a Brighter Future. Their treasurer, Matthew Tester, is listed here. How can I reach him?"

"You can't. How can I help you?"

"Can I talk to Erma Walsh?" She was listed as the sole board member.

"No. She's a very private person. I'm the only one who speaks for the PAC. What do you need?"

"Well, I have a client who loves what the PAC's doing and wants to make a donation to its efforts. Who do I speak with to do that?"

"They don't need any help."

George had expected the initial brush-off. People who traditionally donate to SuperPACs don't call out of the blue and ask *how* to do it. If you have big political money to throw around, you know exactly where to throw it. Patricia Murphy likely understood this. So it was time to sweeten the pot.

"I'm talking a multi-million dollar investment," George said. "Enough to blitz a whole state. Give them even more momentum to wipe that awful Janet Moore out."

"Sir, ABF has all the resources it needs. Thank you anyway." The phone went dead.

Who says no to millions without even getting a name? George wondered. Especially in politics, where everyone was always looking for more money.

George jumped back online to learn more about the woman he'd just talked to. Patricia Murphy, one of two siblings running the small family firm in Wilmington, Delaware. Graduated from University of Delaware law school only four years ago. Specializing in corporate law, but in the grand scheme of the legal world, just a pup.

The best firms in Washington would kill for a client with pockets as deep as ABF's. How in the world had this near-rookie at a no-name firm in Delaware landed it? On the one hand, George knew the answer. ABF had gone with a low-profile firm far from the Beltway to stay under the radar. But still, with so much at stake, ABF would have only placed themselves in the hands of someone they trusted. So there must have been some significant connection between ABF and Murphy. George set off to find what it was.

* * *

LAS VEGAS, NEVADA

The minutes were ticking away on her last chance. Cassie Knowles had chased Bravo around the Strip all day and gotten nowhere.

First it was Paris—the casino, not the city. Bravo had been there greeting casino workers, Vegas's most powerful bloc on Nevada's caucus day, but he'd come nowhere near the roped-in press pool. Even from a distance, though, Cassie had noted his raw talent. Grasping hands, gripping arms, making eye contact, hugging. He posed for one selfie after the next, laughing throughout. And just as striking was the exuberance on the faces of those walking away after their moment with the candidate. Smiles of pure joy.

It was palpable. Bravo had something. Something special.

The second stop, at the Luxor, had proven as futile as the first. Long wait. No access. No questions. At least the pyramid-shaped casino had provided a nice backdrop for her live shot about the attack ads.

Two hours later, Cassie stood in the large arena where the UNLV Running Rebels played basketball. The crowd of 15,000 was cheering as Bravo delivered a stem-winder of a speech.

"College students should not be shackled by college debt for decades after they've earned their degrees," he bellowed from the floor, looking up into the stands. "You've done exactly what we've asked you to do—get an education. Why should it set you so far back economically? Enough is enough!"

The young crowd, a rainbow of ethnicities that perfectly represented the broad Bravo coalition, roared at the red meat.

Strapped with $90,000 in loans from Boston College, Cassie agreed with his rhetoric. But she was distracted, imprisoned in yet another press pen. The pen's location guaranteed they wouldn't be getting close to the candidate here either. How would Bravo try to get out? He would work the rope line, but there was no way to get up there. Then he would clearly go behind the rafters to exit. Then where? With minutes left in his stump speech, she scrambled out the back of the arena. She exited down the stairs, turned left, and made her way around the oval building.

And there they were. Three dark SUVs idled near a service door. Two ropes, a few yards apart, created a temporary walkway that Bravo would presumably follow to his vehicle. A small crowd of enterprising students had already gathered to greet the candidate.

Definitely her best bet, but she'd have to fit in. She removed the press badge from around her neck, hid her jacket behind a bush, rolled up her sleeves, and unbuttoned two buttons of her shirt to reveal her tattoo. She approached the gathering and made her way to the front row, directly behind the near rope. If Bravo worked this side, she'd have her chance. She readied her phone and waited.

Minutes later, the door sprang open. Two secret service agents emerged, followed by Bravo's body person. Then the small crowd applauded as Bravo himself appeared. He squinted in the bright sun but recovered quickly to shake hands.

Good, Cassie thought. He chose to work the rope on her side, and was now a stone's throw to her left. Even better, everyone in the young crowd whipped their phones out, snapping as many selfies as possible. Her phone wouldn't draw suspicion from either campaign flacks or the secret service.

Bravo moved closer, working slowly, grasping every hand he could reach. Close up and in-person, he was far more striking than on television. Dark eyebrows, brown eyes, and olive skin. High cheekbones. Thick, black hair, parted to the right. Not a crewcut, but close-cropped.

About five feet now. Cassie pushed play on her phone's video recorder.

And then came the moment. He flashed his perfect smile and reached out to her. She went for it.

"Congressman, we know you returned months early from your last tour in Iraq, even though it wasn't officially reported that way. Why is that?"

She'd deliberately shouted so that there would be no doubt he could hear the words, no way for him to ignore her. The crowd heard it too, and fell silent.

The congressman froze. Looked right at her, pursing his lips grimly, pupils dilating. Cassie had seen the look many times—the surprise, and fear, of an unwelcome question.

"Wh—? Excuse me?" he said. The Hollywood smile returned. But it was too late.

"Why did you come home from Iraq well before your unit returned in October? And why did the Pentagon hide that fact?"

He had fully recovered now, chuckling as he responded. "I don't know what you're talking about. I proudly served my country." He turned his head, reached out to two young women to Cassie's right, and moved on.

"Are you denying you were back in the summer?" Cassie shouted. "You visited the Kroons. Your unit didn't come back till late fall. Why did—"

A large hand grabbed her left arm and pulled her forcefully away.

"What the fuck are you doing? This is not for press." A stocky, round-faced kid glared at her. He wore a Bravo for President badge but definitely was low on the totem pole.

"Get your hands off me," she said, pulling away from his grip. "He's running for president. It's all public. I asked him a simple question."

"Get the hell out of here."

"I'm leaving. But I want a full accounting of when he left Iraq. The Pentagon says he returned in October with his unit. We have sources saying that's not true, and he pretty much just confirmed it with his reaction."

"What are you, a mind reader? He didn't confirm shit."

"Like I said, we have sources. His reaction said it all. Here's my card. I expect a full accounting by tomorrow or we run the story."

"Who's w—"

Cassie arched an eyebrow and flipped her Republic News card toward his chest. She watched him struggle to keep his expression neutral. The Republic News logo meant she was to be taken seriously.

After gathering her things, she replayed the footage she'd captured with her phone. Bravo's face appeared in the top right-hand corner of the screen, but other than being off-center, the shot was perfect. Most of the clip captured Bravo in his full charismatic glory, but the final few seconds showed his frame-by-frame transformation into a man frozen by a jarring question.

She frowned as she watched it. Yep, Jack was right. Bravo, her dream candidate, was hiding something.

After watching the video twice more, Cassie sent Jack the video clip. She followed with a text. Four words.

Got him. What next?

CHAPTER 6

LAWRENCEBURG, INDIANA

"SESLER? AIN'T HEARD the name in years."

The badge on the stout man's blue shirt indicated his name was Doug, and that he was the sales manager.

"Yeah, do you know him?" I asked, looking down, exhausted from too little sleep.

"I did, I did. Dude drank himself to death."

Damn. Another dead end. Alex had identified the fifth platoon member as Dave Sesler, an Army sharpshooter and former all-Indiana basketball star who'd returned from Iraq to his hometown of Lawrenceburg in October 2007. The town had celebrated his return with a big parade and a glowing profile in the local paper, and this auto dealership was his last known employer. I'd flown to Cincinnati on a 7:00 a.m. flight, taken a cab here, and the curly-haired Doug had greeted me just inside the sales office.

"He's dead?"

"So dead. Dude was pretty much dead for years. But then he took his own head off in a car crash a few years back." His eyes bugged wide as he dragged a finger across his throat, seeming to enjoy his graphic description.

"You don't appear to be upset about it."

"It is what it is. He was a war hero and a star athlete before, but only a drunk after. Went the wrong way on 275 at two in the morning. Lucky no one else died when he did."

"Sad."

Doug shook his head. "Yeah. Sad was that no one cared. He had no one left in his life. He chased them all away."

That really was sad.

"Is there anyone in town who can tell me more about him?"

"Parents are both gone. He's got a younger sister in town. Darla. Married to a local cop. Shouldn't be too hard to find."

* * *

HUNTSVILLE, TEXAS

Cassie shuddered as she wound her way up the driveway toward the foreboding red brick facade of the Huntsville Penitentiary, better known as the Walls Unit. Having witnessed five executions for the *Boston Globe*, including a prisoner convulsing for minutes before flatlining, she detested the death penalty. And yet here she was, dispatched by Jack Sharpe to the nation's execution capital.

From Vegas, she had grabbed the first flight she could to Houston, landing late at night. After a six-hour stay in a Hampton Inn, she'd driven a rented Dodge Charger an hour north. Along the way, Jack had briefed her on Jimmy Cull, who he said was eligible to take visitors. For all his bad luck, at least Cull was in the maximum security section of the Walls Unit, as opposed to death row. The jury had offered him that one measure of mercy after convicting him for murdering his young wife.

After parking and making her way through a second round of security, Cassie stepped into the visitors area. The uniformed woman on the other side of the glass chuckled when she heard the name.

"Jimmy Cull? He never gets visitors. Who are you? His girlfriend or something?"

"My name's Cassie Knowles. I'm with Republic News." She passed her driver's license and work ID through a slot in the thick glass.

"And you didn't call ahead?"

"A colleague did just a few minutes ago. Jack Sharpe? Your people said he was eligible for visitors today. It's up to him if he wants to talk, right?"

"It is."

"Please let him know I'm here to talk about Congressman Bravo and their old unit." Jack had said the unit was proud of Bravo's success. She was gambling that Cull still felt that way.

"It may be a while since y'all didn't make an appointment," the woman said. "And this will have to be a no-contact visit. Have a seat over there."

Without cell service, the wait in the cafeteria-style visitors room dragged. Cassie watched a series of family reunions, women and kids sitting at tables with orange-clad inmates. A few interactions were emotional, but most were casual, just part of everyday life. One little boy cried as his dad got up to leave. All of it was so hard to watch.

Two hours in, a deep male voice announced her name. "Cassie Knowles, please go to window six. Inmate Cull is on his way."

She took a seat under a number six and found herself staring into a large window. Thick cloudy glass separated her from a small room on the other side. Moments later, with a guard escorting him, a giant of a man hopped heavily into the small room, crutch in hand, the lower left leg section of his orange pants dangling empty. His head and face were hairless except for a stringy goatee. And he had enormous round eyes. But all his features were eclipsed by his gargantuan size, both in height and thickness.

Cassie had interviewed prisoners before. Friendly ones. Fierce ones. Crazy ones. She knew you had to win them over from the outset. They each lifted a gray phone from their side of the glass, and Cassie said, "I can see why they call you 'Bus!'"

It worked. He laughed.

"Guess so, ma'am. Haven't heard that nickname in years."

As rough as he looked, Jimmy Cull's deep Texas accent was regal. Firm. What you'd expect from a professional soldier, not from the other side of a no-contact prison window. And as he spoke, his green eyes sparkled, in stark contrast to the otherwise dreary setting.

"Thank you for meeting with me."

"I don't get many visitors. And they said it was about my man President Bravo." He flashed a big smile as he said the name. Unlike most inmates, Jimmy Cull exuded serious charisma.

"So you know he's running for president?" Cassie asked.

"Oh yeah. We get the basics in here. But that's about it."

"He talked about your battle in Iraq the other night. About being there with Sergeant Kroon."

Cull shook his head. "He was amazing that day," he said. "Saved my life."

"That's why I'm here. To talk about that."

"What do you want to know?" he asked, leaning back, folding his arms.

"About him. Your unit."

Cull lowered his head.

"I'm sure it's not easy for you," Cassie said gently. "But we want to know more about Congressman Bravo, especially now that he's running for president."

He hunched toward the window, his enormous hands gripping the table in front of him. "I would never say anything to hurt him." His large nostrils flared as he spoke.

"I'm not asking—"

"The man saved me. And he could save me again."

"Again?"

"Presidents have pardons, right?"

"Yes."

"So if he wins, he can pardon me. He knows I wouldn't have killed my wife. He knows me."

Damn, thought Cassie. That was one hell of a reason not to sell out his old war buddy. "Have you and he talked about your case?" she asked, wondering if that could possibly be the scoop here.

"No. We haven't talked in years. But he knows me. And from what my lawyers have told me, he's the one guy who can get me out of this place. So you're not going to get me—"

"I wasn't asking you to say anything that would undermine—"

"I never would!"

"I understand!"

Cull nodded, seemed to be satisfied.

"Well," Cassie said uncertainly. "Tell me about your unit."

"We were so tight," Cull said. "All the way through. We liked to think we represented America. Big city. Small town. Black, white, Asian, Hispanic. The surge chewed us all up, but we hung together even then. Then the day from hell came. Tony saved me, saved Dontavius, and hung with Tommy as he died. They were so close. I can't imagine how hard that was for him."

"Who? Tony and Sergeant Kroon?"

"Yes. They had a bond. We were all close, but they had a bond."

"Then what happened?"

"We split up. Dontavius and I recovered at Walter Reed. Sesler and Choo came back later in the year."

"We know of Dave Sesler. Who's Choo?"

"Michael Choo. He was a specialist like Sesler. A great guy and a real badass. He went back to New York, I believe."

She scribbled down the name in her notebook. "Jimmy, when was the last time you saw Tony?"

"He visited me shortly after I got to Walter Reed."

Another confirmation that Bravo had come home early. How the hell had Jack Sharpe known to chase this down? *Tread gently*, she told herself. *Don't spook him.*

"So was he home for good then, or on a leave?"

"He didn't say. It didn't seem like he was heading back, or we would have talked about that. That would've been tough. But we basically talked about my recovery. That's all he cared about."

"Did you talk about Kroon?"

"No. Too tough. It's still tough now. I have nightmares about it to this day. And in this shithole, waking up alone, it's only worse. I was fucked in the head even before I got in here, now it's only worse. Sorry for cursing, ma'am."

"No problem," Cassie said gamely. "Shit, I swear like a sailor myself. Tell me about your case."

He bowed his head again. Finally he said, "I came home one night. My wife, the only person who was leading me out of the darkness, was on the floor unconscious, next to our bed, beaten terribly. I tried to revive her but she stopped breathing not long after. I'm the one who called the damn cops and ambulance. But before I knew it, they were accusing me. Anyone who knows me knows I would never have done that."

She shook her head sympathetically. "I'm sure. What do you think happened?"

"I have no idea. Someone broke in. Her face and neck were so bruised. But whoever did it left without a trace. No broken locks or glass. No fingerprints there but mine. The cops had it out for me and got me on a bunch of circumstantial bullshit. I'll admit I got in one too many bar fights, drunk off my ass. But I would never have killed Audrey. She was the only one who made things better."

He lowered his head again. She couldn't hear a sob, but his bald head bobbed up and down. Although she'd been jaded by one too many inmates' claims of innocence, Cull's raw emotion was wearing Cassie down. It was hard to imagine this man killing his wife.

"All I know now is that I'm in here for life, and that a President Bravo is my only hope to get out. And even then, she's gone."

"Have you reached out to him?"

"We sent him a letter after he announced his run. But I haven't heard back. I know if he saw it he'd be on my side."

"Where did you send it? And when?"

"We sent it to his congressional office. Maybe a month after I got into this place."

"Who's your lawyer, by the way? The one who told you Tony could pardon you."

"He showed up from Houston and went out of his way to defend me.

His name is Dean Gamble. Good guy, also a veteran, out of some fancy firm down there. Strauss something."

Cassie wrote the name down.

"Is there anyone else from your platoon you think could help me understand Tony?"

"Just Sesler and Choo. That's it. Dontavius is dead."

"I know. So sad how hard it's been for so many vets."

Cull didn't answer, and Cassie realized what a deep well of pain her statement must have tapped into. She searched for anything else to ask. Nothing.

"Well, thanks for your time, Mr. Cull. Good luck. Hang in there."

As they each hung up their phones, Cull's intense green eyes locked onto her through the window. He clearly wanted to keep talking. Who could blame him? Cassie didn't turn around and walked away.

* * *

LAWRENCEBURG, INDIANA

I stood uncomfortably in the small, cluttered kitchen of Darla Murphy, dreading that her husband would burst in at any moment.

"Dave wasn't never the same after he came home," Darla said. "And our family wasn't either. The superstar who went over there, that boy died over there."

The petite woman spoke to me from the other side of the small linoleum island, her wispy blonde hair flowing halfway down her back. She was extremely pregnant, days from delivery by the looks of it, her lower belly stretching her thin, yellow T-shirt to near transparency. She sliced onions as we spoke, each slice punctuated by the oversized knife striking against the wooden cutting board.

"I'm so sorry to hear that," I said. "It sounded like he struggled with alcohol."

"Yeah. I'm a nurse," she said. "I've seen it hundreds of times, but it's so hard to see your big brother drunk all the time."

"Did he ever talk about the war? His time over there?"

She would not meet my eyes, focused instead on the onions. "Not a word. But he had nightmares. His buddies may have lost limbs, but he lost his spirit. He'd walk out of a room before talking about it."

"He ever hear from any of his combat buddies? From all accounts he was in a tight-knit group."

She looked up, a dumbfounded expression on her gaunt face. "I never heard about them. Never saw them."

"And how long ago was his accident?"

"Two years ag—"

Just then, the screen door to our right was yanked open, its rusty hinges screeching in protest, and a burly cop in full uniform stepped through the doorway. "Darla," he was saying, "why didn't you answer your—" He stopped short when he spotted me. "Who the hell are you?" I watched his right hand move down toward the taser side of his belt.

"Sir," I stammered, raising my right hand. "Sir, hold on. I'm a reporter from Republic News."

Darla tried talking, but her husband cut her off.

"Republic what? And why the hell are you in our kitchen?"

"Bobby, he just wanted to know about Dave."

"And why the hell would you be talking to a reporter about Dave? Or anything?"

"Sir, we're doing a stor—"

"I wasn't talking to you. Darla, why the hell is a reporter in our house?" he asked, never taking his eyes off me.

"Honey, he was just—"

"You've got a lot of nerve conning your way into this house, with my pregnant wife all alone. It's time for you to go."

"I was just—"

"Out!" He took a step towards me, lifting his right hand.

"Bobby! Stop!" Darla dropped the knife and half an onion, then stepped quickly around the island. "I let him in, I'll walk him out."

"Fine. But I want him out of here."

"Come with me," she said quietly, striding toward a narrow hallway.

I followed. The fridge creaked open behind us. At least Bobby and his Taser were staying put.

"I'm so sorry about that," she whispered as we entered a small, cluttered living room. The stench of fully-loaded diapers overcame the onion aroma that had been trailing her.

"It's fine. Cops and reporters don't mix well," I said. "Can I at least ask if Dave left anything behind about his service?"

She stopped just feet from the front door and nervously raked her fingers through her hair. "He had a bunch of papers, pictures, awards and stuff. From his time over there. He kept all of it in his attic."

Finally, some hope. "Do you still have it?"

"No, someone came to collect it."

Collect it? "Who?"

"Someone from the Army came after he died. He said they needed it for the official archives."

Strange. I'd never heard of the Army collecting dead soldiers' papers. "Is there nothing left?" I asked.

"Just that one picture," she said, pointing to a set of wooden shelves built into the far corner of the room. "I found it in my mom's attic last year." Two dead potted plants took up the top shelf. But on the shelf below sat a silver picture frame. A group of guys wearing fatigues.

"Can I take a look?" I whispered. Before she answered, I'd stepped over and between scattered Lego pieces, a few Matchbox cars and one pair of tiny shoes and arrived at the shelf.

Six guys. Kids, really. In fatigues, beaming smiles. In the back row, on the far left, stood Dontavius Jackson, well-built and confident. Just to his right stood an enormous hulk of a guy, blonde hair. A skinnier but equally tall white guy stood to his right. In the front row, from left to right, were an Asian-American man, a young Anthony Bravo, and someone I instantly recognized as Thomas Kroon. All three looked to be about 5'11". Trim. Muscular.

"So that's Dave in the back right?"

She nodded and winced, clearly worried we'd be overheard.

It was the only picture of this crew I'd seen. Beyond the faces, races, and sizes, the poses told a story. This group was close. Confident. Dontavius and the hulking white guy, presumably Jimmy Cull, draped their burly arms across each other's shoulders. Dave Sesler's hands gripped Kroon's shoulders. Bravo and the Asian-American both gave a thumbs up.

I aimed my phone and took a couple photos.

"Darla, what the hell?" Bobby shouted from the kitchen. "Is he gone yet?"

Darla opened the door. "He's walking out now," she yelled, beckoning me frantically.

I snapped three more quick shots of Bravo, tiptoed back across the room, and escaped out the door.

* * *

HOUSTON, TEXAS

Within hours of leaving the depressing visitors room of the Walls Unit, Cassie peered out over the jagged Houston skyline from the highest point possible—the gaudy conference room on the top floor of the JP Morgan Chase Tower. The receptionist had left her there as she alerted Dean Gamble of her arrival.

Long marble table. Dark mahogany walls. Old portraits of dead partners. Baker and Strauss was one fancy law firm, the kind that gave Cassie the creeps. Definitely not the place you'd expect to see lawyers defending violent criminals. Insider trading or fraud, maybe. Or as Cassie had experienced as a teenager, to bail out a well-heeled client who'd run afoul of the law. But an accused wife-killer with no connections? Not a chance.

Dean Gamble strode into the room as Cassie was looking out the window, so she heard his deep twang first. "They tell me you're from Republic News. I was hoping you'd be Bridget Turner."

She turned around quickly. Brown pinstripe suit in a big frame. Perfectly bald head, shiny under the conference room lights. She labored to smile. "Sorry to disappoint. I'm Cassie Knowles. A reporter for the station."

"You're definitely not Turner. I'll get over it. How can I help you?"

"I wanted to talk to you about Jimmy Cull, the guy you defended a couple years back."

"Jimmy? Great guy. What about him?" He didn't sit down, clearly not interested in a long meeting.

Cassie eased into a chair. "I just wanted to know more about his case. It's really good of a big firm like this and a top-flight lawyer like yourself to take on his case."

"Why thank you," he said, sitting down across the table from her. Relenting. "I try to help my veterans when I can. All pro bono. I was an early Iraq guy myself. I got out better than most, so I do what I can for those who are suffering. Jimmy is a great guy who never recovered from the war."

"So you've done this before?" The key question, making clear that this interview was about probing, not celebrating.

"Done what?" he asked, looking right back at her.

"Helped veterans. Helped them defend themselves in court."

He casually nodded. "Sure. Mostly civil stuff. Bankruptcies.

Foreclosures. And charitable stuff. There's nothing like giving back to those who've sacrificed so much."

"Not criminal cases?"

He leaned back ever so slightly. "Hm?"

"You do criminal cases? Before Jimmy?"

"Jimmy's was the first. But when I saw the story, I knew we had to do something. Whether or not he did it, he needed a good defense. That's our—"

"Doesn't sound like you think he's innocent?" Cassie interrupted, leaning in.

"Who knows? It was a weak case, but there was no evidence pinning it on anyone else either. His prints were everywhere. He had some violence in his past. Once against her. We did the best we could." He stared at her for a few seconds. "What exactly are you looking into?"

"I'm talking to people who served with Congressman Bravo. We're trying to know him better as he runs for president."

"Congressman Bravo? That's what this is all about? Then why are you here?" He grinned, but his tone was not friendly.

"I'm just following up on my chat with Jimmy. To be honest, I'm intrigued. You're not a criminal lawyer, but you took his case. And he said you were the one that told him that if Congressman Bravo was elected president, maybe he'd get pardoned."

He tensed up. "Young lady, that conversation was attorney-client priv—"

"—And the client voluntarily waived the privilege when he talked to me."

He backed off. "I told him that because it's true. That's his best hope at this point. It wasn't even worth appealing."

"He doesn't seem to talk much about his service. How'd you know he knew Bravo?"

"He mentioned it at some point. We were reliving our days in battle."

"He doesn't seem to enjoy doing—"

"Veteran-to-veteran conversations are different, darlin'."

Funny, Cassie thought. The prison guard said Jimmy rarely had visitors. He must've forgotten about the heart-to-hearts with Gamble. She moved on.

"He took your words seriously," she said. "He's banking on Bravo winning as his only hope."

"Unfortunately that's the reality. He needs Bravo." He leaned forward in his chair. "Honey, I'm gonna have to—"

Keep pushing, Cassie told herself. A guy like this wouldn't let a young woman get the last word. "Who handled his case for him?"

"I was lead. And some associates. We have the best here. Two Harvard grads assis—"

"Criminal lawyers?"

"No. But smart as hell. He could never have hired better." His head shined a little brighter as beads of sweat accumulated like dew. He was pissed. Time to move on.

"Did your team ever reach out to Bravo about the case?"

"We haven't. Jimmy wanted to send a let—"

"Yes, and never heard anything. You didn't follow up?"

"I figured it made more sense to wait til he actually got elected."

So it wasn't too early to raise Cull's hopes, but too early to actually do anything. What bullshit.

Gamble stood up. "Darlin', I'm going to—"

"Thank you for your help, Mr. Gamble."

"Have a nice day. Next time, send Turner instead."

Cassie laughed and waved a hand. "Oh, she only does the big interviews."

He walked out of the room, leaving her to find her way out.

CHAPTER 7

WASHINGTON, D.C.

"So what do we know?" I asked, thinking aloud. "Enough to do anything?"

The gloomy looks around the table answered my question. We were gathered at Republic HQ the Monday after the Nevada primary, in which Bravo had rocketed to a big win over Janet Moore. Under the barrage of attack ads, she'd barely edged out Pete Nicholas for second. I'd called together the team to review our findings.

Alex described the official Bravo war record and the sad demise of Dontavius Jackson.

Cassie filled us in on Bravo's discomfort in Vegas, and the call from the campaign she'd gotten the next day. "The guy claimed Bravo returned stateside for six weeks before returning to serve out his tour. He said it was some type of leave."

"Then why would the congressman have been so uncomfortable when you asked him?" I asked.

"Exactly," Cassie said. "And why was the campaign spokesman so pissed off about it? He was livid on our call."

She also walked through the fall of Jimmy Cull, and his sketchy, makeshift criminal defense team.

George Vassos chimed in. "The judge should never have allowed a bunch of civil lawyers to represent that guy. Good intentions aren't good enough. This isn't charity work."

"I know!" Cassie said. "Do you mind looking through the case and seeing what you can find?"

"Not at all."

It was good to see George fired up about something, and the rest of the team interacting with him without rolling their eyes. Next, I talked about the Kroons, and Dave Sesler's accident. I laid a large printout of the group photo on the table.

Vassos then reviewed his research on Bravo's reemergence in San Jose. "He reappeared in November. Then he started teaching the next January in the public schools. He got himself elected to the city council the next November and never looked back."

"So there's no trace of him anywhere before that?" I asked.

"Nope. I've looked for any record of him back in the country before October. Registering to vote. Driver's license renewal. Nothing. It all started to happen in November and after."

"Not sure what we have here," I said, scanning the documents and notes strewn across the table. "A hole in Bravo's story for sure, with no clear explanation. But almost anyone who'd know what happened has since died. Definitely not enough to do anything at this point."

Alex leaned over the table, pointing at the photo. "Maybe this is the story. The before and after. It's a case study of our troops' struggles as they return from war. It would make a compelling human interest story."

Cassie waved a hand dismissively. "I didn't sign up for fluff."

She had channeled my thinking. "If we find nothing else, maybe we do that," I said. "Let's at least dig into Choo."

"Choo?" Alex asked. "I forgot to mention that. He's dead. Shot in some bank robbery a few years back. Another dead end."

As everyone dejectedly filed out of the room, I remained at the table, stewing. Something was off. Small discrepancies usually lead to big discrepancies. But running my team around the country on this was burning through time, money, and my credibility. I needed something to break.

Minutes later, my phone rang.

* * *

VIRGINIA BEACH, VIRGINIA

Going for neutral territory, we'd arranged to meet at Scuppers, a greasy spoon a block from the boardwalk. I arrived a few minutes early. Half the diners sported crew cuts, and almost all of them wore a cap, shirt, or jacket with some ship's name on it. This was definitely a Navy town.

My dining partners walked into the place at 10:00 on the nose, clearly father and son but a study in contrasts. I got a much better look at Earl, the Kroon patriarch, than I'd had at their home. He looked to be at least 75. Lanky. Tall but hunched. Cane in his right hand, he walked gingerly, carefully placing one foot in front of the other, studying the floor closely before planting the cane's tip. The son, Logan Kroon, patiently held his dad's right elbow as they approached my table.

I stood up as they arrived. Logan spoke before I could say a word, a big smirk across his face.

"I figured out who you were!" he said. "You're the guy Bridget Turner shredded so bad last year."

I forced a laugh. Heard this all the time. Even though I'd been proven right later, that disastrous interview—Bridget taking me down on national television—was what everyone remembered. My big national debut.

"Yeah. She's tough. Now we've joined forces."

Zero reaction to my happy update.

"Thanks for reaching out, Earl," I said to the older Kroon, whose heavy-lidded eyes made him look like he was still waking up. "Have a seat."

The small talk before and after ordering was short but painful. These were not happy men. All politicians were crooked. The country was going straight downhill. No hope left. I nodded along, trying but failing to build a rapport. The delivery of three plates of fried eggs and two sides of bacon and grits mercifully ended the meeting's gloomy opening. In synchrony, heads down, father and son dove into their meals.

"So what did you want to tell me?" I finally asked, digging my fork into a pile of cheese grits.

Earl looked up from his plate, a droplet of egg yolk embedded in the right corner of his dry, cracked lips.

"That Bravo—" He paused, sneered, glanced across the restaurant, then back at me. His bony Adam's apple elevated an inch as he prepared to deliver his punchline. "—he's queer."

The disgust on his face jarred me almost as badly as the words themselves.

"Excuse me?"

"You heard him," Logan said. "Mr. Big Shot Congressman is gay. He hit on my brother."

"Slow down, fellas," I said. "Give me a little more context here. How do you know this?"

"I saw it," Logan said. "We saw these guys up close and personal for a week. I was with them. It was frickin' obvious."

"I don't know the best way to ask this," I said, wincing for effect, "but did your brother reciprocate?" I gambled that a touchy question might draw out the most honest responses.

"Are you kidding me?" Logan said loudly. "How dare you ask that? Of course not. He was as disgusted as we—"

"No son of mine," Earl interrupted, waving his fork in the air, "no Kroon, would *ever* engage in homosexual activity. We raised him right."

"Can you tell me what you saw, specifically?" I asked Logan.

"I was out with them a ton the week they were all back here. And four or five times I saw Lieutenant Bravo, out of the corner of my eye, try to touch Tommy in some weird way. Unable to help himself."

"And Tommy?"

"He would push him away. He was a lot nicer than I would've been, but still pushed."

"Did anyone else notice?"

"I don't think so. I was young, excited my brother was home, so maybe it was more obvious to me. Bravo did it when others weren't looking. But I saw it."

"Did you say anything?"

"I talked to Tommy late one night. I asked him what Tony's problem was. He told me he was having a hard time dealing with the stress, and not to worry about it."

"Did you tell anyone?"

"Yeah. Told my dad."

"Mr. Kroon, what did you do?" I asked.

"I talked to Tommy, too. The day before he left. I told him he needed to report Bravo and get his ass sent home. There's no room for pervert stuff like that in the barracks, especially in a warzone. Jesus, how was Tommy supposed to fight a war with someone stalkin' him?"

"What did he say?" I asked, ignoring the old man's opinions.

"Not to tell anyone. That he'd take care of it."

"Do you know if he did?"

"My son was a man of his word. That's got to be why Bravo came back early and never went back. No other reason for it. He definitely wasn't hurt, saw that with my own two eyes."

The puzzle pieces snapped together in front of my eyes. *Holy shit*, I thought. Bravo's early return. This explained it.

Logan looked right at me, seeing that I'd figured it out. "Big deal, huh?" He smiled, then tapped his right finger against his temple. Proud of himself.

I refused to satisfy him. "And why are you telling us this now?"

"Are you kidding?" Earl said. "This guy's on his way to being president. People need to know the truth about him."

"And what's that?"

"What's what?"

"The truth?"

"That he's no war hero. That he couldn't keep it under control when his unit needed him. That he pranced home early while everyone else in his unit kept fighting. Why do you think he's in such good shape while others are struggling? It's cuz he got out early."

My muscles tensed. "Mr. Kroon, this man stayed with your son until he died. They were clearly close. You're being awfully tough on him."

The old man leaned back, folding his arms. "And now we know why he stayed, don't we? I wish every day that it was another man with Tommy that day. Not this one." He shook his head. "Makes me sick to think about."

I held back from saying more. No point. I'd heard this kind of talk before, so I knew that the only real way to get through it was to ignore it. "So does anyone else know?"

"Who knows?" Logan said. "When I served, we would have known. But we've never told anyone until now."

"Not even your mom?"

"Nope. We've kept it from her. It would've broken her heart. Still would."

I looked back at Earl. "Will told me that Bravo visited you later. Did it not come up then?"

"No, it didn't. I knew he was home because of it. But no reason to open that can of worms. Tommy was dead. Bravo was out. That's all I cared about. I wasn't gonna give him the satisfaction of even talking about it. And it would've gotten ugly quick, believe me."

I took a long sip from my coffee to avoid saying something I'd regret. "So you called me to make sure people know?"

"Definitely," Logan said. "It's a big story."

These guys were too eager to talk. And no doubt other media outlets would jump on it immediately. I needed to shut them down. "Well, Republic will only cover this if it's an exclusive. You have to keep it quiet."

Logan looked back at me, disappointed. "Okay. If that's how it works."

"Definitely is."

"Anything else you think I should know?" I asked.

"That's it, but that should be more than enough," the old man said, looking down at his now-empty plate, shaking his head. "That man is no hero."

* * *

WASHINGTON, D.C.

"I need to talk to you about something highly confidential."

Alex and I were back in the office kitchen. She raised an eyebrow at me in that way that always unnerved me.

"It's about Don't Ask, Don't Tell. How did it work? Remind me of the details."

"Why are you interested in that hateful old law?" She narrowed her eyes. "Wait. Don't tell me."

I barreled on. "Confidentially, the Kroons believe Bravo was discharged under Don't Ask, Don't Tell. They say he hit on their son, and that's why he came home early."

"Jesus, Jack. So now we're going to drag a man through the mud because he's gay?"

I'd been asking myself the same question for hours, but there was no easy answer. "I don't know what we're going to do yet," I shot back impatiently. "We're reporters. We have a responsibility to verify it, or to tell the Kroons they're off base. They're going to tell someone either way. At least we have a chance to get in front of it because they tipped us off first."

She ran her hand through her hair and sighed. "So you want me to dig into his dismissal file?"

"Yes. And tell me how the policy worked again?"

"It didn't. That's the problem. It was an unworkable compromise. Gays could serve, and higher-ups couldn't 'ask' if they were gay. But if a soldier exhibited or discussed his sexuality, he'd be kicked out. Thousands were discharged until Obama repealed it."

"And how would a discharge under the policy be effectuated?"

"Originally, as a dishonorable or other-than-honorable discharge, which was how gay soldiers had always been kicked out. Then they mellowed over time, so it more often came as a general discharge or even an honorable discharge. Usually 'homosexual conduct' would be cited as the reason, or something along those lines."

"And after it was repealed, what happened to all those who'd been dismissed under the policy?"

"My understanding is that any discharged soldier can request that the nature of his discharge be reviewed. For Don't Ask, Don't Tell discharges, they've been upgrading them to an honorable discharge. And the sexual orientation or conduct of the soldier is struck from the official record."

"So would Bravo's record reflect any of that?"

"Who the hell knows, Jack?" she asked. And with that she all but stalked out of the kitchen, ending our conversation. I'd never seen her in such a sour mood.

CHAPTER 8

ARLINGTON, VIRGINIA

"Ma'am," THE WOMAN said to Alex, "we're closing in eight minutes. You really need to go quickly."

The plump, silver-haired clerk in the Pentagon records office frowned as she pointed up to a large clock behind her. She left the impression that asking for documents at 3:52 in the afternoon was a crime. Still, she handed Alex five expandable legal-size folders, packed full of yellowing pieces of paper. These were the DD-214s of Bravo's platoon—the records verifying the dates of each soldier's service and type of discharge.

Alex cradled all five folders in her arms and walked briskly to a small research room. Rifling through the files as fast as she could, she pulled out the five names she needed. Staff Sergeant Dontavius Jackson and First Lieutenant Jimmy Cull were medically discharged in May 2007 due to their injuries. Specialists Dave Sesler and Michael Choo were honorably discharged in October 2007. And, according to his record, so was First Lieutenant Bravo. But despite the similar date, Alex frowned as she pulled out Bravo's document. It wasn't as faded as the others. Whiter paper. Crisper. Different font. Newer.

Alex hurried back to the clerk, who now stood by the door, jacket on and purse over her shoulder. "Ma'am," said Alex. "Why would one document look newer than the others? Does that mean it was changed?"

"Ma'am, it's really time to leave."

"I have two more minutes," Alex said firmly. "Please answer my question. Why would a document be newer?"

The clerk sighed. "If people succeed in upgrading their discharge, or in correcting some other error, the discharge review board voids the old record and replaces it with a new one."

"And is that old information kept anywhere?"

"No, it's all kept confidential to protect the veteran's privacy. But the new discharge is reflected on the new DD-214. That's all that matters going forward."

Alex thought for a second as the clerk looked at her watch. "Can the date of a discharge be changed, in addition to the nature of it?"

"Possibly, ma'am, if there was an error in the original date. I doubt that happens much, but it could in theory."

"I gotcha. Can I make copies of the—"

"It's 4:00. You'll have to come back tomorrow."

"Ma'am, it's only five copies. It'll take two minutes. I'll be back before you know it."

The clerk hesitated, her forehead creasing into wrinkles. She pointed to a copy machine in the back of the lobby. "It takes only dollar bills. Please hurry."

Alex smiled. A hard-won victory. She had never been one to let herself be out-ma'amed.

* * *

CHARLESTON, SOUTH CAROLINA

It was the first time they'd hit Bravo. Hard.

I was there in person, just an observer this time, in the College of Charleston arena for the much anticipated South Carolina debate.

This was a big moment. Presidential primaries were all about momentum, and South Carolina did one of two things: it gave the campaign with early momentum its final boost to victory, or it killed that momentum. So the big question was whether Bravo could be stopped. On the surface, the answer looked to be yes. The Palmetto State held the fourth contest of the primary, but the first in the South. African-Americans comprised a majority of the state's Democratic voters, giving Michigan's Wendell Stevens a big advantage. But because those expectations were already baked in, unless Senator Stevens wildly over-performed, he would only gain marginally even with a win.

It was the other results that really mattered. Governor Moore couldn't afford a distant third or fourth or her once-promising campaign would be done.

All of this tension exploded into a prime-time gang tackle of Bravo. Hard to tell how it looked on TV, but from fifteen rows back, it was rough. Senator Stevens pounced immediately after opening statements, prompted by a question about experience. "Congressman, this is not personal," he said, shooting a steely glare at Bravo, "but you have no executive experience. And with all due respect, even your legislative résumé is thin."

Looking at the camera instead of the senator, Bravo ticked off some talking points around veterans and gun safety, but his defensive tone and rehearsed answer proved Stevens's point.

Governor Moore, desperate for some traction, piled on. Leaning into her microphone, the skilled prosecutor went on the offense. "We cannot afford a candidate who needs on-the-job training. Too much is at stake."

Next, when the moderator brought up the SuperPAC attacks, Moore unleashed genuine anger for the first time in the campaign. "Congressman Bravo, you should be ashamed of yourself for these attacks," she said, glaring at her opponent. "This is the very kind of secret money you claim to be against. Will you renounce these ads?"

Bravo turned to face Moore. "I have nothing to do with those ads. I don't know who's behind—"

"Congressman Bravo," the moderator interrupted. "These ads began just as you started to rise in the polls. They've been all over social media, Facebook, and TV. Are you telling us you have no idea who's responsible for them?"

"I do not. I am running on my positive vision for our country."

Smirking, Stevens shook his head, not buying it, while Governor Moore laughed out loud.

Finally, Governor Nicholas entered the fray. But unlike the others, he chose the role of peacemaker. "Four good public servants are standing on this stage," Nicholas said, chin up. "It's a shame to see dark money going after any one of us. These ads are beneath us. They should be pulled."

Felt slick and overly indignant to me, but the room responded with sustained applause. Our focus group later affirmed it was the line of the night.

After the debate, back in my hotel room, I watched the ads first hand. Nasty ones just like Nevada. And Americans for a Brighter Future was again behind them. The same ads that had attacked Moore in Nevada appeared again here, but now a second set of ads was also running. Equally tough, but aimed at a new target: Senator Wendell Stevens.

An elderly African-American woman: "Wendell Stevens has been our senator in Michigan for years, and nothing's gotten better. Nothing. Don't believe a word he says." She was sincere. Credible. A powerful ad.

Then a middle-aged former auto worker testified: "I had worked there for years. Had the dignity of a good job. But Wendell Stevens crushed it all." Again, pitch-perfect lines. Tough ad. If Moore's fall in Nevada was a precursor, maybe Stevens wasn't in such good shape after all. Even more importantly, who the hell was behind these attacks? And it wasn't some innocent group pining away for a brighter future.

I sent George Vassos a quick email: "Americans for a Better Future beating the hell out of both Moore and Stevens down here. This is a serious operation. Could change the outcome. Let's dig deeper into it."

* * *

WASHINGTON, D.C.

Damn it, Alex Fischer cursed herself. Another ex-pilot with an ego still soaring above 40,000 feet.

Requiring weeks on the road throughout the year and ridiculous hours even when she was home, the life of a cable news reporter was not conducive to having a family. Her failed marriage was testament to that. Four years into it, when her daughter, Molly, was two, Alex had caught her husband sleeping with a paralegal from his law firm. No wonder he'd never seemed too upset when she'd traveled for assignments. She'd forgiven him that one time. But when she caught him a second time four months later, that had been it.

So at 44, and with Molly shuttling between her ex's Bethesda condo and Alex's Dupont Circle apartment, juggling work, motherhood, and some semblance of a dating life was tough. Alex had more than her share of suitors, and said yes to the few who interested her. But given her busy schedule, bad dates like this one were such a waste of time. Which is why she was scolding herself again on Wednesday night. The sushi and wine were both impressive, her date less so. Naval aviators were generally too cocky for her taste, but a former instructor from Miramar's famous flight school was even worse, it turned out. As good-looking as the dark haired, square-jawed guy sitting across from her was, the rest was too much. Too conservative politically. Didn't want to talk about anything but himself. Wildcat, which he'd explained was his fighter call sign, even ate like a pig, stuffing sushi rolls into his mouth by hand and then talking with that mouth full.

During a rare moment when he was taking a breather, Alex tried to salvage the evening—with work. "You ever have someone kicked out because they were gay?" she asked, pivoting clumsily from his third tale of trainee hazing.

"Sure," he said, oblivious to the conversational left turn. "It's happened a few times."

"Mm," Alex said, nodding encouragingly for the first time all night. "What was that like?"

"Oh, pathetic," he said, scowling.

"Why pathetic?"

"Listen, I don't mind if someone's gay. That's none of my business—"

There's a 'but' coming here, Alex thought.

"—but at least follow the frickin' rules. Follow orders. Christ. These guys knew the terms of their service, and they couldn't hold back. While the rest of us served, they went home. It wasn't very different from going AWOL if you ask me."

"So could you not hit on women when you served? Or have a relationship?"

Wildcat gripped another roll in his right hand and shoved it into his mouth. His chopsticks remained in their paper wrapper, untouched, off to his right. "Oh, I was happy to! Definitely! But I was *allowed* to—" He interrupted his own train of thought to wave down a young busboy walking past the table. "Hey! This beer was warm."

"I'm sorry, sir," the kid replied timidly.

"Don't be sorry," said Wildcat. "Just get me another one."

Alex bit her lip, appalled. She smiled politely at the busboy. "My wine is perfect."

He grinned meekly and walked away.

Alex turned back toward her date. "So what would you have done if being with women had been forbidden?"

"It would have been rough," he said, nodding thoughtfully, chewing more deeply, if that was possible. "But I followed my orders. In the military, you follow the rules. Without that, it all falls apart."

"It seems easier said than done when it comes to personal life."

"Nah. The military is all about sacrifices in your personal life. From the moment you get out of high school you give things up. And you don't question it. No exceptions. Even if you're gay."

"So what do you think now that the policy's gone?"

"It is what it is. Glad I'm retired and don't have to deal with it."

At least he was being honest now. "Could you forgive those who were kicked out?"

"Nah," he said. "It doesn't really change anything. The rules were clear, even if they changed later. They broke them and left us to fight. A discharge is a discharge."

The busboy delivered a new beer bottle to the table. "Here you go, sir."

Wildcat grabbed the uncapped bottle directly from his hand then turned back her way.

Alex kept her gaze on the busboy. "Thank you," she said, smiling. "We'll take two checks, please."

As miserable as it had been, the date had helped for two reasons. First, this blowhard probably reflected common disdain for those who'd violated Don't Ask, Don't Tell, even long after the policy's repeal.

Second, lesson learned. No more Top Guns.

* * *

HUNTSVILLE, TEXAS

The entire purpose of the return trip felt wrong to Cassie, so wrong she hadn't even told Rachel about it. And she told Rachel everything.

At the same time, Jack had a point. She was just tracking down a tip. Basic due diligence. Deciding how to cover it, or whether to cover it at all, would come later.

She walked into the Walls Unit at 3:45, and Jimmy appeared behind the window right at 4:00 and grabbed his phone.

"Hi, Ms. Knowles. You sure came back quickly. I hear you visited Mr. Gamble."

"Oh, did he mention that?" Cassie said, surprised.

"He sure did. Called Monday."

Probably in panic mode, thought Cassie. "Did he say anything?"

"Just never to trust the press. Not to say anything to you or anyone else."

"Anything about what?"

"I don't even know. About my case, I guess."

"But you still agreed to meet with me?"

"I don't get a lot of visitors. And I liked our last conversation. I feel like I can trust you."

Cassie smiled. This was a start. But the next step would be tougher—dredging up dirt from someone hell-bent on keeping it buried.

"Jimmy, I'm concerned about Mr. Gamble. He is not a criminal defense lawyer. Nor were the members of his team."

His expression hardened, but he remained calm. "I was frustrated by the trial, but he and his guys were really smart. Who else would have helped me?"

"Well, the state provides lawyers when you can't afford them."

"I know that. But when he called and offered to bring a bunch of smart Ivy League lawyers, how could I say no?"

"Right," Cassie said, nodding. "I'm just not convinced he had your best interest at heart. Our lawyer—the one we have at Republic—took a look at your case and agreed. He said his defense was incredibly weak, maybe even malpractice."

Cull paused, then slowly began shaking his head. "But why the hell would he have volunteered to help just to screw me?" he asked.

"That's what we're trying to figure out."

They sat silently, and Cassie hesitated. "Jimmy," she said tentatively, "we can't even verify that he was a veteran. There's no evidence that Gamble served in the military."

He threw up his huge hands and leaned toward the window. "But that was the entire reason he said he helped me!"

"I know. But we can't find any record of his service. And that wouldn't be hard—"

"—No DD-214?"

"Nope. I'm curious, Jimmy. Did he know that you knew Congressman Bravo when you started?"

"He didn't seem to. He came in fired up to defend me. The Bravo part only came up later."

"Like when?"

"Ma'am, I can't even remember."

"He told me it was when you guys swapped war stories."

He swatted the air with his right hand. "Swapped war stories? We talked about the war some during the trial, but that was it. The Bravo stuff and the pardon idea didn't come up til after. Why would it have come up during the trial? We thought I'd be found innocent. He only mentioned the possibility of a pardon after I was sentenced, on a call."

This made sense. Gamble's story from a few days ago did not.

"Ms. Knowles, what are you trying to get at?"

The door was now open—time to walk in. "It seems like Mr. Gamble might have been trying to keep you quiet about Bravo, using the pardon as a carrot."

"Keep quiet?"

"Yes. I don't know much about Congressman Bravo. You do. Is there something about his service that he or others would be protecting?"

Cull looked back warily. Then he lowered his hands to his hips and stared right into her eyes. "I told you," he said coldly. "I will never say anything to undermine Tony."

Cassie needed more, even if she hated pushing one friend to out another. "But there is something, isn't there?" she said gently. "My suspicion is that even though he screwed up your trial, Mr. Gamble wants you to protect Congressman Bravo."

More silence.

"Do you know he never sent the congressman anything about your pardon?"

"Did he say that?"

"He did."

Jimmy's shoulders sagged at the news. More silence. Then he leaned toward the glass. "Ms. Knowles, I don't think you understand the bond among soldiers. This goes way beyond my hope of a pardon or whatever Gamble might have been up to. Tony rescued me, leg half blown off, from a battlefield. Saved my life. I will not betray him."

His trust in Gamble had plummeted. And he was speaking as earnestly as a man could. Time to pop the question: "Jimmy, would it surprise you that Kroon's dad and brother think Tony was gay?"

His head shot backward as if Cassie had just jabbed him in the face.

"Yep," Cassie said. "They told us that. Does that surprise you?"

"Of course." But his answer lacked conviction. He was trying hard, but this supremely honest man was failing Cassie's polygraph.

"They said he was kicked out for Don't Ask, Don't Tell. That it's why he returned early."

"I wouldn't know. I was on my way home, without half my leg."

He patted his left knee as he said it, trying to change the subject.

"But would it surprise you if it was because of Don't Ask, Don't Tell?"

He pounded his fist against the small counter beneath the window, shaking both the window and her side of the counter. "I told you, I'm not saying anything to undermine my friend! Stop asking this stuff or I'm out of here."

He was about to walk. New approach. "Jimmy, you're responding as if I'm accusing Lieutenant Bravo of doing something wrong. I happen to be gay myself, married and everything." She held up her hand, wiggling her ring finger, and continued. "I think the policy was terrible. Outright discrimination. People kicked out for violating it were victims."

Cull sat, stone-faced, and then nodded slowly. "I never felt good when people got sent home for being who they were. They're fighting with us shoulder-to-shoulder one day, gone the next. We lost a lot of great men that way. Men that we needed. So stupid."

"Exactly."

"But that's not how a lot of people viewed it. It was a stain then, and still is now."

"So you think it would hurt Bravo?"

"I told you. I'm not going there."

He was done. "Okay. I understand. I really appreciate your time."

"I enjoyed last time better." His voice was much quieter now.

"I did too, believe me. Jimmy, I'd keep this all from Mr. Gamble."

"So now I can't even trust my own lawyer?"

She looked him in the eye, letting his question hang between them. That was also the moment she decided not to inform Jimmy of the worst news of all, something that hadn't occurred to her until George Vassos had reminded her. Cull had been convicted for murder, a state crime. Not even a President could pardon that.

* * *

Cassie, Alex, and I were on a conference call Friday morning to pool our findings on Bravo's platoon. I'd received bits and pieces from them while they were in the field, but I wanted to put it all in one place and see if it amounted to anything.

Alex went first. "The documents I found are vague," she said. "There's no doubt his DD-214 was changed, and that it was likely a discharge upgrade. But does it say why? No. And I don't think we're going to find a record that does. So that's a dead end."

Cassie agreed. "You know I don't like this story," she said. "But I still did my best to drag something out of Cull. His body language suggested he thought the Kroons may be right, but he wasn't going to go any further than that. Nothing to base a story on."

Nothing clear from the records. Nothing definitive from the only living platoon-mate. "And we're out of other people we can talk to?" I asked.

"Looks like it," Alex said. I expected her to gloat, but she seemed as disappointed as I was.

I shook my head. "Unbelievable. What a cursed bunch." The picture of the group had been on my desk for days, and I'd found myself staring at it constantly. "Okay. Let's pause for now. I'll give the Kroons a call and tell them we couldn't verify it. If they take it to someone else, so be it."

They'd done their jobs. Looked into it. Probably could do some more. But this was getting uncomfortable for them. And the trail was weak at best. Part of good journalism is chasing down every lead as far as it takes you. And another part is knowing when to spike a story. This one looked about done, and I knew my team sensed it.

Still, the ghosts in that photo kept nagging at me, challenging me to dig one layer deeper. But one thing was clear—I wasn't going to get anywhere chained to my desk or stuck behind the camera.

PART 2

CHAPTER 9

COLUMBIA, SOUTH CAROLINA

"A TOTAL COLLAPSE," I said dramatically, mic in hand.

The sun was setting in Charleston as the polls closed, and the fall of Governor Janet Moore looked more and more inevitable. My cameraman had carefully positioned my live stand-up so the copper dome and white granite columns of the Statehouse appeared behind me.

Bridget Turner spoke from our D.C. studio. "Jack, she's behind the other three by even more than we predicted. Not sure how she survives."

"And it looks like a tight race at the top," I added. "Congressman Bravo closed on Senator Stevens in the last few days. Nicholas is not too far behind them."

Over the next hour, the vote totals from across the state came in. About a percentage point every three minutes. Stevens hung on to win with 32% of the vote. Bravo closed at 28%. Nicholas at 25%. Moore brought up the rear at 15%.

"She's cooked," I said, getting ready to sign off. "After New Hampshire, who would have expected this?"

"Nobody," Turner said. "From the exit polling, it looks like Congressman Bravo took most of her votes. The young vet takes out the frontrunner. Amazing."

Moore's demise was hard to watch. No one in America was better prepared to be president than Colorado's governor, and here she was, buried at the bottom of the pack. Politics was rough, too often weeding out the best people for the job. And for all the wrong reasons. In front of the Colorado statehouse the next day, white-tipped mountains gleaming in the background, Governor Moore officially suspended her campaign.

* * *

WASHINGTON, D.C.

Cassie couldn't sleep. And it wasn't because she'd gone to bed tipsy, Rachel was snoring, or that she'd spent all night dancing in Adams Morgan. That was her usual Saturday night lineup, and she always slept soundly. It was the bouncer at the last bar. Huge guy. With a bronze bowling ball for a head, he'd looked just like Jimmy Cull. And after seeing him, Cassie couldn't stop thinking about Cull, sitting like a caged animal in that little box of a room.

Sure, she'd been eager to put the Bravo story behind her. Cull's unwillingness to say more had helped her get that done. But it looked like "Bus" had been railroaded. With or without the Bravo connection, this was a story unto itself. And that's what was keeping her up.

At 3:10, she abandoned her futile effort to sleep and walked into the kitchen in a white T-shirt and worn boxers. The T-shirt sleeves were so short, her second tattoo, the one above her left elbow, was on display. She glanced down at it as she lifted her laptop out of her backpack. 8.14.04.10.20. The thick, black numbers—etched in the fancy script that had felt appropriate at fifteen years old—ran up the inside of her left arm. Those digits had kept her going ever since.

Day or night, she always did her best work at the kitchen counter. So she took a seat and hopped online to dig deeper into Cull's trial.

Cull had lived in Temple, Texas, a city small enough, and proud enough of its veterans, that the murder itself had been big news. "Wife of decorated veteran murdered," read the front page of the *Temple Daily Telegram*, along with a photo of the happy couple. Cull looked sharp, dressed in full, formal Army attire—the paper's editors showing their hand that they stood with the local hero. But two days later, the narrative had already turned.

"Cull Questioned in Wife's Death."

It had only gone downhill from there. Stories, presumably leaked by the prosecution, had spilled details of barroom brawls, DUIs, and two reports of domestic violence. Unflattering mugshots had accompanied each new story, turning Cull into a public monster overnight. An out-of-control brute. Always drunk, often violent. The papers had convicted him before the trial even started, so the jury's verdict had surprised no one. The only public outrage had come when Cull was spared a death sentence. An entire page of letters to the editor blasted the two spineless jurors who had refused to budge.

As she perused the stories, Cassie typed out a long set of questions.

Beginning with her own family's case, she'd witnessed enough courtroom dramas to know how they usually went. Cull's trial team had made a number of head-scratching decisions. Why hadn't they asked to move the trial? So much hostile coverage guaranteed a tainted Bell County jury pool. Plus, the prosecutor's rhetoric had crossed the line. The opening and closing had both been over the top, yet no one from Cull's team had objected. Even without a law degree, she knew the prosecutor had gone too far a number of times. And why the hell had Cull testified? They'd torn him apart. Half the questions should have been objected to, but weren't. And then no appeal. Who doesn't appeal?

This was all malpractice at best. And it all went back to Gamble, the non-veteran corporate lawyer who'd leapt into the case.

She grabbed a Diet Coke from the fridge and pulled up a map of Texas. Temple was almost 200 miles from Houston. Not the same media market—not anywhere close. Even though Cassie found nothing in the Houston papers about the murder, Gamble and his team had begun speaking for and representing Cull within days of the crime. It didn't make any sense.

Originally from the suburbs of Houston, Dean Gamble had gone to Texas for undergrad, George Mason Law School, and then had clerked for a federal court in Texas before joining Baker & Strauss back in his hometown. There, he'd focused on government contracts, procurement law, and more general corporate work. He was listed as part of the D.C. office's government affairs team. No clients were listed, but he clearly handled big-dollar stuff. And from the trial coverage, she also got the names of the two associates who'd worked on Cull's case. Both were Harvard law grads, serving on Law Review and graduating Cum Laude. Three years out of school, one was now listed in the corporate law department, the other was no longer listed on the firm directory at all.

The caffeine from the Diet Coke wearing off, Cassie quickly looked into the Texas firm's D.C. outpost, a small seven-partner operation. Like Gamble, the partners were government affairs types representing a variety of clients and industry groups: banks, airlines, government contractors, and others. While the partner in charge, George Lyall, had clearly been around D.C. for decades, the office had only existed for seven years.

So much was out of place in this case. There was so much to dig into.

At least she now knew where to start. She was back in bed at 4:30, spooning Rachel as she fell asleep.

* * *

George Vassos strode to work from the Metro stop at a faster clip than usual.

Long ago, when he'd received his Georgetown Law diploma, his goal had been to make a difference. Surely, he'd thought, his rise against long odds—namely an iffy childhood on the hardscrabble streets of Queens—destined him to accomplish some grand and noble purpose. But his massive law school debts, later coupled with the addiction to his hefty year-end Big Law bonus to support his growing family, had trapped him. The client list had lengthened, the billable hours had grown, and the money had flowed in. But the noble purpose had never emerged.

Each year, he'd asked himself, Is this all my journey's about? Is this the endgame? But inevitably, he'd go back for more. Finally, the move to Republic had been a lifestyle change without the sacrifices that he'd always assumed he'd have to make. He was enjoying more time with his wife, his best friend in the world, while making the same fat salary. So what if he still felt purposeless most days?

But this SuperPAC story had rekindled his youthful yearning to matter. Something was going on. And the amount of money being spent meant it was something big.

Vassos spent his morning back on the trail of Americans for a Brighter Future. The question had nagged at him: how did 30-something Patricia Murphy land this whale of a client? The firm's website showed that she'd been at her family's firm since getting her law degree four years prior, doing little but in-state corporate work. Her brother Ray had pursued the same path three years ahead of her. A ho-hum law career, with no clear connection to anything bigger. What was the hook? Why were they entrusted with something so big? So political? Vassos poked further around the firm's website. Nothing shed light on that question.

Then he read the firm's history.

"Seven years ago, Ray Murphy joined his father, Ray Murphy Sr., to found their family's firm in their home state of Delaware. Ray Sr. combined his years of experience at a powerful Washington firm with Ray Jr.'s entrepreneurial spirit to create one of Wilmington's leading boutique firms. Ray and Patricia now lead the firm following their father's death."

"Powerful Washington firm" caught Vassos' eye. Ray Sr. must've been the hook.

As usual, his obituary included the most detailed account of his life. From Delaware originally, Ray Sr. had also gone to Delaware Law School, but unlike his kids, he'd descended to Washington following a short stint in the JAG corps. He'd spent fifteen years at a mid-caliber D.C. firm, then lateraled to a firm Vassos instantly recognized.

The Progress Group. *Now we're talking.*

The Progress Group had once been the powerhouse of D.C. lobbying. But the firm had shuttered almost a decade ago after a few senior partners cut one-too-many ethical corners. The others had scattered, which must have been when Ray Sr. had returned to Wilmington to join his son. So nothing would've been more important to the fledgling firm than dad's ties back to his former colleagues. Fortunately for the Murphys, Progress Group alumni were as well-connected as they come.

CHAPTER 10

WASHINGTON, D.C.

THREE DEAD PLATOON mates. A fourth in jail for life. What were the odds?

It was the day before Super Tuesday, 22 hours before the first polls would close. I finally had a free moment to piece together what we knew of Bravo's platoon—to make sense of the part that was nagging me. My team's research was spread across my desk. The photo I'd snapped lay off to the right. As I worked, I couldn't avert my eyes from the six faces staring up at me. Young and confident only a decade ago, their lives now over. Haunting. And as Alex had said weeks ago, perhaps the story itself.

Of course returning veterans struggled. With PTSD. Substance abuse. Homelessness and crime. A shocking rate of suicide. One of America's moral failures was how poorly we treated our vets. So on one hand, as tragic as they were, the struggles of Bravo's platoon didn't stand out from the norm. But as I pulled together the different strands of my team's work, one thing did.

The timing.

Two years ago, in early February, Dave Sesler died in that car accident.

Late February, the same year, Dontavius Jackson overdosed on the streets of Baltimore.

Audrey Cull was killed in March of the same year, leading to Jimmy's incarceration within weeks.

A month later, according to Alex, a bank robber shot Michael Choo dead.

These young men had survived the war. Whatever their demons, they'd gone on to survive for years after returning. But within three months of one another, they'd all met their tragic endings.

Except one.

I looked at the photo. At the smiling Lieutenant Bravo, the sole survivor. Unlike his fallen platoon mates, he was kicking ass, charging along a path that might even lead to the presidency. Amid the tragedies, a lottery winner.

I swiveled to my keyboard and conducted a quick search. Didn't take long to find. The headline ran across the front page of the *San Jose Mercury News*: "Congressman Bravo Exploring Presidential Run." Some local experts had thought it was too early for the congressman. A few party elders had claimed it was his time. His constituents had given him rave reviews. All standard stuff, along with two large photos of Bravo, one in uniform, one as a congressman.

But it was the date of the article that stuck out now.

May 4.

Two years ago. One month after the last of his platoon-mates was out of the picture.

* * *

"Ned Livingston here."

Good, Cassie thought. Not a voicemail. "Howdy, Ned how are you?" she asked.

"I'm fine." His voice was nasally and soft. "To whom am I speaking?"

"My name's Cassie Knowles. I'm from Republic News in Washington."

"Um, I don't really talk to reporters."

Only a few moments remained to keep him on the line. He looked like a real bookworm in his attorney profile photo. Unaccustomed to flattery, Cassie hoped, and likely susceptible to it. "As an associate, I don't imagine you do. But today's your lucky day! I'm doing a feature on law firms that dedicate a lot of time to pro bono work. We want to highlight you guys."

"You do?"

"Yes. We watched how much time you and your colleagues put into the Jimmy Cull case. Most firms would never do that. Good for you!"

"Um, that wasn't really up to me. But thanks, I guess."

He was still a sentence or two away from hanging up. Stroke him even more. Go big. "Can you tell me what it was like to defend a murder case?"

"I can't say much because of attorney-client privilege. But we sure did our best. I was new at the time. I'd always wanted to be part of a real trial."

"Because you're a corporate lawyer, right?" Cassie asked.

"Yeah. You don't see the courtroom from our side of things. So when the memo was sent around about this case, I jumped at the chance."

"How did you prepare yourself for such an important assignment? I mean, a man's life was at stake. A veteran, no less."

"Kristina and I—she was the other associate who did most of the work—we crammed our criminal law and evidence rules for weeks before the trial."

"So you worked all day on corporate law, and prepared for this trial at night? Bless your hearts." Cassie forced a smile as she said it, to make her words sound more sincere.

"Sure did. It was hard, but we did the best we could."

"I talked to Dean Gamble earlier. He obviously played the lead role though, right?"

"Of course, but you know how things work at a big firm. The associates do all the legwork and the partners get the glory. But he didn't know much about trying a criminal case either."

Come on out of that shell, Ned, Cassie thought. "So you did most of the trial prep work?"

"Uh-huh, we really did. By the time the trial started, we knew a lot more than Dean did."

"It was a shame that he was ultimately found guilty. But with you and Kristina, I mean you guys are both Ivy Leaguers, and you worked so hard, you've got to believe it was inevitable."

A pause. "We worked hard. So . . . yeah."

"So," Cassie said conspiratorially. "Do you think he was guilty?"

"I really don't. But it was such a tainted jury pool. We were fighting an uphill battle from the start."

"Couldn't you have moved the trial?"

"Well, you're getting into details I can't discuss. Like I said, we did the best we could." His tone had an edge to it. Not anger. Frustration.

"Who's we?"

"Me and Kristina."

"Not Dean?"

More hesitation. And then, reluctantly, he answered. "Of course, him too." His voice trailed off as he said it.

"Ned, again, it's commendable that you did the pro bono service as well as you did. Have you done any more pro bono trials since?"

"No. That was my one go. Truth is, trial work isn't for me. And losing when you think your client is innocent, that's a painful feeling. I don't want to go through that ever again. I'd rather review documents for weeks than that."

"How's Kristina doing?"

"She actually left the firm after the trial. Took the loss hard."

Cassie had already learned that online, but wanted to see his response. She had left Kristina Jones a message minutes before calling Livingston. "Did she really?"

"Yes. Like I said, we put all we had into that case. Losing was painful."

"Where is Kristina now?"

"Went to a small firm in Houston. She actually chose to go into criminal law after that."

"Wow," Cassie said. "Good for her. Listen, thanks so much, Ned. This has been really helpful. I'll follow up if I need to. Meantime, have a good one."

"Uh," Ned stammered, clearly alarmed that the conversation was ending where it was, and at everything he'd just said. "I'd like to—"

"Thanks again!" Cassie said cheerfully, and hung up.

She shook her head at Kristina Jones's career switch. *Next time, try going into criminal law* before *getting an innocent man convicted.*

* * *

"What the fuck you think you're doing?"

The call came from the same Houston area code Cassie had dialed an hour earlier.

"Excuse me? Who is this?" Cassie knew exactly who it was and why he was upset. But she played dumb.

"This is Dean Gamble from Baker & Strauss. Why are you harassing our associates? And what's this bullshit about featuring our pro bono work?"

"Just getting to the bottom of the Jimmy Cull case. Wanted to talk to others who worked on it."

"Haven't you already done enough damage?"

"Damage? What damage have I possibl—?"

"You mean you haven't heard?

The way he asked the question, Cassie sensed that terrible news was coming. She took a deep breath, prepared herself, and spoke slowly. "Heard what?"

"Jimmy Cull's dead!"

Her throat clenched. Dead? That giant of a man? "Are you serious?" she said, trying to remain calm. "What happened?"

"A guard found him hanging in his cell Sunday morning."

"Oh my God. That's terrible."

"Yes it is, Miss Knowles. And I hold you responsible."

"Why me?" she asked, although she knew exactly why.

"We know you visited him last week. He already was at his wit's end. Whatever you said clearly dashed whatever hopes he had of getting out. What did you tell him?"

"That's between us. And how did you know I visited him?"

"I'm his lawyer, remember? The warden told me when he informed he was dead. Whatever you told him, it led him to kill himself. He left a short note about how he'd given up all hope. That he couldn't face the hell of being there the rest of his life."

Cassie didn't know how to respond. Her hands, her whole body, trembled. Maybe it was true. Her questions might have convinced Jimmy that Bravo would never be president because his secret was coming out. Or maybe undermining Jimmy's confidence in his legal team had been the last straw. Either way, she'd crushed a fragile man's hope. And Jack Sharpe had forced her to do it, all for his bullshit story.

She tried to maintain an air of strength, sitting up straight in her chair, hoping to sound more authoritative. "Ned didn't mention he was dead."

"Ned doesn't even know! I didn't have the heart to tell him yet. I've been around a little longer than you, sweetheart. I try to think things through before shooting from the hip. Please do the same." He hung up.

Cassie put her phone down on her desk. She stared straight ahead into her small cubicle, swallowing hard as she pictured Cull's massive figure dangling in his cell. Here she was trying to take on the man, take down this high-rolling attorney, but she'd pushed so hard that Jimmy Cull had ended up dead. She didn't cry much, and steeled herself to avoid doing so now. But a mix of nerves and nausea welled up in the pit of her stomach. She reached for a waste basket under her desk, pulled it under her face, and gagged.

* * *

George Vassos spent the rest of his Monday retracing the disintegration of the Progress Group. Within months, dozens of its lobbyists and lawyers had scattered throughout the D.C. area and beyond. Somewhere in that network was the person who had referred little Murphy & Murphy the largest client in its short history.

When the Progress Group imploded, three partners had been indicted, and a number of others had retired outright, fat and happy. Like Ray Murphy Sr., others had left town to wind down their careers at a more relaxed pace. But most of the junior partners and top associates had lateraled to other D.C. offices, no doubt highly sought after for their thick Rolodexes. To ferret out those with the best political connections, Vassos focused on the lobbyists.

One firm stuck out. It was called DGA, and all four founders had come from the Progress Group, making it the largest combination of former Progress Group partners. DGA was short for Doherty, Graham and Allison, but the "D" was clearly the rainmaker of the group. A quick search found that Steve Doherty had long been one of Washington's high-octane lawyers and lobbyists. He had all the trappings of a D.C. insider, mastering the revolving door of public and private sector pedestals in the Capitol. Alfalfa Club. Council on Foreign Relations. Think tank boards.

Doherty had worked in the Foreign Service before going to Georgetown Law School, four years ahead of Vassos himself. He'd then joined the Progress Group, working there for years. He'd served in a few Pentagon civilian posts during the Bush presidency, then back to the Progress Group, then had co-founded DGA with Mr. Graham and Mr. Allison.

From that perch, Doherty had played a policy advisor role in the successful Elizabeth Banfield presidential campaign, while also raising millions for the winning effort. When she'd won the White House, he clearly could have grabbed a senior slot in the administration or at the Pentagon. But he'd stayed with DGA instead, cashing in. Trade journals described how DGA had leveraged Doherty's connections to line up clients with hefty contracts to produce ships, airplanes, and trucks for the military, then expanded into new technologies. Then, three years ago—the year after the president's reelection—Doherty had fallen completely off the grid. DGA remained, but its founding partner was no longer there, or anywhere. No activity. No articles. No digital footprint whatsoever. But also no indication that he had passed away.

So DGA's partners had been contemporaries of Ray Murphy Sr. at the Progress Group. They were big fish, connected to people with real money, with a major interest in the outcome of the presidential election. And their main partner had now gone dark. Doherty and DGA had to be the tie back to Americans for a Brighter Future. But there was only one way to find out. George dialed the number he'd called the week before.

"Murphy and Murphy," the same receptionist answered.

"I'd like to speak with Patricia Murphy."

"She's on a call right now. May I take a message?"

"Sure. Please tell her Steve Doherty wants to speak to her. Tell her it's important news on ABF."

"One second, Mr. Doherty . . . ," The phone clicked. "She'll take your call." The phone clicked again.

The voice from their last call came on the line, far friendlier this time. "Is everything okay, Steve? How can I help you?"

Vassos hung up.

* * *

Another Houston area code flashed on Cassie's phone. Still shaken by the news on Cull, and desperate to learn more, she answered.

"I'm looking for Cassie Knowles," a smooth Southern female voice said over the phone.

"This is she."

"This is Kristina Jones. Returnin' your call."

"Kristina. Thanks for calling back. I'm looking into the Jimmy Cull case. And the representation Baker & Strauss provided to him."

"Oh." Then silence.

"Are you comfortable talking about it?"

"I signed a non-disparagement agreement when I left the firm. So I can't say much about the case."

"What can you say?"

More silence. "Off the record?"

"Of course."

"Still not much. I can't violate that agreement. I left the firm after the case, which tells you all you need to know." Jones' accent was so thick—*tells y'all y'need t'know*—that sometimes it took Cassie a second to understand her.

But she wanted to say more. So Cassie stayed quiet, letting her fill the silence.

"I'm not gonna lie. I'm now a criminal defense lawyer because I'm heartsick havin' watched an innocent man go to jail for life. I still have nightmares about it."

"So you're sure he was innocent?"

"Heck yes, I'm sure."

"Knowing what you know now, would you defend him diff—"

"I told you. I can't talk about that."

Cassie looked up and across the newsroom, thinking. Like a lawyer at trial, she'd have to get around the objection. "Let me rephrase it this way: If you were first chair in a similar case now, do you think you could get someone in the same predicament off?"

"What predicament, exactly?"

Good. She was playing along. "Let's see. No direct evidence. A hostile community. An overzealous prosecutor."

"Oh, yes. I could get that person off. Any aggressive defense lawyer could."

"Would you push for a change of venue? Move the trial?"

"Of course. No-brainer."

"Would you put the defendant on the sta—"

"No. Never. Far too risky."

"How about if a prosecutor told a jury they could 'send a message' to the community by convicting your client?"

"I'd object, and I'd win that objection. Clear prosecutorial abuse."

"Is that what most criminal lawyers would do?"

"Any good one would. Not doing so would be malpractice."

"And would you appeal a conviction?"

"Of course. 'Nother no-brainer."

"So why would anyone not do all those things?"

"There would be absolutely no reason. No *good* reason, at least. None at all."

"That's all helpful," Cassie said. "Thank you. Have you talked to Jimmy since the case?"

"I haven't. I had to agree not to communicate with him going forward. Or involve myself in any future proceedings."

Cassie couldn't help herself. "Why would they insist on that?"

"You'll have to ask 'em. Read into it what you will."

"Kristina, I have some bad news for you, if you haven't already heard."

"Oh no," she said immediately, her voice cracking.

"Jimmy was found dead two days ago."

"No! Oh my—"

Cassie heard a sharp intake of breath, then faint sobbing.

"What . . . What happened?"

"I just heard the news myself. Don't know much. They said he was found hanging in his cell. And left a note."

"Are they tryin' to say suicide?" Jones said shakily.

"It seems like it. That he'd lost all hope."

"That's bullshit," she said, suddenly angry. "As bad as things got, Jimmy would never have killed himself. He was a strong man, and at the end of the day, an optimist. More than that, he was a proud survivor of Iraq when so many others didn't make it back. Out of respect for those he served with, he would never have taken his life later. Never."

The words buoyed Cassie. Maybe it wasn't her fault. "So you think it's foul play?"

"I have no idea. All I know is Jimmy Cull would not have killed himself. Can I ask why you even know about him?" Kristina said. "About his case? Why would you be reporting on Jimmy Cull?"

"He was in the same platoon as Congressman Anthony Bravo, who's running for president. We're simply trying to learn more about the congressman's time in the service."

"Really? Bravo? I love that guy. Heck, I just voted for him. I had no idea they were in the service together."

That's right, Cassie thought. Texas was voting today. "Are you serious?" she asked. "Jimmy never mentioned it?"

"Not through the trial. He didn't say much about his service. I knew he was hurt in Baghdad, and that's about it."

"Well, Dean Gamble seemed to know about it."

"Ned and I spent a lot more time with Jimmy than Dean ever did, and he never told us."

"Either way, that's why we were talking to Jimmy. But over the course of our conversations the whole trial began to seem a little odd."

"I still can't say more on that. But I'll put it this way—keep diggin'. And maybe that connection to the congressman explains it all. Odd is an understatement."

* * *

"Fasten your seat belts, America. Tonight is going to be a wild ride," Bridget Turner said as our Super Tuesday coverage kicked off.

It was 6:30 p.m., and we were both sitting in studio. We had half an hour to frame the night before the results started flying in. The biggest delegate hauls would be Massachusetts, Georgia, Virginia, and Texas. But they were just the beginning. A treasure trove of delegates was up for grabs in the South—Alabama, Arkansas, Oklahoma, and Tennessee—along with Colorado, Minnesota, Vermont, North Dakota. And sometime in the morning, we'd hear from Alaska.

"We know Senator Stevens has some advantages tonight, just as in South Carolina," Bridget said. "Those Southern states should help him, shouldn't they?"

"You'd think so, but he's taken a lot of incoming attack ads ever since Moore dropped out."

"Any idea who's behind them?"

"Unfortunately, the laws really allow them to conceal who they are and who's paying for them." George Vassos had filled me in earlier on the slow pace of his investigation. His verdict: not enough to report anything. Yet.

"Jack, Colorado, North Dakota, and Minnesota are all caucus states. How does that change things?"

"The turnout in those states will be low, so whoever's most organized usually wins. Moore had a great operation, which helped her win Iowa. So this will be the first real test of who else has a strong ground game."

"And the question for all the states," Bridget said, "is who will pick up most of Governor Moore's votes."

"That's the big unknown. Bravo picked up a bunch in recent weeks, but where will the rest go? Who knows?"

By 7:00 p.m., we did.

"Something's shifting," I announced as soon as we could talk exit polls. "It looks like Governor Nicholas is picking up some steam."

"In what states?"

"Everywhere."

Nicholas had leapt ahead in Massachusetts with 45%. Bravo was second at 30%. Stevens followed with 25%. The three were tied in Boston, but Nicholas won big in western Mass. The Massachusetts pattern repeated elsewhere throughout the night. In neighboring Vermont, Nicholas reached the low 40s, well ahead of the other two. In Georgia, while Stevens won as expected, it was tight. He garnered 38%, while Bravo and Nicholas were tied at 31%. Virginia also reflected Nicholas movement. He finished slightly ahead of Bravo, 39-35. Stevens was way back.

"It looks like that last debate and Moore's exit really boosted Governor Nicholas," I explained to the TV audience. "While the others were squabbling, he stepped up and called for unity." I hated giving him credit for what was a blatantly insincere move, but it had worked.

Bridget jumped in. "Let's see if that continues for the upcoming states."

It did. Same pattern. Stevens won Alabama and Arkansas, with Nicholas not far behind and Bravo way back. But Nicholas edged both of them out in Oklahoma and Tennessee. With huge support from Hispanics, Bravo won Texas with 50% of the vote, scoring the biggest delegate haul of the night. But in the states with caucuses, Nicholas prevailed. He won easily in Vermont, Colorado, and North Dakota.

By a little past 11:00, the theme of the night was clear.

"All three candidates picked up delegates tonight," I said. "They each won states. But Nicholas won the night. His momentum in South Carolina has catapulted him to unexpected wins across the country."

"Can you explain why?" Bridget asked.

"Three things seem to be happening. With Moore out, and the blowback against Bravo for those ads, Nicholas seems to be picking up a lot of her votes. Stevens and Bravo are splitting the minority votes. And it looks like Nicholas has the best ground operation when it comes to caucuses."

The last point surprised me. There had been no activity indicating that Nicholas had a strong operation in caucus states. Would have to look into that.

"Sounds like a nice combination for him," Bridget said.

"I'll say. Maybe the winning combination."

At last, three hours later, Alaska came in. The final caucus of the day.

Nicholas won easy.

CHAPTER 11

BALTIMORE, MARYLAND

THE THREE-INCH NEEDLE was still sticking out of Dontavius Jackson's tattooed arm when the firefighter had dragged him out of the Taco Bell bathroom.

The grisly police photo of the husky, lifeless body did more to wake me up than the black coffee I'd been downing all morning. I'd taken an early train ride north and was sitting at a small desk in Baltimore police headquarters, reviewing Jackson's file. The completion of Super Tuesday finally allowed me to dig into the downfall of Bravo's platoon.

A cook on break had found Dontavius in the bathroom stall, and the first responders had arrived quickly. A firefighter had injected Narcan, but even that miracle drug had not revived him. His forearm looked like a pin cushion, meaning he'd shot a lot of heroin and should have had a high tolerance. But the toxicology report explained why he'd overdosed anyway: Dontavius had not injected standard heroin. Knowingly or not, his final hit had involved a lethal cocktail of heroin laced with its far more powerful, synthetic cousin.

"That fentanyl was more lethal than any we had seen before," said Dr. Juanita Brown, the chemical specialist who'd signed Jackson's report, as I sat in her office. "Someone went to town making that batch. Would've killed an elephant."

Nasty stuff. When I'd left Ohio, county morgues had been struggling to keep up with the spike of overdose deaths resulting from new synthetic painkillers like fentanyl and carfentanyl. A single dealer could spark dozens of overdoses across a community. A few years back, one bad batch in Akron had killed eight people in three days.

"Did the batch turn up in other bodies?" I asked.

"No, thank God. We had other overdoses in the weeks that followed, but none showed traces of that mix."

"Surprising."

"Definitely. And a relief. Must've been an isolated sale, or Mr. Jackson brought it from elsewhere."

"Would that be typical?" Of course it wouldn't be, but I wanted to hear her explain it.

She shook her head. "Not at all. Dealers usually sell to their whole network. And the reason you find people dying in restaurant bathrooms is because they take the hit almost immediately after buying. They're so hooked they can't wait. So traveling would not be typical."

Plus, Jackson was destitute. No way he was traveling far. "Were there any other baggies of heroin found on him?"

"Nope. That poison he stuck in his arm was all he had."

"And you never found the dealer who sold it?"

"No. The cops pushed hard given the risk of an outbreak. But they never tracked it down."

As I got up to leave, an image of Mrs. Jackson flashed in my head. She had said it was the war that killed her grandson. An understandable sentiment—it certainly played a role in his demise. But the coup de grace had come from a single dose of a drug designed to kill, sold only to him.

Dontavius Jackson had his problems. Maybe he'd been on the road to a short life either way. But his death looked to be a well-disguised hit.

* * *

WASHINGTON, D.C.

Looking up from the next urinal over, the bespectacled, combed-over lawyer craned his head, eyes wide with surprise.

"Brent?" George Vassos repeated from a foot away, big smile on his face.

They stood side by side in the Old Ebbitt Grill's bathroom—a fancy one: mints, bow-tied attendant and all. Vassos had tried to meet with Brent Graham at his law firm, but had been shooed away twice. This was one place the slippery lawyer couldn't escape without risking a mess.

"Who wants to know?" Graham asked. It was not a friendly response.

"It's Al Chambers. We met a few years ago."

"Did we?" Graham asked, frowning.

"We sure did. I'm good friends with Steve Doherty. We were classmates from law school. I bumped into you guys a couple years ago."

Vassos had tracked down the name of one of Doherty's Georgetown Law classmates. No idea if they were acquainted—it's a big school—but if they researched it, the name Albert Chambers would at least check out.

Graham turned back toward the wall in front of him, facing slightly down, as did Vassos. The challenging part of this strategy was that men aren't comfortable engaging in long urinal-to-urinal conversations.

Silence and a slight shaking signaled Graham was wrapping up, so Vassos did as well. They both approached the sink. Vassos did a double take as he looked at himself in the mirror, hardly recognizing his clean-shaven face. Then he looked at Graham's reflection, and restarted the conversation as he pumped the soap.

"How is Steve anyway? I've been meaning to call him. I've got a major client I might want your team's help on."

No better way to catch a lawyer's attention than dangling a substantial client his way. But Graham didn't bite. "He's no longer with us. He left a couple years ago." As he answered, he smoothed long strands of dark hair forward from the back of his head, in an apparent attempt to cover his shiny bald head.

"Is that right?" Vassos asked. "What's he up to?"

Graham stopped combing, and turned from the mirror to look directly at Vassos. Sizing him up. "He went in-house with one of our clients."

"Maybe you guys could help me out then. It's a major matter."

"Involving?" he asked, finally curious.

"A large contractor is looking to sell its latest vehicle to the Army. A light supply truck. Big opportunity."

"Sure. We can talk about it. You have a card?" he asked, completing his comb-over with the focus of a surgeon.

"I don't. Why don't you give me yours and I'll follow up."

Graham pulled a business card out of his pants pocket.

Vassos returned once again to his old classmate. "I'll get Steve to vouch for me. What company's he with?"

Graham shot back another stern look. "I'm not at liberty to say."

"I see. Classified stuff. I understand."

Graham said nothing as they walked out of the bathroom.

Vassos, trailing behind, stopped in front of the attendant.

"Mint?"

* * *

TEMPLE, TEXAS

Cassie stepped into the rundown coffee shop and spotted a thin brunette in a corner booth.

"Are you Kristina?" Cassie asked.

"I sure am," Kristina Jones replied in a mild drawl, beaming a pretty smile. "Cassie, I presume. Welcome to Texas."

"I wish it were for a better reason."

"Me too."

For the third time in weeks, Cassie was back in the Lone Star State. The Cull family had taken possession of Jimmy's body to arrange a proper funeral, and today was the day. Since Kristina also planned on attending, she and Cassie had arranged to meet an hour before the reception.

"You learn any more about his death?" Cassie asked after sitting down.

"Not really. I'm hoping to talk to his family today and see if they know anything. And who knows who else will show?"

"Is Ned coming, from Baker?"

Kristina shrugged her shoulders. "I figured this would be a lot easier if Dean wasn't here, so I didn't tell him. And I doubt the family reached out to them."

Good call, Cassie thought.

When they'd finished their Cokes, Kristina drove them through the modest streets of Temple, which looked like so many other small towns Cassie had covered in recent years. Then they pulled into the funeral home. If he had died in Iraq, Jimmy Cull would have been buried as a hero, parade and all. But the parking lot of the funeral home was nearly empty.

After walking through the main door, Kristina led the way over to a bearded, heavyset man in a black suit that was sizes too small. He looked a lot like Jimmy, just inches shorter.

"John, I am so sorry," Kristina said softly.

He smiled, then reached out for an embrace. Kristina practically disappeared into his corpulent frame. "You're sweet to come, honey," he said. "Y'all—you and Ned—fought hard for Jimmy. Y'all really believed in him." *Yer sweet ta come home. Y'all fawt hard fer Jimmy.* He had the deepest Texas accent Cassie had ever heard.

"I did," Kristina said. "And I still do. How're your folks?"

"We were shocked when we heard the news. But the way we look at it, Jimmy died when Audrey was killed, and died again when he was sentenced. Big bro was a warrior. He wasn't meant to live in a cage."

"That's true. But John, you and I both know Jimmy would not have killed himself."

John hesitated and looked over at Cassie.

"Let me introduce you," Kristina said. "John, this is Cassie Knowles from Republic News. She's a fr—"

A sour look swept across his face. "And why the hell are you here? You were the one harassing my brother."

"I wasn't—" Cassie said.

Kristina raised her hand. "John, she's a friend. We've talked a lot. You know I wouldn't have brought her here otherwise."

"But—"

"After all we've been through, don't you trust me?" Kristina asked slowly, calmly placing her hand on his shoulder.

He paused, nodded, then turned back to Kristina. "We can't imagine he would've killed himself either. But who knows what the hell happens—" He stopped talking and looked past Kristina toward the parlor's foyer. "Wow, Warden Crawford himself just walked in."

A tall, gray-haired man strolled into the room. With his wide, white mustache, tan three-piece suit, bola tie, and dark cowboy boots, the man was right out of a Texas postcard. Cassie couldn't help but smile—this was exactly why she'd made the trip. She never would've had a chance to engage the warden of the Walls Unit formally, yet here he was.

With all eyes on him, the warden strode across to one corner of the room, shaking the hands of an elderly couple. Their appearance—both large, the woman even taller than the man—made it plain that they were Cull's parents. Minutes later, the warden approached Kristina, John, and Cassie. He reached out to John and grasped his hand.

"I'm deeply sorry," he drawled. "Jimmy Cull was a fine man." *Ah'm deeply sorra. Jimmy Cull was a fahn man.* His twang rivaled John's. "My men liked him. They respected him. Respected his service to our nation."

"Thank you, warden. We're honored you would come."

"I wanted to pay my respects. I served in the Airborne myself."

John and Kristina nodded silently, and an awkward pause ballooned among the four of them.

"Warden, we were just talkin'," Kristina said. "Were you surprised he would take his life?"

"Darlin', this is not the place—"

"Warden," John cut in. "It's fine. I'm curious too."

"Well," he said uncertainly. "Then, yes, I was surprised. He didn't seem the type. But y'all would never believe how the Walls can affect a man. I've seen other suicides that I never would've predicted either."

Cassie kept quiet, avoiding eye contact. He'd clam up if he knew she was press.

The warden posed his own question. "Have y'all talked to his lawyer from Houston?"

John and Kristina shook their heads. "No, sir," John said. "Why do you ask?"

"From what I can gather, he was the last person Jimmy talked to. He stopped by Saturday morning. I reckon he knows what was botherin' Jimmy. Our guard said they had one intense conversation."

Cassie fought back her urge to react, but Kristina didn't hide her surprise. "Dean Gamble visited Jimmy the day he died?"

The warden's sleepy eyes opened wide. "He sure did. Y'all didn't know that?"

John looked over to Kristina. "No, I didn't."

"I'm surprised he's not here," the warden added.

"I'm not," John said angrily. "That slick lawyer didn't give a shit about my big brother. He never fought for him."

The warden nodded. "I was surprised he came by to visit at all. We hadn't seen him in more than a year."

Cassie desperately wanted to ask questions, but couldn't. Fortunately Kristina understood the dilemma and kept the inquiries coming. "How did he respond when you told him Jimmy was dead?"

"We only call immediate family for deaths in our prison. So we wouldn't have talked to him. We leave it to the family to tell others."

"Not even his lawyers?"

"No, ma'am. We have a strict family-only policy. John, you and your parents are the only ones we told."

"Yes, sir. We got the call Sunday morning. But we've kept it in the family."

"There you go, darlin'," the warden said, turning back to Kristina. "Y'all should call Mr. Gamble and see what he says. See what Jimmy told him that Saturday morning."

A mournful tune signaled the onset of the service. The warden lowered his head as he stepped away. "Again," he said, "my deepest condolences."

* * *

WASHINGTON, D.C.

George Vassos rapped his fingers on the wood desk as he waited in the DGA conference room Friday morning. Something was wrong.

He had called Graham's number Wednesday afternoon as he'd promised, scheduling today's visit. In the meantime, the digital team at Republic had set up a phony website to complete his cover. The real Chambers was mired in a small law firm in Kansas City, but the new website would pop up first in case anyone checked.

The receptionist had chewed her lower lip as she led Vassos to the conference room, signaling trouble from the get-go. And now he'd been sitting there for close to half an hour.

A short, stocky man finally ended the silence, walking through the door. A bowl-cut of brown hair capped his ruddy, pock-marked face. This was not Graham or Allison. And he was not smiling. This guy was security. Major league security.

"Sir, who are you?" the man asked.

The hostile question forced a quick decision. Keep lying, or fess up. This early in the conversation, lying felt like the right move. "I'm Albert Chambers," Vassos said. "I'm here to meet with Mr. Graham. We arranged it the other day."

"We know that's bullshit. You know that's bullshit. Who are you?"

Was he bluffing? It still wasn't clear. "Like I told Mr. Graham, I'm an old friend of Steve Doherty, I met Mr. Graham through him, and was trying to track him down for a big project. Maybe I should talk to Steve directly? He'll explain it."

The big guy crossed his arms. "Mr. Doherty has no recollection of you."

"We weren't best friends. We overlapped. Jesus, I was offering to bring work here!"

The man looked at him quizzically, then glimpsed down at his phone. Someone was watching. Instructing.

Vassos gestured down to his large gut and smiled. "Listen, I don't look like I did back then. Let me talk to Steve and we'll figure it out."

The goon looked down at his phone again. "You're not talking to anyone." His tone made it clear a decision had been reached. "You're done here. You can walk out with me, or we can call the police. Your call."

No way this guy was calling the cops.

"This is outrageous. Where the hell is Mr. Graham?"

The man shook his head and stepped toward Vassos. "You can't say I didn't warn you."

Vassos stood, holding up both hands, palms out. In three quick motions, the man grabbed Vassos' right arm, twisted it down and back, and spun him around. Vassos cried out as the pain shot through him. It felt like his forearm was about to twist out of its elbow socket.

"What the fuck? What kind of a law firm is this? Let go of me!"

"You agree to leave, and I won't break your arm."

"Okay, okay. I'm leaving."

The twisting pressure on his arm eased, but the man still gripped it firmly above the elbow, bent behind his back. He pushed Vassos out the conference room door and along a different hallway than the one he'd come in, away from the front lobby. Good. The new route at least would offer a second opportunity to check out the place.

Every firm in Washington proudly displayed its Beltway trophy case—photos of partners plastered on walls, yukking it up with politicians, ambassadors, and other D.C. bigshots. And even though he had left, the short, mousy Steve Doherty was at the center of this firm's display. In one, Doherty stood with Henry Kissinger. Another with Colin Powell. Then came both Bushes, both Clintons, and two with President Banfield and her husband. A number of foreign leaders and longtime Senate leaders also made appearances. Sometimes they were in formal settings. Other were more leisurely: fishing, golfing, hunting, tennis. Usually, the photographs were signed by the most famous subject of the photo, the true value of each trophy.

"Good to be with you, Steve," signed Kissinger.

"Thanks for your friendship, Steve," wrote Bush 41.

"I wouldn't be here without you," signed President Banfield.

Vassos, who'd been in countless D.C. law firms, studied this boutique's display of major-league access. But it was one of the least prominent photos that stuck out most, and made the whole painful trip worth it.

Near the firm's back entrance, amid a series of dated photos with people he didn't recognize, Vassos looked past it at first. But two large, eight-point buck caught his eye. Impressive. Next to them, looking ten years or so younger, knelt Steve Doherty, a rifle over his shoulder.

Then Vassos noticed the second hunter, kneeling on the other side of the two deer from Doherty. He was more fit than your typical politician, and his crew cut and square jaw made him look tough as nails. It took a moment, but then he recognized him. Not because of how important the politician had been at the time—just a back bencher in the House of Representatives then—but because how relevant he was at the present.

And the signature on the photo confirmed it: "Good shootin', Steve. Come back often. Pete."

Kneeling in the photo, also gripping a rifle, was a smiling Pennsylvania congressman, soon to be elected governor of Pennsylvania, still sporting the same crewcut today.

Peter Nicholas.

Seconds later, Vassos' large chaperone shoved him through the back exit. "You can take the back stairs to get out. Don't come back." The door slammed behind him.

The eight-story descent taxed his out-of-shape legs and back, so much that when he got to the bottom, he limped through the stairwell door and into the lobby. But neither the pain nor the odd looks from passersby wiped the big smile from his face.

Finally, a breakthrough.

CHAPTER 12

WASHINGTON, D.C.

"WRONG PLACE, WRONG time. You see it all the time around here." The NYPD 33rd precinct's deputy investigator chomped on a piece of gum as we chatted on the phone. I could hardly hear him over the din of cops talking, eating and laughing in the background.

Nice guy, but his answer made no sense.

"What do you mean, wrong place, wrong time?" I asked. "He was a security guard, shot on duty."

A colleague from New York had faxed me the file. Michael Choo had been working the main security desk of the Century Building in midtown Manhattan when an escaping bank robber had shot him dead.

"Security?" said the investigator. "Nah. After 9/11, you can't get into a building without showing your ID at the front desk. So they've dressed a bunch of people up in uniforms to sign people in. Good gig, yes. Security? No." The smacking of his lips as he chewed was nearly as loud as his actual words. "The funny thing is that bank had its own security guard. The perp had already gotten past him, and was in good shape for a clean getaway. But then he ups and shoots your man. I'm tellin' ya, wrong place, wrong time."

He was right. The robber could have run back out the bank's main entrance onto Sixth Avenue. Instead, he'd used the inside exit, which headed into the building lobby where Choo was posted. A much tougher escape route versus a crowded street.

"Where was he hit?"

"Right between his frickin' eyes. Can you believe it? That perp was either lucky or a hell of a shot."

"Any witnesses see the shooting?"

"It happened so quickly no one saw it. People heard it, saw the perp run, then saw Choo lyin' in a pool of blood. And then, like good New Yorkers, they kept walkin'." He laughed.

"Was Choo's gun out?"

"Nah. It was still in his holster. Poor sucker."

"And you never figured out who did it?"

"Nope. That's the funny thing. Most small-time robberies like that are a hot mess—an addict needing quick money, sloppy as hell. But this perp was a pro. He knew how to keep from being recognized, avoiding the cameras. And then he just disappeared."

He paused.

"That poor guy survived three tours in Iraq, but died in New York for a measly eight grand."

I thanked him and shook my head as I ended the call. He'd captured the tragedy of it all perfectly. But he'd misread the motivation. The bank wasn't the prime target of the crime. Michael Choo was.

* * *

RICHMOND, VIRGINIA

"Logan is missing."

"Excuse me?" I asked.

"Our son Logan is missing."

I found myself at a diner north of Richmond, looking at the stressed faces of Earl and Francine Kroon. The couple that had been so hostile the first time was now desperate for help, having called me three hours before and insisted that we meet in person.

"What happened?" I asked.

"He just disappeared," Mrs. Kroon said, shuddering. "Three days after we last talked."

"Where did you last see him?"

Old Earl Kroon spoke up. Far more politely than at Scuppers.

"I talked to him shortly after you told me you weren't doing the story. He was angry."

I paused, looking sheepishly at Mrs. Kroon.

"Don't worry," she said softly. "I know."

"You do?" I asked.

"Yes," she said, gesturing toward her husband, gently placing her thin, wrinkled hand over his. "As he now understands, I know a lot more than my husband does, and have for a long time. A mother knows her boy, let's leave it at that."

Mr. Kroon sat quietly. They'd clearly had a heart-to-heart about their son.

She continued. "We think Logan called another reporter to push the story. Maybe more than one. And then no word from him in days. No one has seen him at work, and there's no trace of him at home."

"Do you know who he called?"

Mr. Kroon spoke up. "He was gonna call that Stone guy from FOX News. The one we like. But that's the last we heard from him."

Jesus, not Rob Stone. He'd run hard with a tip like this. "So what can I do to help?"

"You're an investigative reporter," Mr. Kroon said, leaning forward. "We figured you'd know what to do."

Appreciating the newfound respect, I leaned in, lowering my voice.

"Have you noticed anyone suspicious lately? Since we first started talking?"

"I can't say that I have," Mr. Kroon said. "And we would notice. Not a lot happens in our neighborhood."

"Logan's call might've triggered something. You probably should head out of town for a bit. This may get dangerous."

"Okay. What about Logan?"

"Rob Stone's an old friend. I'll check with him, see what they talked about, and see what he did with the information."

Mr. Kroon reached out and gripped my hand. "Thank you," he said quietly.

* * *

WASHINGTON, D.C.

Crotchety George Vassos may have finally earned his keep. Governor Nicholas was vaulting to the lead thanks to the SuperPAC's blitz of attack ads. And thanks to George's handiwork, we now knew that Nicholas went back years with some bigshot lobbyist connected to those ads. This was our best lead so far.

But one hunting photo only proved so much. How deep was the connection between Steve Doherty and Governor Nicholas? In politics, the best way to measure that connection—financial support—is just an online search away. With a few free hours before a scheduled flight, I dug in myself.

Before being elected Pennsylvania's governor, Nicholas had served three terms in Congress. Four times in those six years, Steve Doherty of the Progress Group had donated the maximum allowed to the Nicholas for Congress Committee: $10,800 in total. Pretty standard for Washington.

But that was just the start.

On each of the four occasions Doherty gave, ten other Progress Group partners also had contributed. This meant that the Progress Group either had been "bundling" checks, collecting them from numerous others, or they'd been hosting an event for the congressman.

Next, I looked to see what other checks had come on the same day as the Progress Group checks. These would likely reflect more Progress Group fundraising. Not surprisingly, Progress Group days had been big days for Nicholas's campaign coffers. Dozens of checks had come from executives and corporate PACs from across the country. Booz Allen. Halliburton. Airspan. Boundary. Blackwater. General Aviation. Bell Helicopters. DroneTech. Patriot Technologies. Dynacorp. And others.

I recognized some of the names and double-checked the others. It was the *Who's Who* of the defense contractor world: law firms, engineering firms, equipment manufacturers, lobbyists. And each time Nicholas ran, they'd piled hundreds of thousands of dollars upon him. These outfits would only give at such a high and consistent level for one reason, and a quick search confirmed it: within weeks of his first election, Nicholas had snagged a plum seat on the Defense Subcommittee of the House Appropriations Committee. There, Nicholas and his colleagues had doled out billions of dollars in defense contracts to the very firms that supported his campaigns so generously. The first checks had arrived only a month after Nicholas joined the committee. The rookie's new friends had thrown him a welcome party almost immediately. And that friendship and support had only grown during his time on the Hill.

So that was a decade ago. What since? I'd never researched Pennsylvania campaign filings before, but the Pennsylvania site was as easy to navigate as the federal website. Notably, around the time Nicholas ran for governor, Steve Doherty had gone dark, along with a number of other Progress Group principals. But the network of donors Doherty had brought together pumped in more campaign cash than ever. When Nicholas first ran for governor, they'd ponied up $800,000 for his campaign. For his reelection, they'd pulled together $1.3M. With no contribution limits in Pennsylvania, checks had come in all sizes. $1,000. $5,000. A number of $10,000 and $25,000 checks. One had reached $50,000.

Given the millions it takes to run in Pennsylvania, their support would have provided a major advantage over other candidates. And for the contractors, supporting that initial governor run made sense. Even as he ran, Nicholas still sat on the armed services subcommittee, and still voted on their contracts. And he would owe them more than ever. But ponying up for his reelection campaign made less sense. As governor, he could no longer help them. And Lord knows they don't give out campaign checks as thanks for past favors.

No, this was neither generosity nor a thank-you. It was an investment. An investment for the future. For another office, one from which Pete Nicholas could provide an exponential return.

CHAPTER 13

CINCINNATI, OHIO

I ALMOST PUKED AT the sight.

The photos of Dave Sesler's cadaver were worse than any horror movie I'd seen. Only a few slivers of skin and tendons connected the upper and lower halves of his neck.

I'd snuck away Thursday afternoon to complete my scavenger hunt through the wreckage of Bravo's platoon, and now sat in a small cubbyhole in the Hamilton County Sheriff's Department in downtown Cincinnati. Even though Sesler had lived in Indiana, he'd crashed just over the Ohio border, so this large sheriff's department had jurisdiction over the fatal accident.

Beyond the gruesome photos, the record itself raised more questions. I'd known Sesler was tall from the first visit—6'3"—but the coroner had recorded his weight as 265 pounds, which meant he must have really ballooned up after his time in the service.

Given this size, what really stuck out was Sesler's blood alcohol level: .22. A whopping number. Definitely a level that would cause someone to drive the wrong way on a highway. But also a level so high that other aspects of the accident didn't add up. First, at .22, how had Sesler driven more than 20 miles from Dempsey's, the last bar where he'd been seen? You can hardly walk at .22. If you haven't already passed out, you're close. It would be a miracle to drive two miles without wrecking, let alone 20. Second, hitting a blood alcohol level that high would be no easy feat for a guy Sesler's size.

I would know. A decade ago, I'd allowed myself to reach 250 pounds, little of it muscle. I also drank too much back then. I was so big it'd take five or six beers before I'd feel a thing, so I often surpassed that amount in one sitting. My low point had been getting pulled over leaving a local dive—lost my license, and almost my job. The receipt showed I'd drunk a dozen beers over two hours. But I'd only blown a .12, which kept me from losing my license for good.

"Good thing you're so huge," my lawyer had joked at the time, pissing me off. Sesler had been equally blessed with girth. For someone of his weight to hit .22, he would have to drink a lot more at a faster pace.

I took out my phone to do some quick calculating. Sesler's sister said he'd downed five beers at the bar. That would've put him at .056. Nowhere close to .22. In the police report, the Dempsey's bartender confirmed her account. "Served five beers in two hours. Typical amount. Didn't seem that bad. Walked out on his own. Left at 11:15 p.m."

I returned to the accident report. The estimated time of the accident was 12:20 a.m. Unless Sesler was already wasted when he walked into Dempsey's, this sequence meant he'd drunk at least a dozen beers in the hour *after* he'd left the bar.

Just didn't add up.

* * *

As I took a cab back to Indiana, my phone rang. The Kroons, again.

"Jack, our house has been trashed," Mrs. Kroon said, her voice trembling. She had clearly been crying.

"What do you mean?"

"While we were out for a few hours, someone ransacked our house. They went through every room, including the attic."

"What would they have been looking for?"

"I have no idea." She paused. "Wait! Tommy's letters during the war. That must have been what they were after. I'll be right back."

A minute later, she returned, audibly sobbing. "They took them," she said, nearly hysterical. "All of his letters. Gone."

"What was in—"

"Everything. They were like a journal of his service."

Damn. Why hadn't she said something about letters before?

"They were my best memory of my son. When I was alone, I'd read them all the time. It was like he was still with us."

"I'm really sorry, Mrs. Kroon. Did they talk about Tommy's relationship with Congressman Bravo?"

"Oh yes. In detail. They were so sensitive. So honest. I never showed them to my husband for that reason." She paused, then spoke more firmly. "But the final ones, which came home after Tommy died, are probably what got the congressman kicked out of the Army. Whoever gathered his belongings and sent them back here would've known their secret."

That explained it.

"Ma'am, you need to get out of there right away. Don't tell anyone about any of this. Stay with relatives. Don't go back to Virginia Beach."

"Don't worry, Mr. Kroon is packing our stuff now. We're staying with our son Will."

"Good idea. Call if you need anything. Mrs. Kroon, did anyone know about those letters?"

"I never told anyone."

* * *

LAWRENCEBURG, INDIANA

"No can do. I ain't talkin' about that shitty case again. The cops drilled me for months. I'm done. I don't need any more attention."

The only way to confirm my hunch was in the same smoke-filled dive where Sesler had spent his final evening, arriving around the time that he would've been there. But this stout, shaggy-haired bartender was hostile from the start. From my drinking days in Youngstown, I knew the type well. If the police were this guy's enemy, I'd take his side.

"Were the cops trying to blame you for it?" I asked.

"You bet they were," the bartender said, spitting as he spoke. "They've been trying to shut me down for years."

"Why shut down a neighborhood bar like this?"

"The neighbors," the bartender said, laughing. "They're always complaining about noise and trash, piss and puke in their yards. Like they didn't know they were moving in down the street from a bar. They object to my liquor license every year. Cops wanna make 'em happy, so they jump on a DUI—"

"I'll take another, Gordooo," said an old man sitting three seats down, slurring his words. Gordo impassively grabbed a bottle of whiskey from its bottom and filled up the small glass.

I waited for him to finish pouring. "So you think Dave Sesler was sober when he walked out of here?"

"I'm not sayin' he hadn't had a few. But for him, it was a light night. He could handle it."

"Four beers? Five?"

Gordo, who hadn't stopped pacing behind the bar since I'd entered, froze, cocked his head, and looked right at me. "Is this some type of investigation?"

I smiled. *Stay casual. Be his friend.* "Not of you. Tell you the truth, I think he must've gotten drunk after he left."

"Exactly!" Gordo cried, pacing once again. "Here, he had just five beers over two hours. And he downed a plate of fries in between."

"He ate here, too?" All those carbs would've made it even tougher to get that drunk.

"Yeah, the guy had blown up in recent months. He could put away the fries, burgers . . . you name it. "

"Gordo!" the other patron slurred loudly. "Hook me up!"

Gordo filled him up again, then turned back my way.

"I'm tellin' you, those five beers were nothing."

"Did you mention all this after he died?" I asked.

"Of course!"

"They didn't listen?"

"They didn't care. But think about it. For a guy that big to blow a .22, it would take two twelve-packs. Hell, he would need to *shotgun* two twelve-packs."

Bingo. Gordo had figured it out too.

* * *

WASHINGTON, D.C.

Cassie didn't intimidate easily, but her right hand quivered as she gripped the phone. As she always did when she was nervous, she scanned the black numerals etched above her elbow and took a deep breath.

8.14.04.10.20.

Those who noticed the tattoo always looked twice, but never asked. Rachel was the only one alive besides Cassie who knew what the numbers represented: the precise day and time that a drunk driver had knifed into her parents' Chevy. The collision had killed her mom instantly and had sent her dad into a coma from which he'd never recovered, destroying Cassie's childhood just as she'd turned fourteen.

Losing her parents had been bad enough—as doting as her uncle and aunt had been, Cassie had still struggled to sleep for years—but watching the drunk driver, a bank CEO with a documented drinking problem, get off scot-free thanks to a high-priced legal team had forever jaded her about America's justice system and its rigged power structure. From the moment the foreman had pronounced the words "not guilty," she had dedicated her life to evening things out for the little guy. For hard-working people like her mom and dad. Like Jimmy Cull.

On the other end of the call, someone picked up, and Cassie asked if she was speaking to Warden Hale Crawford.

"You sure are," he said. "Who are you and how the hell'd you get my number?"

"John Cull gave it to me, Warden," she said. "I'm sorry to bother you but I need your help."

"You didn't answer the first question. Do we know each other?"

"Not really. I was the one with Kristina Jones at Jimmy Cull's funeral. I'm actually a reporter but had gotten to know Jimmy—"

"A reporter?" Crawford said, audibly disgusted. "Just wait one—"

Cassie pushed hard to save the call. "Remember before the funeral, how we talked about Kristina calling that lawyer, Dean Gamble?"

"Yes, ma'am," he said warily.

"It was your idea, as a matter of fact."

"If you say so."

"Well, she called, and now I haven't heard from her in days. I've been calling non-stop."

"Maybe she's busy, darlin'."

Cassie shook her head, doodling the word "darling!" on her notepad to avoid responding to it out loud. "Her phone goes right through to voicemail. Something's wrong."

"I'm a jail warden, not an investigator. Why are you call—"

"Because you can get it looked into right away. Warden, this may be part of a bigger pattern where people have lost their lives. Including Jimmy Cull himself."

He chuckled. "Let's not get carried away, darlin'. But I'll see what I can do."

Carried away? Jimmy was dead and now Kristina was missing. Cassie was way beyond carried away.

* * *

Back in the office Friday, I went online again to learn more about the donor network that had bankrolled Governor Nicholas. What had they done beyond dumping millions on the current presidential frontrunner over the past decade?

First, no surprise, the assortment of lawyers, lobbyists, PACs, and contractor executives had given to many other politicians beyond the governor. All members of congressional leadership, both Republicans and Democrats, had benefitted. And like Nicholas, all members of the key committees and subcommittees had also been enriched. That's D.C. for you—get on the right committee, dole out the right contracts, and watch the campaign dollars come in.

Notably, like a number of other veterans in Congress, Congressman Bravo had received a steady flow of checks from these donors. Nothing like Nicholas, but he certainly had been on their radar.

Next, I sorted through the network of donors to see who'd given the most. First came the lobbyists of the defunct Progress Group. Even after the group broke up nearly a decade ago, many "alumni" had continued their support of common candidates from their new posts across Washington. This was a powerful, permanent network, but I looked closer to size up which of the contractors and companies were most eagerly giving. Who were the leaders and who were the followers? Who had the most at stake? For the most part, the giving had been relatively even. Engineering firms such as Booz Allen. Manufacturers such as Halliburton and Patriot Technologies. The security firm Blackwater. Others. They'd contributed at about the same frequency and level year in and year out, with no single entity sticking out. But that had changed halfway through President Banfield's term. One company began to emerge above the others.

DroneTech.

The company's PAC and top executives, based out of San Diego, had first begun giving to Nicholas and others a decade ago. A thousand here, $2,500 there, often on the same day as Progress Group donations. Standard stuff. But a few years in, their giving had skyrocketed. Committee chairs and back benchers, Republicans and Democrats, all were recipients of the company's largesse. And no one had received more than Nicholas. DroneTech contributed $25,000 as he ran for reelection to the governor's mansion, one of the largest donations of that campaign.

In politics, that's a big investment, one meant to secure an even bigger return.

* * *

"DroneTech?" Alex asked as I stood over her desk. "They're the Wild West of contractors."

"Looks like they've become one of the big players in the industry," I said.

"The biggest," Alex said. "After the president starting rolling out her 'soldierless army' strategic plan, they exploded. They started with drones, but now provide equipment and robotics to support all types of activities."

"That extensive?"

"Oh yeah. Especially in places like Afghanistan, Syria, and Iraq, drones and military robots are doing a lot of the work these days. They were everywhere the last two times I was embedded in Iraq. As the president likes to say, you can't blow up a drone with a roadside bomb."

"Do you know who's behind the company?" I asked.

"Yeah. A guy named Doug Hansen leads it. Navy SEAL in the first Iraq war—the good one. Then joined the CIA. He barely survived a roadside bomb himself, lost most of his right leg, recovered, and then dedicated himself to changing the way we fight wars. He claims it's to protect soldiers but it's also making him billions along the way."

Hansen's name hadn't appeared in Vassos' financial reports. "Is he political?" I asked.

"I don't think of him as political. Just intense. He often testifies on the Hill. He's a real tough guy, but also a charmer—seems to get along with everyone."

I laughed. "The company's PAC gives to them all, so I'm sure they appreciate him."

Alex nodded. "I'm not surprised. You don't expand as quickly as they have without political backing, from the president to the approps committees on down."

CHAPTER 14

YOUNGSTOWN, OHIO

"HEY," I SAID to Mary Andres, feigning outrage, "where'd my front page go?"

After Abacus, the *Youngstown Vindicator* had placed a framed front page of my scoop in the lobby leading to the newsroom, the last in a long line of the paper's most historic front pages. But it was no longer there.

Andres, the ornery boss who'd edited my stories for years, laughed as we ended our bear-hug. "You have your own wall now, Jack," she said, pointing to my left.

She wasn't kidding. The near wall of the newsroom was now a shrine to the *Vindicator's* coverage of the scandal. The original framed page along with numerous other follow-up stories, large color photos of my and Mary's cable television appearances and the many awards we'd won for our coverage.

So much pride in our big moment. Not just the paper, but the whole community. If only they knew what I'd left out.

It was Monday afternoon, and I'd been trekking around northern Ohio since late Saturday to cover the next stage of this wild primary. Tuesday, which we all were now calling the Big Ten Primary, would be a decisive day. Tired of watching the Southern states get all the glory on Super Tuesday, a number of Midwest states, who were rivals in everything from football to jobs, had come together in a surprising show of solidarity and scheduled their primaries on the same day. Ohio, Michigan, Pennsylvania, Illinois, Wisconsin, and Indiana—big, diverse states with many overlapping interests. Alone, each was important. Together, they were a treasure trove of delegates. As a proud Ohioan, I'd loved the idea.

Bravo, Stevens, and Nicholas had been crisscrossing the Big Ten states since the morning after Super Tuesday. Snow had blanketed the Midwest over the weekend, but hadn't stopped them from hitting every diner, church, bingo hall, and VFW hall they could find.

"What are you seeing on the ground here?" I asked Andres.

"On the ground? What you'd expect. But on air? It's just brutal. Stevens is getting clobbered by attack ads, mainly by outside groups. That one group is especially nasty. And Nicholas television ads and yard signs are everywhere."

"What about Bravo?" Super Tuesday had taken him down a notch.

"Bravo has been quieter, but the millennials love him. I think he'll run up big numbers on campuses all over the state, and with progressives generally."

"Any predictions?"

"What? Are you fishing for content for your fancy primetime broadcast, Jack?" she said, grinning in a way that let me know she was only half-joking.

I shrugged and smiled.

"You know better than anyone that there are two Ohios," she went on. "I think Bravo and Stevens split the dozen big counties. But Nicholas probably takes the others by enough to win." The "others" referred to the 76 other counties—mostly rural, mostly Republican—that made up the Buckeye State.

I nodded, agreeing fully. In fact, Andres had just summed up the race in all six states of the Big Ten primary. Stevens and Nicholas had advantages in their home states of Michigan and Pennsylvania, of course, but more important was the urban-rural split in each state. Because even though the majority of Democrats lived in the Big Ten's handful of large cities, the blue-collar votes in the broad swath of rural areas would add up. In a head-to-head primary, a candidate winning big in the more progressive, young, and diverse urban areas would likely beat out the candidate who won in the rural areas. Or at least it would be close, depending on how the votes broke down. But this was not a head-to-head race. It was a three-way primary. So while Bravo and Stevens were arm wrestling for every vote in those urban areas, Nicholas had the rural areas mostly to himself.

"Of course Senator Stevens will win Michigan," I said. "But yeah, the Stevens-Bravo battle is really boosting Nicholas. Plus, as dour as he is, he's well organized on the ground. Never would have predicted this six months ago."

"Never," Andres agreed. "And I'm telling you, the ads hitting Stevens are pounding his numbers down. Nonstop and nasty."

Broadcasting live from *The Vindicator* an hour later, I relayed this basic summary of the race to the country, which I was sure Andres would give me a lot of guff about the next time I saw her. "Governor Nicholas looks to be in great shape going into the Big Ten primary," I said in closing. "A big win here and he may not look back."

Which also meant our time was running out.

* * *

WASHINGTON, D.C.

"We can't find her anywhere," Hale Crawford told Cassie when he called her back late on Monday. His voice was far more serious than it had been on their prior call.

"Did you go to her home?"

"A sheriff friend did. Her car's still in the garage. The landlord let us into her apartment. There was no sign of her, but also no sign of a struggle."

"Was her stuff there?"

"She hadn't packed to go anywhere if that's what you're askin'. Her purse was still there. But no keys. They must've been on her. All signs of an abduction, and a professional one at that."

I knew it, Cassie thought. "What can you do?" she asked.

"The local sheriff is on it."

"Please have him investigate that Houston lawyer, Dean Gamble. Kristina was going to confront him about the Cull case." Cassie explained her suspicions about Gamble, trying to sound as rational and un-panicked as possible.

"We'll be sure to talk to him," the warden said. "We don't have any other leads."

"He knew about Cull's death even though no one had told him," Cassie said. "Now Kristina's missing. You definitely need to talk to him."

* * *

"I'll be home by 8:30 at the latest," Vassos said to his wife, Helen, as he walked out of Republic's studios just before 8:00 Monday night.

"Dinner might be a little cold," she said patiently, as always. With their kids off to college, he had promised her that the move to Republic would cut down on the late-night, big firm hours they had endured for two decades. And things had gotten better, although not as much as promised. The past month had been especially bad. Still, she never complained.

"You know I like it cold. See you in a few."

Helen said goodbye the way she had since they first started dating at seventeen. "Be careful."

Vassos hung up his cell phone as he stepped onto the M Street sidewalk. It was nearly dark as the escalator took him deep under the D.C. streets. The red line stopped within blocks of his home in Friendship Heights, just south of the Maryland border. They could afford to live in the tonier burbs of Maryland, but preferred the culture and vibrancy of D.C.

Vassos leafed through *The Washington Post* on the ride home. He skipped the now-dated news section, skimmed the editorials, and devoted most of his time to the sports section. The Yankees were off to a good start, and the Knicks were muscling their way into the NBA playoffs after years of losing. He stepped out of the subway car and rode the long escalator up to the street. He'd never been one to walk up an escalator for time's sake; his nose remained buried in the paper. His home was only six blocks from the station. The leisurely walk to and from the Metro stop comprised his exercise each day, as he'd been assuring Helen for years despite his growing gut.

The first two blocks along Connecticut Avenue were lit bright enough that the headlines in the Style section remained readable, but once Vassos turned the corner onto DuBose Street, which lacked streetlights, he tucked the paper away in his computer bag.

An engine turned on just behind him. He glanced over his shoulder to see a gray van, now idling. Strange. Its lights were still off. Then, rather than driving away, the van began driving alongside him. Still no lights.

The rest played out in slow motion.

Footsteps echoed from behind, two sets of hard-soled shoes clicking along the sidewalk—at a faster pace than his own. They were gaining.

Then two men emerged from behind a tree in front of him. Thick builds. Dark suits. Standing in the way.

Vassos' breathing accelerated as he realized what was happening.

Then came the rolling roar of the van's side door sliding open. The footsteps behind him sped up, and the two men in front whirled directly toward him.

While he'd never been an athlete, Vassos had always been physically strong—you had to be where he grew up. But four men and whoever was in the van would be too much to overpower. So he reeled to his right, the only direction available, to see a residential yard on a slight grade. He sprinted a few feet into the wet grass before a thick arm reached around his chest and pulled him back. He grabbed the hand to push it away, but the arm didn't budge. Now a left arm reached around his back, squeezing him with a powerful bear hug.

"If you make this hard for us, it will become much harder for you." The deep Jersey accent came from his left.

Something pinched the back of his right shoulder. Seconds later, his legs tingled, went completely numb, then buckled beneath him. Two more hands grabbed him from behind.

Everything went dark.

CHAPTER 15

Alex Fischer shivered as she walked alongside Colonel Jim Shirey, who was well concealed in a tan fedora, slacks, and trench coat. It was a cool spring morning, and they were strolling amid the white granite slabs of the World War II memorial on the National Mall. She'd called him first thing in the morning, but once she'd asked about DroneTech, he insisted on meeting in person.

"You don't want to get into this stuff. Trust me, Alex."

She laughed. "Colonel, that's what you say for every story."

"This time I mean it. For my own sake and yours, I can't say much."

Alex knew Shirey well. He was serious about not being a source, and wouldn't waver. Time to try a tactic that almost never failed with older, protective men. "Colonel, we're doing the story either way. So you can either help me do it right, and steer me clear of trouble, or I can walk the minefield all alone. I hope you'll help me."

Now Shirey laughed. "You're putting a gun to your head and telling me you need my help to not pull the trigger?"

"Not quite. I'm pulling the trigger. But you can help me fire in the right direction."

"You got me there." He sighed, looked around for a moment, then took a deep breath. "It's a shit show over here on DroneTech. Total civil war within the Pentagon. But the president's top brass like it and the politicians love it. So it keeps growing."

They stepped away from the memorial and paced slowly along the reflecting pool toward the Lincoln Memorial.

"That's what I've always heard," Alex said. "I know it's cutting down on casualties in the field. So who'd be against it?"

"The three stars. The leaders in the field. The thinkers at the War College. And not that anyone cares, but the State Department. Running wars through drones and robots sounds good on the surface, and may make it easier back home for the politicians due to fewer casualties, but it's a terrible direction long-term."

"Why's that?" Alex asked, genuinely curious. She'd interviewed so many injured and traumatized vets in recent years. Why not keep them out of harm's way whenever possible?

"Slippery slope," Shirey said. "It changes the entire nature of war. With such a low barrier to entry, we risk getting into a more permanent war footing. Permanent, *secret* wars. And they gin up a fierce blowback on the ground, inspiring generations of terrorists who hate us. DroneTech may make billions selling these things, but the long-term repercussions are frightening—but of course that leads to even more drone sales." He paused, then added, "And the newest DroneTech technologies are downright scary."

"How so?"

"The older drones at least required a human pilot back in San Diego to operate them, deciding who to bomb and when to fire. The newest generation removes humans entirely. We call them 'autonomous weapons.'"

"Autonomous? As in the weapon itself decides who to kill?" Alex asked.

"Exactly."

A typical Pentagon euphemism for a terrible idea. "What's the speculation on what will happen to all this when President Banfield leaves office?" she asked.

"It all depends on who replaces her. Get a president who's against it, naming the wrong top brass, it could all end quick. Get one who's for it and it gets locked in as our country's primary military strategy for years to come."

"So this election's big for them?"

"This election's *everything* for them."

"Funny. The issue hasn't come up once in the presidential campaign."

Shirey chuckled and gave her a sidelong look. "Come on, Alex. Since when have the big issues been the focus of our ridiculous elections? Either way, I can guarantee you that Doug Hansen and his team know exactly where these candidates stand. They make it their business to know."

Shirey went quiet as they reached the end of the reflecting pool. They climbed a slight hill and crossed a road to reach the steps of the Lincoln Memorial. As they stared up at the pensive fourteenth president, Shirey asked, "Do you know where the candidates stand on this?"

Embarrassingly, Alex had no idea and said as much.

"Maybe you should ask them."

* * *

CLEVELAND, OHIO

"George has been missing for hours. Please call me."

Helen Vassos's Brooklyn accent was the first voice I heard on Tuesday morning as I checked my messages from my Cleveland hotel. Unfortunately, I had slept soundly, and was getting the message hours after she'd left it.

But that was just her first, left at 11:00 p.m. At 1:30 a.m., she'd called again. "Jack, it's Helen. Still nothing. Please call."

At 7:00 a.m., a final message. Her voice strained. Desperate. She clearly had been crying. "The police are here. George never returned. *Please* call."

I dialed the number back right away. "Helen, it's Jack Sharpe. I'm so sorry I missed your calls. Fill me in."

"George never came home last night," she said, her voice husky, tired. "He stayed at the office a little late, was going to be here by 8:30 or so, but then never made it."

Shit. All George did in life was come to work and go home to Helen. That was it. He was not a guy who'd just disappear.

"Helen, I'm so sorry," I said again. "What are the cops saying?"

"Not much. They're looking into the Metro video, seeing if George made it back to the neighborhood at all."

"They check with any hospitals?"

"They did. Nothing." She took a deep breath, then continued. "Jack, what's he been working on lately? He's been so intense at home the past few weeks. He even started shaving and going into work early. He was looking into something big."

"Some political stuff. Possibly related. I'm stuck here in Cleveland for tonight's primary, but I'll have Republic's security people stop over. And keep me posted on what the cops say."

We hung up, and I stared at the wall of my hotel room. Helen was right. From calling that Delaware firm to seeing the old Nicholas photo, George had been consumed. His disappearance had to be connected.

It also confirmed he was onto something. Which meant *we* were onto something.

* * *

WASHINGTON, D.C.

"The fella just up and flew the coop," Hale Crawford told Cassie when he called her back Tuesday.

"Who did?" Cassie asked. She had just sat down at the Dupont Circle Starbucks when the phone rang.

"That slick lawyer," the warden said. "Cull's lawyer. I've been tryin' to track him down since you and I last talked, but he's nowhere to be found."

"Any sign of where he went?"

"No ma'am. We got a search warrant of both his office and home. Nothing amiss. Too clean, really. And his partners swear he just quit comin' to work last week."

Gamble must have cleared out knowing Kristina's disappearance would lead to him. "Did his partners know anything?"

"They really didn't. He did his own thing in that office. They all said he was closer to the D.C. outfit than the people in Houston."

Damn. Cassie hadn't had time to dig further into the satellite office up here.

"Ma'am," the warden went on, "on another note, y'all were right. Jimmy Cull's death is highly suspicious."

Even bigger news. "You find something?"

"Sure did. We looked back at our tape of the day he died. When Gamble visited—"

"You have tapes of that? I assumed that would be protected by attorney-client privilege."

"Oh, it is. We shut off the audio for attorney visits. But we have cameras on those visitor kiosks 24/7. They had a big argument. Jimmy was pissed, pointing at him, throwing his hands in the air. The lawyer hollered back. I don't know what they were talking about, but they carried on for an hour."

"I know exactly what they were talking about. Jimmy knew the guy was a fraud, and had purposely thrown his case."

"Whatever it was, was ugly. We also eyeballed the tapes around the time of the supposed suicide." He let the sentence hang for a moment.

"And?" Cassie asked, heart pounding.

"We found they were tampered with. Either by someone on the inside or someone who hacked into the sys—"

"My God. What did they do?"

"So our guard discovered Jimmy in his cell after lights on at six. When we first reconstructed what happened by replayin' the tapes, there was no noise in his cell all night. The video of the hallway outside his cell showed nothin' but one of our guards makin' his rounds. So the suicide theory checked out."

"And then?" Cassie asked, gripping her half-empty coffee cup tightly.

"When we eyeballed it more closely, we saw that the prior footage had been spliced in. Someone replaced the feed into Jimmy's cell, as well as the hallway leadin' into his cell, for about two hours after midnight. The spliced footage hid whatever happened in the minutes that Cull died, includin' any sound. And, assumin' someone entered his cell to kill him and stage the suicide, they removed the footage of that person enterin' and leavin'."

"Oh my God."

"Yep. Then one of the guards on duty that night up and disappeared a few days ago. We're interviewing everyone who was there that night to learn what we can."

"Have you ever seen anything like this?"

"I've seen lots of things, darlin', but nothing like this. Not even close. Whoever pulled this off is damn sophisticated. We're talking a military-style operation." The warden was quiet as his words hung between them. "Young lady," he said, "I don't need to tell you this but I will. Be careful. And at this point, I'm asking you not to report any of this."

Ugh. Nothing offended a reporter's sense of duty more than those words, especially from a public official. It usually made a story more likely, not less. But with no idea where this was heading, there was no sense in defying him.

Yet.

* * *

"Soldierless army." "Autonomus weapons." "DroneTech."

Alex's search of those terms unleashed a torrent of websites, documents, and reports about the heated debate Shirey had described. One side argued that drones spared soldiers' lives and limbs while accomplishing important missions, the other argued it was a slippery slope toward permanent war and human rights violations. They didn't necessarily break down along party lines, either. Often the differing viewpoints reflected life experience.

What didn't pop up were presidential candidates opining on the subject. Not surprising. Alex would've remembered that. She even typed in each major candidate's name into her search. Moore. Nicholas. Bravo. Stevens. The Republicans. Nothing. After scrolling through dozens of stories without success, she took her hands off the keypad. She thought for a second, then typed in a new name.

Bill Lopez.

Bingo. It ran in the *Des Moines Register*.

Bill Lopez, governor of New Mexico, the early favorite in the Democratic primary, had weighed in during the paper's editorial interview. His strong opposition to President Banfield's approach was one of the answers the newspaper highlighted in its account of the hour-long session.

"I understand the appeal of drones," said Lopez, "and I think they have their place in our military arsenal. But I think President Banfield's plan goes way too far. We don't want to become the world's policeman, with drones serving as our traffic cops worldwide. And the concept of 'autonomous' weapons scares the hell out of me."

Perfect. Exactly what Alex was looking for.

She quickly scanned through *Register* stories from November and December. Theirs was the most important endorsement before the Iowa caucus, so any serious candidate would have sat down with them as Lopez did, and likely would have been asked the same questions so that readers could compare their answers. She found summaries of the *Register's* interviews with Moore, Bravo, Nicholas, and Stevens. None mentioned drones. But this didn't mean they hadn't been *asked* about drones, just that their answers hadn't made it into the story.

Moments later, Alex was on the phone with the *Register's* editorial editor. "Did you guys record your full candidate interviews from the primary?"

"We always do," the woman told her. "We actually have videos for all of them."

"Great. I assume you asked them the same basic questions."

"We tried to. Sometimes the interviews go in different directions, but we worked off the same script of questions for each one."

"Great. Drone warfare came up in the story on Governor Lopez. Did it come up in the others?"

"It should have. We definitely asked about it routinely. I can email you the video files as long as you credit us if you run anything."

"Of course," Alex said. "Send 'em my way."

* * *

CLEVELAND

"Jack, they're saying this was a highly professional abduction," Helen Vassos said over the phone, her voice far calmer, more alert, than a few hours before. It was almost noon.

Damn. I'd held off panicking my crew in the hopes George would turn up.

"Are you with the police now? Can I talk to them?"

"Sure."

A high-pitched Boston accent came over the phone. "Sergeant Murphy here, chief investigator for the D.C. police."

"Thank you for your attention to this, Sergeant."

"A national reporter nabbed from a D.C. street? We don't love the press, but that's a big deal for us. We've called the FBI too, but we're keeping it all under wraps for now."

"So you think this was a professional job?"

"Textbook."

"How so?"

"Everything about it. These guys were efficient. Quiet. Spotless. They knew his route home, when he'd be walking from the Metro station to his house. But we've scoured the video. It doesn't look like he was followed on the train that night."

"Where'd they grab him?"

"Just after he turned onto his street, where they knew it'd be dark. He ran into a neighbor's yard, and a couple guys grabbed him there. They cleaned up the site, but the grass told the story."

Definitely pros. "So they must have followed him before?"

"We assume so. They knew exactly where to grab him. Anywhere else and we'd have something on camera, or someone might have seen something."

Every detail made this scarier. "Sergeant, this is a key member of our team, and a good man. What can we do to help?"

"At this point, there's not much. We have his photo plastered all over our precincts. But whoever took this much care to grab him is not gonna let him see the light of day. We should talk as soon as you're back in town. We need to know what he was working on."

Not a chance. "Will do," I said. "Back tomorrow."

CHAPTER 16

WASHINGTON, D.C.

As promised, the email from the *Des Moines Register* came in just after 1:00 p.m. Five video attachments, each file named after a candidate. Alex opened the Lopez file first. She knew that finding when in the interview the topic of drones came up would save time reviewing the others.

The video was grainy, but the audio was clear. Three *Register* journalists sat on one side of the table, questioning the salt-and-pepper-haired New Mexico governor sitting across from them. Alex skimmed through each question and answer, eager to find the one on drone warfare.

At one point, twenty minutes in, Lopez became especially animated, his arms waving in the air as he leaned over the table. Alex slowed the video to normal speed to see what they were discussing.

"The attacks from that SuperPAC have been outrageous!" Lopez told the ed board, holding a flyer in one hand with his photo on it. "Completely false! But this garbage has landed in every mailbox in the state, not to mention on everyone's Facebook page."

"So you deny the charges of corrup—"

"Of course I deny them," he said, pounding his fist on the table. "They're totally made up. This is just some dark money group smearing my good name because they're worried I'm going to win."

The governor visibly calmed as they moved onto the next question. Twenty minutes later, the editor in the center asked the third question in a row on national security issues. "Governor, what do you think of the president's strategy of aggressively using drones to do much of the traditional work of the military? Her 'soldierless army' approach?"

Lopez provided the answer that appeared in the later story, but with more passion than the written words had conveyed. "I understand the appeal of drones, and I think they have their place in our arsenal. But I think President Banfield's plan goes way too far." He paused. Sighed. "We don't want to become the world's policeman, with drones serving as our traffic cops worldwide. And the concept of 'autonomous' weapons scares the hell out of me."

He then added perspective that the story later left out. "My biggest worry is that using drones will tempt us to do more than we ever would otherwise. Before we know it, we're running operations in countries all over the world from some office in California."

His interviewers nodded, then moved onto a question about China. The interview ended promptly at 60 minutes.

Alex opened Governor Nicholas's file. Thirty-five minutes in, same drone question: "Governor, the president has aggressively pushed her 'soldierless army' concept to minimize casualties. It's quite controversial. Will you continue it?"

The former Marine paused, looking at each of the three questioners. "When I was in Congress, I served on the subcommittee that addressed this issue," he said. "It's a balancing act. Drones are useful in so many ways, and will undoubtedly become a more important tool on the battlefield, but having been on the ground, I certainly reject the notion of a 'soldierless army.'"

Alex smirked. He'd pulled off the perfect political dodge, which was exactly why she had so little use for politics. The questioner reacted the same way. "That didn't really answer the question. Whatever it's called, will you continue it? Expand it?"

"I'm a veteran. This is not political for me," Nicholas shot back self-righteously. "We will, of course, use drones. I will review that use carefully and balance the competing interests in doing so."

His folded arms signaled he was done with the topic. What an unpleasant guy.

Next came Senator Stevens. Forty-four minutes in, he didn't mince words on the topic. "I may be old school, but the idea of trying to do soldiers' work with so-called autonomous robots concerns me deeply. My fear is that the overuse of drones will put more Americans at even greater risk in the long run."

"Fair enough," nodded the questioner, moving on to the China question.

Alex jotted down Stevens's words.

Governor Moore had a different take than the others. "The concept scares me, and I oppose it on that ground alone," she said. "But equally troubling is the interweaving of contractors and military leaders in the operation of these drone systems. All the while the contractors give donations to the politicians who support the concept. It's an enormous conflict of interest fueled by big bucks. We have to break this relationship up, and put the military back in charge of these decisions at all levels."

Alex jotted the words "interweaving" and "conflict of interest" on her notepad, added a "$" symbol, and then clicked on the final file: Anthony Bravo's. As sharp as he usually was, Bravo could not have been duller than he was throughout the hour of this interview. His long-winded answers made the pace far slower than that of the others. They only got to foreign policy questions after 52 minutes, and had to wrap up after only the first one. The reporters never got to their question about the soldierless army strategy.

* * *

Three bronze G.I. statues peered over Colonel Shirey's shoulder as he waited on the cement bench.

Appropriate, Alex Fischer thought as she approached. As a young officer in Vietnam, Shirey had taken part in the humiliating pull-out from Saigon. Now here he sat, like the somber figures behind him, looking toward the long, low marble memorial wall set humbly in the ground not far away.

She sat down next to him, but he kept his gaze forward. "We've got to stop meeting like this," she joked.

"You're digging even deeper into trouble, Alex," he said bluntly. "You need to be careful."

Alex shivered as a strong breeze blew through, nearly knocking Shirey's fedora off and sending her hair in all directions. "What do you mean?"

"I mean you should stop."

She shot him the most serious look she could muster. "You know I can't. And I won't. What is so dangerous?"

He continued to look straight ahead as he responded. "This issue of DroneTech being too intermingled with the military is a major problem. But those who still care don't know what to do about it."

"Tell me more."

"Decades ago, private contractors sold us the equipment, technology, you name it. They'd train our military personnel on how to use them. Then we'd take it from there. Now, they never leave."

"Are they operating their own drones?"

"Yes. Their people and our people mix together at all levels. They work side by side every day. Except for their official badges, you can't tell the difference, or who's in charge."

"That sounds like a terrible system."

"But it's even—"

Two large men passed directly in front of them. Shirey stopped talking as they walked by, leaning back against the bench. Alex could see his discomfort out of the corner of her eye. He waited until the men were out of earshot before he continued, his voice lowered. "It's more incestuous than that. Many of DroneTech's top people and 'consultants' are ex-military, hired immediately after retiring. In the culture of the military, those stars don't fade when you retire."

"Great, so the private contractors outrank the active military. What a mess. Where does this all take place?"

"For the soldierless army stuff, DroneTech's headquarters are in San Diego. So most of the work is co-located out there. Both on the naval base and in private DroneTech facilities."

"Does anyone talk out about it? Internally? On the Hill?"

"Not anymore. So-called embedded contractors have become standard operating procedure. Hell, the next generation of Pentagon leaders don't know anything different, or how extreme it's gotten. And with all the money flowing to the politicians, they don't say anything either. Especially with—"

He stopped talking as another strong gust blew through.

"—especially with what happened to those brave enough to have done so."

"Wait," Alex said. "What happened?"

The colonel turned and looked right at her. "A few on the Hill complained a couple years back. They called for hearings. None of them survived their next election."

"Really?" she asked. "Who?"

"Senators Brewer in Florida and Little in North Carolina. And a couple House members. Look it up. They took a stand, and for each, it was their last."

"Senator Brewer got caught up in this?" Marshall Brewer was someone Alex had interviewed several times. He'd been one of the most knowledgeable people on the Hill on national security. But then, out of nowhere, the voters of the Sunshine State had tossed him. Alex remembered reading the surprising news, and, frankly, not paying it much mind.

"He tried to. Turned out to be the last thing he did in politics." He looked back at the Vietnam Wall, dotted with the names of fallen comrades and an occasional flower laid upon the ground. "No one has uttered a word since."

CHAPTER 17

GENEVA-ON-THE-LAKE, OHIO

"I HEREBY SUSPEND MY campaign for the presidency of the United States," Wendell Stevens said from the center of my TV screen.

After an early jog along Lake Erie, I watched the announcement over fried eggs and coffee from my cottage in Geneva-on-the-Lake. I'd driven here directly from Cleveland, despite having to be back in D.C. the very next day. Given the pace of life at Republic, even a one-night escape to my summer home felt like a vacation.

Like Moore's dropping out, Stevens' move was inevitable. The night before, except for Stevens' win in his home state of Michigan, Governor Nicholas had swept the Big Ten primary. Just as we'd predicted, he'd run up big numbers in the rural parts of each state while his two rivals battled to a draw in the major urban areas. The rout was on. Senator Stevens now stood in front of Detroit's famed Joe Louis monument, an enormous, dark fist punching the air, only yards from the Detroit River. A fitting image. His wife and three grown children flanked him, along with his 86-year-old mother.

"We fought the good fight," Stevens said gamely. "And we congratulate the remaining two candidates. What a ride it was!"

But if the speech was all smiles and hugs, the interviews that followed took a different tone. "You must be disappointed by all those attack ads," one young local Detroit reporter asked, holding the mic up close to Stevens. A strong question, forcing an answer and cutting off any dodge.

"Oh yes," Stevens said. "I was fighting a ghost, hidden yet fiercer than either Congressman Bravo or Governor Nicholas."

"You think it's why you lost?"

"It made a huge difference. If the same ads had been run against my opponents, they'd be the ones stepping out today. Not me."

"But couldn't Governor Moore say the same thing?"

"Absolutely. Same with Governor Lopez. And that's the problem.

Outside groups can control the outcome through dark money regardless of who the candidate is."

The scrum of reporters tried to pivot to their own questions, but the local scrapper pushed on. "It looks like Governor Nicholas is going to win the primary. Will you support him?"

"I will respect whoever ultimately wins. I think both the congressman and governor would make fine presidents."

The senator was doing his best to be gracious. But the narrow-eyed glare and clenched jaw made it clear that the old boxer was fuming about the outside money that had knocked him out—and wondering who was behind it.

Fired me up to watch it. This decent man deserved better.

* * *

WASHINGTON, D.C.

"Some grassroots groups went nuts in the caucus states," Cassie said from the doorway of my office. "They really pushed voter turnout."

She'd stopped by just after 4:00, an hour after I got back from Cleveland. Late last week, I'd asked her to figure out why Governor Nicholas was performing so well in caucus elections.

"What do you mean, nuts?" I asked.

"A bunch of different organizations sprouted up over the past six months, pushing tons of people to the caucuses. That surge in voting helped Nicholas win."

"So that's why we didn't see the Nicholas organization do it?" It was half question, half statement.

"He didn't seem to do any more than anyone else. But these groups did."

"Do you have any of their materials?"

"Yeah. Here's the one from Minnesota. What's funny is it doesn't push for Nicholas at all. His name never appears. It just encourages people to caucus."

"Not a surprise. That's what keeps them legal. And you wouldn't need to say Nicholas anyway."

"You wouldn't?" Cassie asked.

"Nah. Demographic modeling can take care of that. Target the voters that the models say will vote for him, get them to show up, and you win without ever saying his name."

Cassie nodded. "And of course in these low turnout caucuses, any unexpected surge for one candidate could make all the difference."

"*Will* make all the difference. These are mom and pop operations. Not well run, not well attended. And inconvenient for many voters to get to. So if you get people there, you'll win." With so little turnout, and because they're run by volunteers, caucuses were especially vulnerable to big money, third-party influence and sophisticated campaign tactics.

"Were you able to find where the money came from?" I asked.

"No. These groups were all nonprofits. Charities. Apparently they don't have to report that, or how they spent it."

I knew that Americans for a Brighter Future could only spend up to half its money on direct political activities. The rest had to go to nonprofit work like so-called public education. These voter turnout activities would qualify for that.

"Same story for the other states?" I asked.

Cassie took out a number of other flyers. Kansas, Maine, and Nebraska. She held them up like a deck of cards, each boasting color photos and bold type stressing the importance of attending the caucuses.

"Same deal," she said. "Nowhere do they advocate for anyone by name."

"Amazing." Compared to the politics I grew up so passionate about, where each candidate ran his own show, modern campaigns were truly out of control—including beyond the control of the candidates themselves.

CHAPTER 18

WASHINGTON, D.C.

"CAN'T THINK OF a less appropriate place to announce you're quitting," I muttered to my cameraman.

With their two kids flanking them, Congressman Bravo and his wife, Isabella, looked like JFK and Jacqueline Kennedy, standing a few steps down from the top of the Lincoln Memorial. An enormous crowd surrounded them, along with a row of cameras toward the front. We were all shooting live.

"We are so proud of the campaign we've run," the congressman said after lengthy introductory thank-yous and appreciations. "But it has become clear that there is no path to the nomination. Today I am suspending my campaign for the presidency of this great country."

To say that the move came as a surprise would have been an understatement. Of course Bravo was way behind in the delegate count, and continuing on definitely would have been a grind. But with the messy and crowded field narrowed to two, he had finally gained a one-on-one opportunity against Nicholas. And head to head, the math changed dramatically. In upcoming states, the diverse coalition of voters that had supported Bravo, Stevens, and Moore likely would have consolidated behind him. He had a long way to go—all the way to the final primary in California—to catch the governor, but there was now a mathematical chance. A path. Moreover, staying in for the long haul would have squared with recent history. In the last three presidential elections, the final two candidates had always duked it out until the end. We in the media had been eager to see the final showdown.

But here Bravo stood, stepping away, handing it to an underwhelming rival. Odd move for a guy rocketing upward in recent months. Dark explanations were already spreading.

"Rumors are swirling that Governor Nicholas and Congressman Bravo have cut a deal," I explained over the air after Bravo's press conference. "Is

Bravo dropping out because Nicholas is going to pick him to be his vice president? We'll see what happens in the coming weeks."

They would make a great team. Both veterans. Older generation and new. Diverse. And of all the candidates, the two had never really had cross words. That, too, now seemed odd. How do two candidates spend months as rivals, with the presidency at stake and amid a fierce field of other contenders, and never criticize one another?

* * *

The "embedded contractor" concept that Jim Shirey had mentioned sounded like trouble, so Alex spent her afternoon looking into it. The documents she found made for a walk down memory lane.

The major change had come with a company named, ominously, Blackwater. A wealthy former Navy SEAL had created the "private security" firm in the 1990s, providing security to a variety of government agencies. The CIA had been a major initial client, as had the State Department and its embassies. During the Iraq war, Blackwater's footprint had grown rapidly. Billions in contracts funded thousands of "civilian warriors" in the battle zone, more than actual American forces and as heavily armed. They engaged in combat directly, often inflicting more casualties, more brutally, than their counterparts.

While Blackwater had been the most high profile contractor, its model of outsourcing had spread quickly. Over the course of the war, private contractors did everything from building dining halls and training Iraqi police forces to loading weapons onto aircraft and transporting fuel and ammunition. Despite a lot of criticism and taxpayer dollars spent, the real advantage to the new model had been political: by relying so heavily on private contractors, military leaders and politicians back home didn't have to call up hundreds of thousands of troops and reserves. And deaths of private contractors did not bring the same publicity or anguish as deaths of uniformed soldiers.

The next generation of embedded contractors had come from within the intelligence world. Private companies became directly involved in the collection and analysis of digital and electronic intelligence. Surveillance. Public awareness of this trend had exploded when Edward Snowden leaked a treasure trove of information about national intelligence gathering. Snowden's disclosure had stunned the nation not only for what it revealed about the scope of domestic surveillance but for the revelation that private contractors like Snowden were working interchangeably with governmental intelligence officials.

Finally came the rapid proliferation of drones and autonomous weapons, which had followed the rise of DroneTech. Like Blackwater, the company had been founded by a SEAL, Doug Hansen. Started small, then had exploded in the later years of Iraq and Afghanistan operations.

Not only had DroneTech embedded itself within military operations, its technologies had allowed it to box out many of the other contractors who required actual personnel. Why use trucks and truck drivers to transport when you could use a drone? DroneTech wasn't just another military contractor embedded within military operations. It was a contractor rendering many others obsolete, absorbing a broad swath of functions and activities. And so, running most of its work from San Diego, it had grown rapidly.

As she reviewed these reports, Alex was taken aback by the ferocity of the fight over DroneTech's expansion. Journalists, watchdog groups, retired military members, and many politicians spoke out against the creeping danger of private actors making profits by executing so many critical military and national security functions. The lack of checks and balances.

But the defense was equally fierce. Columnists, retired military, academics, all making the case that the approach saved money and saved lives. Left unacknowledged by many of these groups was the benefit of shielding the public from the costs of war. An op-ed in the conservative *Washington Times* summed up the position: "Expanding the use of DroneTech will provide two major benefits. First, DroneTech provides enormous economic efficiencies. Second, DroneTech's latest stable of products will dramatically minimize losses in the field."

Like many of the analyses defending DroneTech, the op-ed cited a variety of studies over the years. But curiously, all those studies traced back to the same Washington, D.C. think tank.

She'd have to pay it a visit.

CHAPTER 19

"GEORGE IS *GONE*?" Cassie said incredulously.

"What the hell is going on, Jack?" Alex said. "What are the cops saying?"

"Why do you think I called the meeting?" I asked, loudly enough to shut down the two-sided attack. "It's clear he was abducted by professionals."

"But why would they abduct him for looking into a freaking SuperPAC?" Cassie asked. "It's not like they're a secret."

"I think they have something bigger to hide," I said.

Alex narrowed her eyes at me. "Like what?"

"I've been digging into Bravo's platoon. All those deaths. There's no way these were accidents, or coincidences. These were hits."

My two top reporters looked at me like I was nuts.

"That would be one hell of a plot, Jack," Alex said.

"I know," I said. "It was. And a cynical one too."

"How so?" Cassie asked.

"Given what happens to veterans in this country, whoever did this assumed people wouldn't notice a few troubled vets succumbing to their vices. After all, it happens every day. And sadly, they were absolutely right. No one noticed or cared."

I walked through all three cases. No way Sesler could've reached .22 on his own. No way Jackson ingested such a lethal opioid strand with no other trace of it in the Baltimore area. Choo was the victim of a precise hit, not the unlucky casualty of a random bank robbery. And they all died within a few months.

"Only a month after Choo dies," I continued, "stories begin popping up about Bravo running for president."

Cassie leaned forward in her chair, warming up to the theory. "The Cull case fits the same pattern. They framed him and left him defenseless once the trial started."

Alex still wasn't sold. "But Jack, veterans *do* succumb to their vices.

Every day. Why couldn't that have happened here? What would be the point of killing these guys?"

I didn't hold back. "Someone was desperate to get rid of anyone who was close to Bravo in Iraq. And needed to get it done before he formally announced his candidacy for president."

Silence followed. They could see it made sense, but they didn't really want it to. Then I delivered some more bad news: "Here's the thing. Vassos wasn't looking into Bravo like you guys were. He was poking around at that SuperPAC. We thought they were separate, but his abduction means they're probably related."

Alex nodded. "God, I hope not. The people behind that SuperPAC have enormous resources. They're tied right into the military."

"Jesus!" Cassie cried. "The warden in Texas said the way they staged Jimmy Cull's suicide looked like a *military-style* operation."

"Listen, we're not sure what we're up against," I said, trying to calm them down. "But this is a dangerous story. Be careful who you talk to. And call me if you see anything suspicious. The D.C. Police have also been—"

"—D.C. Police?" Cassie cut in angrily. "If Alex and that warden are right, what the hell are they going to do about it?"

A fair question without a good answer. "The sooner we get this story out, the better. They're trying to kill it before anyone else knows. Once it's out, we're all a lot safer."

"Easy for you to say!" Cassie said.

"Excuse me?" I asked, raising my voice.

"*We're* the ones in the trenches putting our lives on the line. No offense, Jack, but you're popping around doing fancy stand-ups and in-studio analysis."

I leaned over the table, close to saying something I'd regret. There were so many—too many—ways I could respond. About death threats covering the mob and corrupt politicians in Youngstown. Having my son and his wife followed and threatened. Being knocked out and kidnapped by Russian goons less than a year ago because I'd insisted on chasing down a big story. In short, I'd earned my stripes.

But there was no point in arguing.

I took a few moments of silence and responded as calmly as I could manage. "I'm going to do all I can to get good security. But our best security is to get the story out."

* * *

ALEXANDRIA, VIRGINIA

Unsure why the hell I was sitting there, or where this was going, I asked the question to break the ice: "You hear anything on Logan?"

Seated around me were the older Kroons, Will Kroon, and Will's wife, who had welcomed me to her Alexandria home with a warm smile and a glass of water.

"We haven't," Francine said. Her wrinkled face looked more tired than upset, her eyes a pinkish-red. Earl Kroon shook his head somberly.

"Any other visitors to your home that you know of? Or indications of who broke in?" I asked.

"The police said no one's come back," Will said, his skin paler, dark shadows under his eyes. "And no evidence was left whatsoever. No fingerprints. Nothing. These guys were pros."

"I can't believe he took Tommy's letters!" Mrs. Kroon interrupted, sobbing. "They're all I had left of him."

Will looked over at me, shaking his head dismissively. "We'll always have our memories, Mom," he said. "Just like before." Then he turned back my way, his face tightening. "Jack, we invited you here to ask you what you know. This all started when you knocked on my parents' door a few months back. It's gone downhill ever since. What do you and your colleagues know, and what have you been—"

This I had not expected. "Are you blaming me?" I asked. "Us?" Will opened his mouth to answer, but I didn't wait. "We had put this to bed. Your brother's the one who kept pushing this, on us, on Rob Stone. Whatever's going on, we didn't cause it."

Will raised a hand in defense. "Calm down, man. I'm not trying to blame anyone. We just want to know what's going on. We have a right to know. We, they, are part of this," he said, gesturing to his parents. "What are you guys doing?"

I was about to answer, then hesitated. This guy had just gone from concerned to pushy. "What do you mean?" I asked.

"Where are you taking this story?"

That's not how it works. "With all due respect, I'm not at liberty to say."

"Jack, our son has disappeared," Francine said. "We've been robbed. We're scared. Please help us."

I smiled sympathetically at her, attempting to be polite. She was harder to say no to. "All I can tell you is we're doing our job. There are multiple angles to this story, and we are chasing them down at our own risk. But it must have been Stone's questioning, not ours, that led to Logan's abduction. One of our reporters was also grabbed right off the street, as was a lawyer who apparently knew too much. No one's heard from them either."

"That's terrible," Will said, though he seemed unmoved. "What were they looking into?"

Pushy. Again. "I told you, I'm not at liberty to say. Let's just say it's a complicated story."

"What's with the games, man?" Will spat back at me, now flushed. He was losing it. His wife looked down at the floor.

"No games," I said. "In journalism, we don't reveal what we're working on. And given what's happening, it's best if you don't know any more." I stood. "Probably also best if I go now. Stay safe. I'll be in touch if there's something more I can share."

The Kroons stayed in their seats, staring as I walked to the front door.

"Thank you, Mr. Sharpe," Francine said softly as I opened the door. But I didn't turn around.

A steady rain fell as I navigated out of the neighborhood. Rush hour had ended a few hours before, so it was a quick trip up the parkway, along the Potomac. I drove by Reagan National Airport, then past the Pentagon on my left. I exited toward Memorial Bridge, the grandest of the welcome mats into the District from Virginia. As I often did when taking this route, I glanced to my left, up at the well-lit landmarks of Arlington National Cemetery.

Suddenly something large and solid smashed against the passenger side of my Explorer. A vehicle—I couldn't see it, but I knew that it had to be there—had pummeled me from out of nowhere.

I lurched left, crossing the median. I tried to veer right, back into the curve that guided traffic onto the bridge, but couldn't budge. Looking out the passenger-side window, I learned why: a large SUV was pinned up against the passenger door of the car.

I twisted the steering wheel even harder to the right, but that didn't help. The SUV didn't budge, pushing me further left, now fully into the oncoming lane.

Through the wet windshield, the bright headlights of oncoming cars suddenly blinded me, 30 yards away and bearing down fast.

New plan.

I slammed on the brakes as forcefully as I could.

The sudden stop caught the driver of the SUV off-guard, and the dark vehicle careened forward and to the left, flying across the median only feet in front of my hood.

The rain and darkness blurred what came next. But the sequence of noises told the story.

High-pitched shrieks of tires skidding along the slick road.

The initial thud of the head-on collision, followed by the crunch of metal eating into metal and the shattering of glass.

Car alarms blaring, and the hissing of fluids and air exploding from the engines of each destroyed vehicle.

Another thud followed, as a second car must have careened into the wreck. A second car alarm blared.

I braced my arms against the steering wheel, assuming I was about to join the pile-up, but nothing happened.

Ironically, the SUV that had initiated it all had shielded me from the collision a few car lengths in front. And since I was in the wrong lane, no one hit me from behind.

My first instinct was to help the crash victims. But given how this had started, I decided against it. I maneuvered into an opening in the lane I had been forced from, and drove over Memorial Bridge as quickly as I could.

PART 3

CHAPTER 20

WASHINGTON, D.C.

I THUMBED THE SEND button on my phone, and my message appeared in a text bubble on the screen: *I need your help.*

This was a desperate move on my part, but with George missing, my team wigged out, and that SUV targeting me, I definitely needed help. But not just any help. Cassie was right—what the hell were the D.C. police going to do? This was way above their pay grade. On the other hand, while bringing in the FBI would add real firepower, they'd want to know everything, keep it secret, and freeze us out of digging deeper. The story would be over. Plus, President Banfield's FBI was notorious for leaks, and if word ever spread up the chain and out to DroneTech, we'd still be in danger.

I hadn't been bullshitting Alex and Cassie. To be safe, it was on us to push the story *more* aggressively. Go on offense, get to the bottom of it, and get it all out there. Which posed another dilemma: if DroneTech was really behind all this, walking through their front door to find more would be a suicide mission.

So I needed help, and I was choosing the only viable path to get it. An option that risked exposing the secret I'd spent the past year trying to bury. And if that secret—the truth behind Abacus—ever came out, I'd be packing my bags for Youngstown, though even the *Vindicator* wouldn't hire me back.

But Oleg Kazarov was the only person I knew who could save the day. The Russian energy mogul was the only one with the capacity, and perhaps the interest, independence, and security to get involved. And the only one who would do so without telling a soul.

It helped that Kazarov owed me. The man who'd rigged an American election had gotten off scot-free for one reason—I had let him. I'd had good reason to do so, none more important than saving my life and that of my family. But it still had been one hell of a favor. And in Russian culture, that chit matters. Friends are friends and favors are returned, as he himself had explained to me over our breakfast. "That is the honorable thing," he'd said. Time to call on his honor.

* * *

First, a beefy man with a brown crewcut limped into the ornate private room where I sat waiting. Close behind, smiling from ear to ear, strolled Stefan Holmberg, Oleg Kazarov's consigliere. The tall, blonde Swede had flown me to London a year before, and was the last man to walk out of Abacus on its final day in Russian hands. And eight hours ago, he'd texted me back that he was prepared to meet on behalf of Mr. Kazarov at the Hay Adams Hotel.

"Good evening, Mr. Sharpe," Holmberg said.

My heart raced as his voice reminded me of a stark reality. This duo would kill without hesitation, and thanks to their handiwork I was the last person outside Kazarov's network who knew what he'd done. Here I was trying to convince them to stick their necks out to *help* me when they'd be better off getting rid of me.

"Good evening," I said, standing to greet them. "Thank you for getting here so quickly." Without the hassles of commercial travel, London to Washington was apparently a quick trip.

"This is Boris Popov," Holmberg said. "He heads up our security unit."

"Thank you for coming too, Mr. Popov," I said.

He nodded and grunted. The title confirmed it. There was no doubt this was the man behind the murders that had covered up the Abacus scandal.

"He speaks little English," Holmberg said. "Tell me, Mr. Sharpe, how can we help you?"

We sat down at the wooden table, a glass of ice water in front of each of us. Popov stared straight ahead, like a dog listening to a whistle, as I detailed the election, the disappearances, and our suspicions about what was happening. As serious as I was, Holmberg reacted like a child taking in an adventure tale—smiling, nodding, frowning at moments where I described actual killings but then recovering quickly. Even a few laughs. As I finished, he appeared downright ebullient.

"I have seen many efforts to win elections over the years," he said, rubbing his hands together. "But this is a plot truly worthy of the world's greatest superpower."

"Mr. Holmberg," I said, "this could not be more serious."

"I understand," he said, now somber as well. "Mr. Kazarov is a very busy man. What are you asking him to do?"

"We need protection. These are serious people, and I need to keep my team safe. Second, we need to infiltrate the operation, something I have no ability to do using traditional journalistic tools."

"Of course not. But what do you mean by infiltrate?"

He knew exactly what I meant. "I would like to understand their plot. Find documents that prove it. Then tell the story to the whole country."

"Are you asking us to engage in cyberespionage?" he asked, feigning innocence. Wanted me to say the words. Hell, he was probably recording this.

"Let's call it a private investigation, but yes. I assume you have the ability to do so."

"Oh yes. We have some of the most skilled people in the world."

"That's why I called. Russia seems to be a good training ground," I said.

"Oh, we have experts from far beyond Russia. But why should we do this for you? Hack into a high-risk military enterprise for no good reason? Not wise business practice."

I had prepared for this moment. "Tell Mr. Kazarov I can think of three very good reasons." The Abacus scandal had allowed the Russian to construct three major pipelines pumping oil and gas out of the Midwest.

Mr. Holmberg clapped his hands. "Three very good reasons indeed. He will enjoy that explanation."

"Enjoyment is not agreement," I answered firmly. "Honor means that favors are returned. Mr. Kazarov himself explained that to me."

Holmberg's smile disappeared. He said a few words to Popov in Russian, who mumbled something back, his thick lips barely moving. "How many people must we protect?" Holmberg asked.

"Three. Myself and my two team members. And we need it immediately."

He spoke again to Popov, who nodded back. "It can be done. They will be ready by tomorrow."

"And the surveillance?"

"Only Mr. Kazarov can decide. If the people are as dangerous as you say, there is risk that they will discover our work. We will let you know."

I handed him a file of Alex's papers summarizing DroneTech,

Americans for a Brighter Future, and other items. "Here is all the information. I think you'll know what to do with it."

"Indeed our people will. We will be in touch."

With that, he left the room. Popov limped a few feet behind him, grunting with each step. I studied his exit. Not capable of chasing down and killing Joanie Simpson with that limp, but easily could've been the one who poisoned Oliver Ariens.

* * *

I'd never regretted choosing the Georgetown townhouse that didn't *have* the garage. The decision had saved me $600,000. And even if there wasn't an available parking spot right out front, the walk to my front door was usually pleasant. But after almost being run off the road a day ago, the short walk now scared the hell out of me.

Following my meeting with Holmberg, I had headed back home. But as soon as I turned my battered Explorer onto the iconic cobblestone side streets of the old neighborhood, paranoia set in.

A sedan turned left behind me off Wisconsin Avenue. As I rattled along for two blocks, its distinct, square-shaped headlights bounced as well, about fifteen yards back. When I turned left on 36th St., so did the trailing car.

My townhouse front door was halfway down the block, but I drove right past, took a right at the next intersection, and drove another block up. Facing the regal gates that separate the Georgetown neighborhood from the school's campus, I turned right onto 37th Street.

The car had followed me all the way to this point and had paused at the same stop sign, but now turned left instead of right.

I slowly drove around the block, scouting for parking spots while also checking to see if the car was still there. Didn't see anyone.

The closest space I found was on P St., two blocks from my house. After turning the car off, I sat quietly, scanning up and down the street.

Several car lengths in front of me, a couple walked arm in arm. A block behind, three young men walked my way. Talking loudly, stumbling, they looked drunk but harmless. No doubt returning home from the bar scene. And across the street, my elderly neighbor walked her poodle as she did every night.

All clear.

I got out of my car just as the drunk kids passed, grabbed my small laptop bag from the backseat, and began the short walk home just a few feet behind them. They were definitely wasted, but provided an extra layer of security.

Unfortunately, the three kept walking straight as I turned left onto 36th. My street.

After a few more yards, I first noticed them. Parked not far from my front door. I didn't recognize the car itself, but the taillights were the same square shape as the headlights that had trailed me.

My heart sped up as I got closer to the car, but I kept walking, looking straight ahead, reassuring myself all was fine. Maybe it was a different car. Or simply another neighbor who'd been trying to park and had found a better spot than I had.

Feet from the car, I could see that the driver was sitting still, facing forward. Worse, someone was in the passenger seat. Besides lovers, who sits in a car together at 10:30 at night? And these two were definitely not making out. I paced faster, past the car. Reached into my pocket to feel for my house key among the many options on my overcrowded key chain.

A car door creaked open behind me. My chest tightening, I ended all pretense of courage and broke into an outright sprint.

I pulled out my key the moment I reached my door, fumbled twice to get it in the lock, whipped the door open, jumped through the doorway, and slammed it shut behind me. Far louder than I meant to.

* * *

"Is that you, Jack?"

I jumped at the sound of the woman's voice coming from up the stairs. And then I remembered I had a visitor. One I had invited.

"Sure is," I said, feeling my heart rate slow. "You made it in okay?" I tried to play it cool, but the loud door slam and my heavy breathing had signaled something was up.

"What the hell happened?" Alex asked from above.

"I don't want to scare you, but I think I was being followed."

"Geez, and I came over here because you promised it'd be safer!"

True. That had been my reason for inviting her over. Or at least the one I'd given. Alex and I had spent months alternating between playful bickering and mild flirting. Knowing she lived alone, I'd casually offered my guest bedroom as a more secure place for her to stay than her Dupont Circle apartment. When she'd accepted, I'd reacted casually, keeping it to myself that my heart had skipped a beat.

I jogged up the stairs. She was standing at the top, dressed in black leggings and a gray Vanderbilt sweatshirt, her hair in a long pony tail.

"Go Commodores!" I said it louder than I'd meant to. Nerves. Still breathing heavily, I approached the second-floor window behind her. I pushed apart two slats of the drawn hallway blinds to look for the car, and leaned up against the window. The space it had occupied was now empty, and another car, an Audi owned by the lawyer across the street, was in the process of snagging it.

I looked back at Alex, who stood right behind me. "A car followed me as I drove home, found the best spot on the street, watched me walk by, and then left," I said. "Not good."

"Well, you're safe now," she said calmly.

* * *

I'd worried for weeks that events would beat us to the punch.

This event did, and it was a big one.

The advisory promising a "major announcement" hit the wires at 9:00 a.m., and the surprise news conference started at 10:30. We didn't have time to send anyone to Harrisburg, so we just aired the pool feed live—as they had surely intended. Cassie and I watched from the conference room, each of us looking rough.

"There they are!" Cassie said, pointing at the television set. "Amazing."

Governor Nicholas, his wife, Congressman Bravo, and his young wife and kids, all stood together in front of the Pennsylvania statehouse. Music blaring in the background, a crowd of about a thousand rallied for several minutes before Nicholas began speaking.

The governor, looking upbeat for once, cut right to the chase. "From the moment this campaign began, I have searched for the perfect running mate. The man or woman who could help me lead this country."

On his right, Mrs. Nicholas looked as unhappy as usual, but a foot to Nicholas's left, Bravo beamed with every word.

"It's become clear that the man I was looking for was right next to me much of the time. He, like me, is a survivor. Of politics. But more importantly, of the battlefield, serving our country. So today we are going to get started. I am proud to announce that my running mate, and the next vice president of the United States, will be Congressman Anthony Bravo from California."

Amid another round of cheers, Bravo stepped to the podium. The moment he did, hundreds of Nicholas/Bravo signs waved in the air. Perfectly scripted.

Alex walked into the conference room just as Bravo was about to speak. I nodded at her, poker-faced—nothing had happened but a late-night conversation, but we'd agreed to keep the visit our secret. Then I turned back to the television.

"Thank you, Governor," Bravo said. "I am honored that you have selected me to join your ticket." He grabbed his wife Isabella's hand, as she placed her other hand on her younger son's shoulder. A family made for a postcard.

"American families are looking for strong leadership," Bravo said. "New leadership. To be as strong as we have always been. But they are also looking for us to lead in new directions in this challenging age."

New directions? The way this Nicholas-Bravo team had come together was definitely new, and not in a good way. It was disappointing to see Bravo falling right into line.

"I am proud to accept, and will be proud to serve," he said, raising his wife's hand like a prizefighter. "On to Cleveland!"

As the television cut back to regular programming, I picked up the remote and turned it off.

"Well, there it is," I said to Alex and Cassie. "Wish we had beaten them to the punch. But if what we suspect actually happened, we have until Cleveland to do something about it."

"Do something?" Cassie asked. "More than just reporting?"

"Well, yes. This ticket, brought together the way it was, cannot possibly stand."

* * *

Given the way George Vassos had been plucked off the street, I was looking forward to having a team of thick-necked Russian goons protect us. But the team Mr. Popov brought to our offices in the afternoon—thin, young, all smiles—looked more like our summer intern class.

"You know how serious the people we're investigating are, right?" I asked my new guard, Arthur, after introductions. Slightly shorter than my own 6'2", and at least twenty pounds lighter, Arthur was somehow the team leader. Tan, with a thick mane of jet-black hair combed back and falling to his shoulders, he looked more like a C-list Hollywood actor than an elite bodyguard.

He smiled back. "Mr. Sharpe, have you heard of the Alpha Unit?" he asked with only a hint of an accent.

Sounded vaguely familiar. "No."

"It is the Russian special unit for counterterrorism. Think of your best Navy SEALs, but trained to stop attacks of terror. We are all from Alpha Unit. Mr. Kazarov hired us specifically to protect you. You have nothing to worry about."

Reassuring, but still. "I was expecting . . . larger people."

"We don't all look like Mr. Popov. But that is good for you because we run much faster," Arthur joked, looking over at his far larger supervisor. "In fact, our strategy is to blend in. Not look like security at all. If their intent is to attack you, why invite more firepower?"

He paused. I nodded my acceptance.

"Mr. Sharpe, let me say again, you have nothing to worry about."

"Good."

He smiled. "May I say, you looked very worried last night."

"Excuse me?"

Now he laughed. "But it's good to know you can run fast when you need to. Not faster than me, but fast enough."

"Ah, I get it. That was you in the car."

I liked the guy already.

CHAPTER 21

"IOWA WAS THE key," I announced excitedly as Cassie walked into the conference room. I'd been marking up spreadsheets and state maps for two hours when I'd finally had a breakthrough and called her in.

"What do you mean?" she asked. "Didn't Nicholas lose there? Bravo too?"

"Yes, but the Iowa caucuses were the key that unlocked it all. The first true barometer of where Nicholas was performing well demographically. Once they knew that, they had all they needed." The color-coded maps were strewn across the conference room table. I grabbed the map of Iowa. "See the red counties? Those are where Nicholas won in Iowa."

Cassie took the map out of my hand. "That's a decent amount of counties, but it looks like Janet Moore won the most." Her counties were colored blue, and included Des Moines, Cedar Rapids, Davenport, Sioux City, and Iowa City.

"She sure did, which is why she won the state. You see those numbers?" With my black Sharpie, I'd handwritten a number over each county.

"Yeah."

"Those represent the voter turnout for each county." Most of the numbers were in the mid-to-high teens. A few in the lower twenties.

"Wow," Cassie said. "Those are low."

"Yes and no. Caucuses have notoriously low voter turnouts. Only the true die-hards show up. Those are about what you'd expect."

"Of course. They're still lower than I would have thought."

"Importantly for Moore, though, the turnout numbers are pretty even across the state."

She nodded.

I reached for the map of Minnesota. "Now check out this one."

Cassie looked at it for a few seconds. "No more blue counties."

"That's right. Moore was out by Minnesota."

"It looks like they're replaced by purple and yellow counties. Did Bravo and Stevens win those?"

"You got it. They largely filled in where Moore lost. But what do you notice about the turnout number?" The purple and yellow counties generally showed numbers in the teens. But Nicholas' red counties were in the high thirties, with a few topping 40%.

"That's a huge spread," Cassie said.

"Actually, the purple and yellow are about average for Minnesota. Outside of Iowa and Nevada, states like Minnesota, whose caucuses have rarely mattered in the past, see turnouts in the low teens."

"So it's the Nicholas counties that are high?"

"Yes. Historically high, for caucuses at least. Still not that high for a regular primary."

"So basically, the outside groups used the Iowa results to see where Nicholas did best, then selectively pushed turnout in later caucuses to secure big victories."

"You got it."

"So you can really push it if you're organized. Run up the score where you need to."

"Absolutely. Think about it: Minnesota has more than 5.5 million people. Usually, only 200,000 or so vote in the Democratic caucus. Upping the number to 350,000 like they did this year changes the outcome, especially if you do it in counties that are predisposed to one candidate. And in Minnesota it's even easier because you don't have to be a registered voter to participate in a caucus. Just need to be voting age, and attest that you are a Democrat."

"So that's how they won?"

"Sure is. Same story everywhere else." I spread out the other maps, all caucus states that Nicholas had won, including Colorado, Kansas and Maine. "Sky-high turnout in Nicholas's counties. Standard low turnout in the other counties."

"And Nicholas won each time?"

"Decisively."

"And those non-profits I found could do this all legally?" Cassie asked as I stacked all the maps into one pile.

"Legally?" I laughed. "It's not just legal. It's treated as charity work. They got a tax deduction for doing it."

* * *

Mr. Kazarov is prepared to meet.

The text came through in the late afternoon. The answer I'd hoped to hear, but also one that made my stomach churn. Kazarov was a brilliant man, but also deadly, with many overlapping interests and agendas. The meeting brought real opportunity, but also risk.

When? Where?

He wishes to meet you tomorrow.

London again?

No. He is at his dacha.

Dacha?

His summer cottage. Near St. Petersburg.

Talk about walking into the lion's den, unprotected. *Russia?* I replied. *I can't go to Russia. My team needs my help.*

Your team is in good hands. Mr. Kazarov will only meet in person. Be prepared to leave in three hours.

Glad they were in good hands. The question now was whether I would be.

* * *

ANNAPOLIS, MARYLAND

Alex recognized the thick white mustache from half a block away. An old Navy man himself, the former senator stood on the pier, slightly hunched in a tan bomber jacket and blue slacks, tall silver masts lined behind him.

"How are you, Ms. Fischer?" he asked as she reached him, removing his hat.

"I'm well. How are you, Senator?"

"I've never been better, probably because I'm no longer a senator," he said, smiling.

They both laughed, but it was such a sad answer. Alex had been in D.C. long enough to know better. Politicians didn't recover after the fall from the rarefied air of the Senate to everyday citizenship. Despite his half-hearted quip, his career-ending loss in a shocking primary upset would eat at him for the rest of his life.

"I can only imagine," she said.

"Let's take a walk, shall we? How can an old codger like me be of any help?" He angled his left elbow out toward her, and Alex placed her hand on the inside of his thin arm. One slow step at a time, they walked down the pier, the white spire of Maryland's state capital towering over buildings to their left while boats of all shapes and sizes bobbed along a wooden dock to their right.

Brewer pointed to a large, two-masted sailboat anchored 50 yards from shore. "That old schooner's been in this harbor for decades. She's a beaut."

With her landlocked Missouri upbringing, the best Alex could do was nod and parrot the lingo. "She sure is." She then jumped to the topic at hand. "Senator, you took a brave stand a number of years ago against the embedding of private contractors into military operations, particularly in the areas of drones."

His pace didn't change, but his polite smile disappeared. "I did, indeed. Someone had to say something."

"And my research leads me to believe it cost you your office."

He nodded slowly. "Worse than just my office," he said, frowning. "It cost me my good name. My career in public service."

Now there was the more honest pain of a defeated politician. Several sleek boats were docked to their right. Mini ships—no masts, fancy satellite dishes on top, one with a helicopter on its deck. Brewer turned to look at them, shaking his head.

"Those power cruisers are taking over this place. Why go with noise and fuel when you can sail quietly wherever you need to go?" He pointed at a boat a few hundred yards in the harbor, one triangle sail up, moving slowly from left to right. "I don't get it."

Alex got it. A guy's fancy power boat had once been the only highlight of a short relationship. Still, she nodded respectfully. "So you agree you lost because you stood up to DroneTech and others?"

"Young lady, this is something I never discuss." His voice wavered and his left arm tensed up. This was not a comfortable topic for someone who otherwise exuded a stately confidence.

Alex waited.

"The issue never came up in the campaign," Brewer said. "But yes, I'm convinced the forces I challenged planned every step of that campaign, and funded most of it, whether it was by way of the other candidates or those ridiculous ads against me."

"Including *both* other candidates?" Alex asked. Her quick research had revealed he'd faced two primary opponents, a woman and a man. The woman had bested him by two points while the man trailed well behind.

"Of course," he said impatiently. "They squeezed me from both ends.

I'd never have lost if I'd faced just one. I believe they were *both* recruited for the sole purpose of knocking me out. The same thing happened to my old friend George Little, who also stood up."

"Stood up for what?" She knew the basics, but wanted to hear him explain it.

"This is all on background, right? You'll keep it quiet?"

"Off the record, actually. I'm just learning for now."

"We stood up to keep the contractors from total immersion in the military's chain of command. It was unseemly when Blackwater did it, obscene when I took it on, and it's even worse now."

"And what happened when you stood up?"

"They got to everyone. No one would stand with us. A bunch who said they would ultimately caved under pressure. So we were hung out to dry."

As they approached the end of the pier, which abutted the closed gates of the Naval Academy campus, a dozen seagulls scampered to and fro in front of them. Several took off, cawing loudly, flying straight out over the water.

"And what's happened since?" Alex asked gently.

The senator stopped and pivoted, looking back up the harbor they had just walked past. "It's only gotten worse. The president is letting it all happen, and after seeing what happened to guys like me, Congress will never try to stop it. This can only be halted from the top. Our best hope was Governor Moore, but now she's out too."

"Governor Moore?"

"Oh yes. Ending these practices was a key priority for her. She called a few times about it. Lopez and Stevens weren't bad either, but Moore was the key."

"You know them? Even though they're Democrats?"

"Young lady, in my position, you know everybody. And some things are bigger than party. The sad part is that Moore had the guts to do it. So did Stevens. But like me, they lost."

"Right. In a crowded primary where a lot of independent money was spent. Sounds familiar." She let the sentence hang to see how he responded.

"I know what you're getting at. But mine was one state. You're talking about the entire national primary process. That's a lot harder to pull off."

She turned toward him, but he kept his gaze on the boats in the harbor. "You can't tell me you don't see the similarities."

"Of course I do. I actually brought it up with Senator Little. Watching what happened to Governor Moore reminded me of our own races. The debates. The attack ads. The squeeze. The biggest difference is that Nicholas and Bravo were real candidates."

"What did the senator say?"

"He didn't want to talk about it," Brewer said. "I've always been impressed by Bravo, by the way. Still have hope for him."

"Has he ever taken a position on DroneTech?" she asked, recalling his odd *Des Moines Register* interview.

"Not that I know of. But Nicholas? He's as diehard as the president, I'm afraid. He always kissed up to those guys on the Hill—one of the worst when he was there—and they've rewarded him ever since."

"Why haven't you spoken out during the campaign, Senator?"

"Honey, I'm damaged goods. No one wants to hear from me."

"You don't think your voice would matter on this now?"

"Sadly, I'm not sure anyone's voice matters on this. Like so many of the most important things in Washington, this is insider baseball. And money. These days, you win elections on shallow things that don't matter, not the real issues."

"That's depressing to hear, coming from you."

A sudden ruckus from behind caused them both to jump. All at once, the rest of the seagulls flew past them, then over the water, wings flapping loudly.

"Tell me about it," Brewer said. "I'm sitting here because it's the truth." He finally averted his gaze away from the water, turning toward her. His brown eyes now bore in on hers intensely, a glare she recalled from when he had ruled over committee hearings. "You probably know this, but you should be very careful covering this story. These guys don't mess around."

"So I've learned," Alex said coolly. "I have 24/7 security at this point. Some bodyguard named Olga is watching us right now and I can't even tell you where she is." She laughed as she said it, to leave the door open to the possibility that she was joking. "But why do you say that?"

"I saw things that raised alarm bells. A little blackmail here, extortion there. When a whole lot of people left me out to dry—good people stepping away at the key moment—I wondered what DroneTech had on them. Hell, I became convinced that one of my opponents only ran because they had something on *him*."

"Really?" She'd normally dismiss this as paranoia, but Senator Brewer was as level-headed as they came.

"Really. Either way, they certainly have the capacity to do a lot of damage. And I'm not talking about nasty television ads."

* * *

WASHINGTON, D.C.

"I've got some bad news," Warden Crawford said, without preamble.

Cassie braced herself. "About Kristina?" she asked.

"'Fraid so."

"She's dead." She wasn't asking, but stating a fact. Her voice sounded more bloodless than she intended.

"She is indeed. Saddest thing. But how she died is downright scary."

The warden explained that Kristina had been found on the side of a country highway on the outskirts of Houston, barely breathing. Still in the tight jogging clothes she had worn the day she disappeared.

"Her folks pulled the plug in the hospital. A brutal blow to the head had sealed her fate hours before. There was no comin' back."

"Any signs of what could have happened? Besides that final blow?"

"Not at first. Her body and clothes were clean of any evidence. It looked pretty straightforward."

"At first?"

"Yes. But she was a donor, and her folks wanted to donate her organs. They saved her heart, kidneys, her pancreas, and a lot of undamaged tissue."

"That's nice, but what does that have to do with her cause of death?"

"It's what they couldn't save. They had to reject her lungs. They looked fine at first, but on close inspection, damage was found that was way out of place." He paused. "You heard of the term *pleurisy*?"

"No."

"Me neither. The doc explained it. It's an inflammation of tissue in the lungs. Somehow she had it bad. Her lungs were a mess."

"How do you get it?"

"That's why they were puzzled. When they looked for the typical causes—a viral infection, sickle cell disease, certain types of drugs—they didn't find any. For someone her age, so healthy, it appeared out of nowhere. So they dug deeper, and found serious damage to her esophagus and larynx."

Cassie grew tired of the buildup. "So what was it?"

"Cassie, they think Kristina may have been waterboarded. It's the only thing the doc thought might explain that pattern of damage in someone with her good health."

Cassie jolted upright in her chair. Waterboarding conjured images of a bearded, grizzly terrorist in some secret foreign prison, not a healthy all-American woman from Texas. Then the chilling image of torture quickly led to another fear: whoever had done this to Kristina was looking for information. What had she told them?

The warden accurately read her silence. "Ms. Knowles, this means you're probably in danger," he said.

Cassie laughed. "You think?"

"You should assume she told them about your conversations. What you know about Cull and Gamble, and what y'all were looking into."

"Truth is, I already do assume that," she said, trying to sound tougher than she felt. Thank God for the lanky blonde Ukrainian bodyguard sitting a few yards away.

CHAPTER 22

STAFFORD, VIRGINIA

STAFFORD REGIONAL AIRPORT in Virginia to St. Petersburg, Russia. 4,500 miles. And far too much time for me to dwell on all that could go wrong.

Holmberg wanted to keep my exit as low profile as possible, so departing from the 5,000-foot runway made more sense than Dulles or Reagan National. Arthur dropped me off at the small strip at 5:00 p.m., and Kazarov's black Gulfstream waited outside the sole hangar. I boarded, the entire cabin to myself. Minutes later, we took off into the perfect May evening. Knowing that we would meet as soon as we landed, I fumbled around to open the pull-out bed and slept the entire way.

Eight hours and eight time zones later, the plane descended sharply as the high sun beamed off the waters of the Baltic below. Thousands of small islands dotted the gleaming water as we crossed over the southern edge of the Finnish mainland. Looked like a summer paradise now, but the winters down there must've been hell.

Minutes later, as we dropped through 5,000 feet, the plane banked hard to the left, providing a postcard-perfect view of the iconic bridges, canals, and spires of St. Petersburg off the right wing. Moments after crossing over land, we touched down, coming to a jarring stop at an airstrip no longer than the one we left in Virginia. Large evergreens surrounded the field, masking the fact that one of the world's great cities was only miles away. A black Mercedes met me at the plane, and we—just myself and the driver—exited through an imposing fence.

From what I could tell, we were driving away from the city. Seagulls circled high above. Tall pine trees, or the occasional spruce and birch, lined both sides of the bumpy road, filling in more densely the further we went. Every mile or so, a small wooden cottage appeared deep in the wood. Most were so small and rundown it looked like we had traveled back in time. The road curved to the right, and the occasional clearing to our left revealed the deep blue water of the Gulf of Finland lapping up to a shoreline that offered a mix of sand, scattered pines, and hulking granite boulders and rock formations. As we paralleled the coast, far larger cottages and homes replaced the small cottages from before. Some featured old architecture that had been refurbished; others, new builds that you'd find in the Hamptons. No doubt, Russia's new rich were buying up the place.

After several more miles, we turned left, waited as a large iron gate opened, and headed down a long driveway through even thicker woods. A wooden spire emerged between the trees. Then a second one, well to its left. A few moments later, the entire dacha came into sight, bookended by the two towers. Its brown oak façade created a rustic feel, but counter to Holmberg's description, this was not a cottage. It was a palace.

The car stopped in front of the main doors. I walked up the stairs, and just as I hit the top step, the door opened. Standing directly inside was the same butler who'd welcomed me to Kazarov's London estate one year ago.

"Welcome, Mr. Sharpe," he said. "We have been waiting for you." He ushered me to a screened-in porch area, where I took a seat and waited.

* * *

"Welcome to Komarova." Holmberg reached out his wiry, tan arm for a handshake.

"It's beautiful."

"Oh, yes. For centuries this was the summer escape for the great Russian poets, artists, and musicians. And it's now become the most popular place for the new capitalists and government leaders to build their summer dachas."

"I noticed."

"Mr. Kazarov was one of the first. Between the fast boats and the fast cars, we are not pleased that so many have followed him."

Sounded like the Great Lakes. "How long has—"

"Mr. Sharpe"—*Meester Sharpe*—"you have a problem." The tall, thin Oleg Kazarov burst into the room, talking loudly in his blend of Russian and British accents. I'd forgotten how bleak a figure he cut. The beady, dark eyes. Sharp nose. Pale skin. Oily brown hair.

I leapt to my feet to greet him, but he gestured for me to sit back down. He did not return my smile. "I know I do," I said. "Thank you for meeting with me to help solve it."

"And when I say *you* have a problem," he said, "I mean your country."

I hadn't heard it that way, but didn't say so. I was not interested in one of his lectures. "What have you found?" I asked.

During the Abacus scandal, Kazarov had taken great pleasure in highlighting the flaws in America's democracy. His familiar grin returned now. "The corruption of the enterprises you have brought to our attention is as deep as any we have encountered. Your country now resembles the Russian government's way of doing business."

I sat quietly. A bogus comparison, but not a reason to interrupt him.

"But worse," he went on, "is that corruption has infected all levels of the largest and most lethal military on the Earth. So it is a risk not only to your country, but to the world. This is a very dangerous direction."

"I understand. That is why I reached—"

"I originally agreed to help because friends help each other. But now I help because I want to eliminate this grave danger."

Good. The more motivated, the better. "What can we do?"

"You must expose this, and do so early enough to prevent the election of Governor Nicholas."

A side door creaked open as the butler entered the room, ramrod straight, carrying a circular tray. He placed a white teacup in front of each of us, then poured from a silver teapot. He placed several small bricks of sugar next to Mr. Kazarov's cup, then left as quietly as he entered.

"Why do you think I reached out to you?" I asked, smiling. "Can you help me?"

"I don't know," Kazarov said. "The members of my digital team have successfully breached major companies and governments all across the world. They have gathered much information that has helped me succeed, and in other cases, crippled competing enterprises—"

"Perfect," I said. "They're who we need to help us—"

"The team attempted to penetrate DroneTech," he said. He leaned forward, wrapped his spindly fingers around a sugar brick, then dropped it into his teacup. He lifted the cup a few inches above the table, and gently swirled it.

"And?" I asked.

"They failed. Their systems were better protected than most national defense and intelligence agencies we've encountered."

"I guess that's not a surprise, since they essentially operate as a defense agency."

"You are correct. But still, it was an impressively robust system. So we decided to look for a backdoor entrance. We attempted to breach the campaigns of Mr. Nicholas and Mr. Bravo." He lifted the cup to his mouth and sipped quietly. A loud slurp came from my left, from the less-refined Holmberg.

"Good idea," I said. "Campaigns can be sloppy in protecting against hacks."

"Yes, they typically have been easy targets. But not in this case. My best people could not penetrate the Nicholas campaign. Or even the Bravo campaign. Their security was as strong as DroneTech's. In fact, they appeared to be the same protections."

"The same?"

"The signatures were identical. This is strong evidence of collusion, but not helpful for our purposes." He placed the cup back on the table.

"And the SuperPAC? Americans for a Brighter Future?"

"If they have a separate system, we can't find it. It is probably housed within DroneTech somewhere."

"What do you do in a situation like this?"

He lifted the cup again. I sat quietly as he sipped, longer this time. Still, not a sound.

"Mr. Sharpe, we have not faced a situation such as this."

"Okay," I said, impatiently. "So what do we do?"

He returned the cup to the table. Another loud slurp from Holmberg. "We need another backdoor. And a way to open that backdoor. Once in, we can find everything we need."

"Is that why you brought me here?"

"It is." He suddenly stood. "It is a beautiful morning. Let us walk."

* * *

Walk didn't quite capture what followed.

Friends who'd spent time in Moscow had once told me Russians enjoyed picking mushrooms. But unless you experienced the pastime in person, you couldn't imagine the vigor and energy invested in the hallowed mushroom hunt. And it was a *hunt*, waged as aggressively as we in Ohio targeted deer, with the elegance and style Montanans brought to fly fishing.

After we donned heavy boots and dark fleece jackets, the butler handed each of us a wicker basket and a small knife, apparently essential tools in the mushroom-picking process.

"There are many types to pick," Kazarov explained, gleeful like I'd ever seen him. After exiting the back of the dacha into the heavy woods, we walked along an overgrown trail. "The most important choice," he said, "is which are the good ones and which carry the poison."

I shrugged. "How can you tell the difference?"

"There are many mushroom books and guides, but a good mushroom hunter knows by sight. By instinct."

Just as he said it, Kazarov leapt forward, loping to a spot well off the trail. He reached down behind a bush, spinning his right arm as if he was swimming the backstroke, his second and third fingers separated widely like a scoop. Then he brought the knife down with his left hand. A moment later, his right hand reemerged, holding up the largest mushroom I'd ever seen—it looked more like a small potato on a stem than a large fungus. He tossed his find into his basket and walked back to us.

"I assume that one is safe?"

"Oh yes. It is a beautiful specimen, especially so early in the season. This week's rain has helped."

We resumed walking along the trail. Unsure of the social etiquette of mushroom hunting, I kept quiet.

Kazarov didn't. "Mr. Sharpe, who else might know about the plot?"

"There are several law firms that have been involved. I think they were in the documents I sent."

"Yes. We attempted to penetrate them, but they were equally secure."

"And the individual attorneys? Mr. Doherty? His partners?"

"They are very careful. No separate accounts. No use of social media. So no opportunities there either."

"How about in the military itself? The Pentagon? Surely there must be some holes there."

As I finished the sentence, Holmberg jumped off the trail to his left. Displaying none of the gracefulness of his boss, he reached down with both hands and sliced. He then raised his right hand to show us what looked to be a small donut, which he then tossed into his basket.

"A milk cap," Kazarov said admiringly. "Splendid. Yes. There are many weaknesses in their systems, but none where DroneTech is concerned. We found nothing."

Kazarov bounded off the trail again, this time to the left, plunging much deeper into the woods. He came back a minute later holding what looked like hors d'oeuvres I had eaten once at a fancy Cleveland restaurant.

"Puffballs," he announced. "A delicacy!"

"Forgive me, Mr. Kazarov," I said, "but how did you see them way back there?"

"With time, one develops an eye for hidden wonders others cannot see."

"I see." This, I thought, essentially summed up his conquest of the natural gas throughout Eastern Ohio. I stopped talking and focused more intently on the ground, scanning from left to right a few dozen yards in front of me. At the foot of a large oak tree to the right, a streak of tan stuck out from the mocha-colored dirt. I took a few steps in that direction, and spotted three mushrooms that, although slightly smaller and flatter at the top, looked similar to the potato mushroom Kazarov had first picked. The one he had been so excited about.

I set off quickly to grab the targets before anyone else. Hearing the two men following me, I broke into a sprint. Knife in my left hand, I reached down with my right for the grab.

"Stop!" Kazarov yelled.

I stopped on a dime, afraid my aggressive behavior had violated mushrooming protocol.

"Do not touch those!"

"Why not? They look just like the one you picked earlier."

"Mr. Sharpe, those mushrooms are among the deadliest you will find."

"You're kidding."

Holmberg set me straight. "He is not. Those are Death Caps. It is believed that just such a mushroom killed Peter the Great's mother. She picked one not far from here."

"Good company, I guess," I said, laughing.

Neither responded. Poisonous mushrooms and dead tsarinas were apparently no laughing matter.

Two hours later, our mushrooming came to a halt as we exited the thick woods and reached the beach. While our baskets brimmed with every color, shape, and size of fungus, our brainstorming on how to hack into the DroneTech operation had been less successful. As we headed up the sand and rock beach to return to the dacha, Kazarov pushed one last time.

"Please press your team," he said. "Look again into the research they've conducted. We must find the weak link into their system. Then notify Arthur. When you do, we will exploit it."

* * *

WASHINGTON, D.C.

Who knew the most secure hotel in Washington was the lowly Fairfax?

"This is where foreign visitors who require best security stay," Olga had explained to Alex. Short, compact, with a tight blonde ponytail and more makeup than she needed, the Russian bodyguard reminded Alex of the tiny Soviet gymnasts she'd watched as a kid.

Jammed among embassies up and down Massachusetts Avenue, the extra layer of security made sense. Emissaries and foreign visitors demanded it, aware that their every move was watched as they visited their nation's most important outpost.

Alex had slept soundly her first night there, but the text message that greeted her in the morning quickly brought her back to reality. A 703 number.

Shirey here. We need to talk.

The colonel never texted. She looked at her hotel's landline, and sent that number back to him. *Call this number from a secure line.*

Seconds later, the hotel phone rang. The usually calm Shirey wasted no time on pleasantries. "They asked who you were."

"Who did?"

"Some higher-ups. Serious brass. Someone saw that you had signed into the archive section, and were nosing around in the files of Bravo's unit."

"That's right," she said. "I had to sign in there. What did you tell them?"

"That you're a good reporter. That you've been a friend, and helpful at times. And that you don't cause trouble."

"All lies!"

"Exactly," he replied, laughing. "They wanted to know what you were working on. I said I had no idea. That you and I kept up regularly, but you held things close to your vest."

"That's pretty much true."

"Alex, here's the problem. If these guys know, DroneTech knows. Dangerous people know. Doug Hansen dresses up nicely when he needs to, but word is he's a real psychopath. He plays for keeps. You need to be really careful—don't leave a paper trail anywhere, because they will find it."

She'd completely forgotten about the archive sign-in sheet. What other traces of her work had she left out there? Nothing came to mind. After hanging up, she dialed her ex.

"Morning, Mike. Hope you're well. Is Molly up?"

"Sure is. One sec."

A few seconds passed. "Mommy, are you at that hotel?"

"I am, sweetie. Is Daddy taking good care of you?"

"Yes. But I want to come home."

Hearing the sweet, sad voice pained her. She missed her too. "Sweetie, I have to stay at this hotel for a couple days. When I'm done, you can come home."

"Okay. Love you, Mommy."

"Love you. Please put Daddy back on."

A few seconds passed, then he returned. "Everything okay with you?" he asked.

"Like I said, we're doing a tough story. I really appreciate you doing this. It may be a few more days though."

"Not at all, Alex. I'm glad to help. Just stay safe for all of our sakes."

"Will do. Thanks, Mike."

She hung up.

Funny. They'd gotten along better after the divorce. Mike was more reliable and loyal than when they were married. And a great dad. She hated not being up-front about how dangerous things were getting.

CHAPTER 23

OVER THE NORTH ATLANTIC

EVEN IN LUXURY seating, my quads and calves ached the entire flight home. Picking mushrooms had kicked this old quarterback's ass. Looking back, the hunt had been almost three hours of lunges. Not a bad workout.

On the plus side, the long daytime flight home meant rare quiet time to catch up on work. And as Kazarov had stressed, job one was to find a back door into the DroneTech network. The company itself was impregnable. The campaigns were airtight. The law firms were protected. So how to get in?

I had only skimmed Alex's files previously. Now that I had time to read them more closely, Kazarov's alarm made sense. The DroneTech model threatened to change the entire way the United States conducted war, with no checks standing in the way but billions of profits to be made. And eight years of another supportive president would cement it all into place permanently. Hence, the no-holds-barred effort to place a champion in the White House.

But what also emerged from Alex's files was how robust the public defense of this unseemly arrangement was. Reminded me of the fight over climate change. Energy companies and their leaders had funded endless efforts to undermine the scientific consensus that human activity contributes to rising global temperatures. Over time, those never-ending attacks had muddied the issue with the public, and given politicians cover for voting against the clear science.

Likewise, despite the obvious risks of the DroneTech arrangement, an army of credible and high-profile surrogates had mounted a spirited defense. Retired generals, academics, former congressmen, and talking heads, all fighting DroneTech's battle for them on multiple fronts. Testimony. Conferences. Articles. Studies. Television appearances. And these advocates always came armed with compelling data to support their case. Cost savings and efficiencies. Enemy casualties inflicted. And best of all, American lives saved—the magic number, cited again and again.

After digesting the reports, I thumbed through the footnotes. Where were all these guys getting their supportive facts? And that's when I found it.

One Washington-based think tank appeared repeatedly. Its paper from three years ago had been the source for the cost-saving estimate. A different study had derived the casualty estimate. A third paper had calculated the estimate for lives saved. Again and again, one think tank produced the treasure trove of data that DroneTech's surrogates drew on whenever they marshaled the company's defense. But what stuck out was not that a single institution enjoyed a monopoly on defending DroneTech. No doubt, like the climate debates, the company and its leaders had bankrolled the self-serving research and received a tax write-off for their investment.

And it was not that the think tank was located only a few blocks from our offices. Right under our noses.

What stuck out most was that two months ago, I had been sitting comfortably in its main conference room, amicably meeting with one of its top analysts. The prime source of all that data, cited in footnote after footnote, was the Defense Policy Institute. The same think tank where Will Kroon spent his days analyzing modern warfare.

"My God," I whispered to myself, remembering our first meeting. Thomas Kroon's brother had been as welcoming as can be, eager to scoop up every detail he could. I had fallen right into his lap, including showing up at his house and being followed home. The son of a bitch had even tried to have me run off the road. I'd been played.

But now came the opportunity for payback.

The monitor in the cabin showed that we were just over the edge of Greenland. The plane had been bouncing through mild turbulence for the past few minutes, but, impatient to report my finding, I unbuckled my seatbelt, walked to the cockpit door, and knocked. A bearded, dark-haired pilot opened it, his bushy, raised eyebrows communicating that he didn't appreciate the interruption.

"Is there a way to contact Mr. Kazarov from here?" No doubt Kazarov's own plane would have a secure line.

Saying nothing, the pilot pointed to a gray phone to the left of the cabin's main door. He closed the cockpit door before I could even thank him.

The plane bounced even more roughly as I stepped toward the phone, knocking me a couple feet past it. I steadied myself and lifted the receiver, but there were no numbers to dial. It simply started ringing. On the third ring, it clicked.

"Holmberg here. Are you not satisfied with the flight?"

"A little bumpy, but Kazarov Air is great as always," I said. "I found something. We should look into a Washington organization called the Defense Policy Institute. They appear closely linked to DroneTech."

Holmberg went quiet for a few moments, no doubt asking someone else how to respond. "The team already looked into the Institute as well. It was protected just like the others."

Strange they hadn't mentioned that. But I pushed back. "We may have an 'in' with them. We've had contact with one of their analysts and his family. It might present an opportunity."

As I said it, the plane jolted far harder than before, almost knocking me over. With my free left hand, I reached up to the ceiling, pushing against it to steady myself.

Over the phone, silence. Muffled voices. Then the Swede spoke again. "Is the analyst our friend?"

"He is not. But his family may be, and they need our help."

More voices. Then he was back. "An opportunity indeed. Arthur will have instructions when you land."

The plane bounced violently as I hung up. I grabbed hold of the back of each seat as I headed to my own, my sore legs aching with every bounce.

I sat down and buckled up.

* * *

WASHINGTON, D.C.

Alex walked back from the mini bar with a Chardonnay in one hand, a bourbon in the other. Sitting on the end of the bed I was lying on, she handed me my glass.

"Thanks," I said as we both looked at a television set airing the political news of the day. "I'll get the refills."

Back at the Fairfax after my return from St. Petersburg, I'd just dozed off with the lights on when she'd knocked on my door. Her evening visit was a welcome escape after a long day. But her visit the other night went unacknowledged, and I didn't know if that was a good or bad thing.

"All good with Molly?" I asked, unable to tell her about my trip.

"Yep. Mike is a saint. But I miss her."

"I'm sure. Hopefully this will be over soon."

"God I hope so."

Footage aired of Nicholas and Bravo barnstorming the country. The Bravo bus toured across Ohio's northern cities, drawing big crowds at every stop. Nicholas trekked across Virginia, North Carolina, and Georgia, now swing states where his veteran status was a big plus. Wherever Nicholas campaigned, his wife stood only feet away. She rarely spoke, and never made solo appearances.

Isabella Bravo was her polar opposite, jetting all over the country on her own. This week, she was making a swing through Florida, meeting with groups of young moms like herself. And as tonight's lengthy footage captured, when given the mic, she was as strong a performer as her husband. With her jet-black hair, emerald-green eyes, and always chic outfits, she spoke with passion and had an obvious personal touch with everyday voters.

"Wow. She's good," Alex said. "So poised."

She really was, especially given the circumstances. "You think she knows?" I asked.

"About what's really going on?"

"Yes."

"I guess it depends on their marriage, but I can't imagine she doesn't. We wives know."

I agreed. "What would you do if you found out that your husband was in the middle of some wild plot like this?"

"Now that's a tough one. I hope that I'd do my best to stop it. But I wouldn't want to hurt my family either, especially my kids."

I'd been idly asking questions. But her answer sounded right. Got me thinking. "Maybe we can help her find that balance."

She turned toward me with a smile, her long ponytail flipping behind her. "Somehow I knew you were going to say that."

* * *

ALEXANDRIA, VIRGINIA

"Mr. Kroon has left."

"Good," I said. "Alone?"

"Yes, alone," Arthur, who was playing lookout, replied. "His parents must still be in the house."

"And you're sure no one followed?"

"I am sure."

Minutes after Will Kroon had left his home, I knocked on the door, hoping my first visit hadn't been a fluke—that, as in Virginia Beach, Mrs. Kroon would answer.

The patter of faint footsteps approached, a good sign. The door clicked and opened. And then she appeared, wet straggly gray hair falling to her shoulders, wide-rimmed glasses magnifying her wrinkled eyes, fluffy white bathrobe wrapped around her small body.

"Oh my goodness," she said, smiling. Embarrassed. "What are you doing here?"

I raised my finger to my lips and handed her a note I'd written in the car, asking for a time when we could talk privately. Her initial response would show everything. Hesitation? Suspicion? Or had I built enough trust with her that she would reply with no doubts?

She raised her right hand and mimicked writing. *Good.* I handed her the pen I'd brought, she placed the piece of paper against the wall, wrote something down, and handed it back.

I take a short walk every morning at 10. Can meet you then?

Perfect.

I gave her a thumbs-up and walked away. The hour-long wait would let me look into something that had bothered me all morning.

* * *

When incumbents were booted from office, they blamed everyone. The campaign staff screwed it all up. Other politicians on their ticket dragged them down. Some other person got in the way of their otherwise smooth path to reelection. Everyone's at fault but the candidate himself.

That's how we'd reacted when my dad lost decades ago. Softened the blow.

So when Alex had described her long talk with Senator Brewer—and his theory about why he'd lost—I'd dismissed it as the typical finger-pointing of a jilted incumbent. Brewer had stayed a term too long, lost a step, and the voters had opted for new blood. Sad for him but that's how it went.

But after sleeping on it, I'd reconsidered. Brewer was a serious guy, more self-aware than most politicians. Even more importantly, his description of that final, losing race felt familiar. As Governor Moore had learned, multiple opponents and outside attacks can wreak havoc on a front runner. Was Brewer's Senate loss a forerunner to the presidential primary? A dry run?

Worth checking out. And from Alex's telling, the key figure in it all was the third-place finisher in that Florida primary. He hadn't gotten a lot of votes, but those he did get were likely critical—the difference between Brewer eking out a narrow victory and losing. This guy's spoiler role had been similar to Bravo's, but without any clear reason to have played it. Why run at all? Sitting in my car, I hopped online to find out.

Chuck Groppe hailed from Melbourne, Florida. He was a longtime wrestling coach who'd gotten himself elected to the Florida House at 46 years old. Eight years later, facing term limits, he'd unexpectedly won a seat in the Florida Senate when a financial scandal ensnared his opponent. After winning, Groppe again displayed the same lack of ambition and prowess that had marked his two terms in the House. A total zero.

Then, out of the blue, this lifelong backbencher had announced that he would challenge Senator Brewer. The news surprised the Florida media not only because he was such a longshot, but because he was not running "from cover"—he would have to sacrifice his safe state senate seat in order to run. No one could figure out why he'd choose this kamikaze mission. And he never explained it.

Once in the senate primary, he waged an intense campaign on one issue: guns. You name the gun control measure, he was against it, even tagging Brewer as a "gun grabber" because he had supported adding childproof locks to certain types of guns. While Groppe lost badly, exit polling showed that a big chunk of male voters, voters who likely would have voted for Brewer, had loved Groppe's gun rhetoric. Losing those voters had cost Brewer the seat.

Such an odd candidate. So strange that he'd run at all.

I texted Arthur: *Have you ever been to Florida?*

* * *

How hard would it be to convince a mom to rat out her own son? Time to find out.

"That's a fast pace you keep, Mrs. Kroon," I said after she opened the passenger-side door. I had driven behind her for a few seconds before she'd stopped.

"Why thank you, Jack," she said, big smile on her face. "I actually was a varsity athlete a hundred years ago!"

"Oh, stop," I said, smiling. "But that is impressive."

She sat in the passenger seat, breathing quickly, as we drove around the block. I wanted to secure her trust by being friendly, but I also genuinely liked her. Tough old lady, especially with all she'd been through.

"So what is it you want to tell me?" she asked. "Any news on Logan?"

I'd spent all night planning my answer. Get her to help, give her hope for Logan, but don't come between a mother and her son. No one wins that battle. "We have a lead," I said, "but it's very complicated."

"How so?" she asked.

"It involves Will. His workplace, actually."

She cocked her head as she looked over at me. "Will?"

"We found evidence that his workplace may be involved. That he may be in danger too."

Worry lines creased her forehead. "We need to tell him."

"Mrs. Kroon," I said, pausing for the big moment, "we can't tell him. That's why I'm telling you while he's gone. They're watching his every move, but not yours. They may want to grab him just like Logan."

My stomach tightened as I said it, nerves on edge. Didn't feel right to mislead her. Plus, if she didn't buy it, she'd go right to Will and blow it all. Everything was in the hands of this sweet old lady.

"What can we do to stop it?" she asked.

"That's why I wanted to talk to you. If we can access their computer network, we might be able to protect Will, as well as figure out where Logan is."

Her frown deepened. "I'm still confused. Why would we not tell Will about this? He would know what to do."

"Because he's the one they're watching. If he looks into any of it, they'll know. With you, they won't."

"Okay," she said, her nose crinkling with skepticism. Still work to do. Go deeper.

"Mrs. Kroon, did you notice that long scratch on the side of my car as you entered?" I asked. "That's from the other night. Someone tried to kill me when I left here. Almost ran me off the road. And all because they're watching Will, and they believed I was giving him information that night."

Her mouth opened wide as I told the story. "That's horrible. I'm so sorry. All because you're trying to help us?"

"Yes ma'am. I'm afraid so."

She clenched her jaw. "How, specifically, can I help?"

"First, we think that they are tracking Will's every move, including his emails and computer files. But there's a way we can check for that."

"Okay," she said.

"Does he have a computer at home?"

"Yes, in his home office. He's always in there at night, typing away. My boy never stops working, even through all this."

I took a small envelope from my left breast pocket, then pulled out the black zip drive and small piece of black tape Arthur had handed me earlier. "All we need you to do is take this little device and stick it into the slot of the computer where it fits. Is it a laptop?"

"No. It sits on his desk."

Even better. "The slot should be right under the monitor. Put this in for a minute. Then take it back out and destroy it. Also, attach this piece of black tape to the back of the monitor."

She looked closely at the zip drive. "That's it?"

"That's it. For his own good, don't tell Will. If no one's tracking him, we'll know it and move on. If they are, we'll be able to figure out who and break into their system."

"Which should help us find Logan?"

"Exactly."

She pursed her lips together as she reached for the door handle and pulled. "I will get it done."

She stepped out the door and resumed her brisk walking.

I smiled for a few seconds, but that moment of satisfaction ended once I read the text that had come through while they were talking.

He's back! Arthur wrote. *The son just pulled up to the house. Leave quickly.*

Why would he come home? I wrote back. Dumb question. How would Arthur know?

Maybe you were seen.

Stay there and see what happens.

Now she just got home.

Damn.

I quickly drove out of the neighborhood. The national election now rested in the hands of Francine Kroon of Virginia Beach.

* * *

As Arthur was driving me to the airport, I dialed a familiar number. "I need a favor," I said.

"Sure you do," Mary Andres said. "What's going on?"

Groveling to my old boss was my best option. I needed her help, but didn't want to say why.

"It's complicated, but the basics aren't. I need you to set up some type of women's forum with Isabella Bravo."

"As in the wife of Anthony Bravo, candidate for vice president?"

"That's right."

"Why would she do a forum with the little old *Youngstown Vindicator*?"

"She's doing them all over the place. You guys are as strategically located as it gets when it comes to swing voters. If you set it up right, my guess is she'll come."

"Okay," she said, clearly not sold on the idea, but I could work on that later.

"And then I need to be able to get one of my reporters in there."

"Okay. Why don't we co-sponsor it? Republic and the *Vindicator*, together."

Time for my curveball. "That's the kicker," I said. "I don't want anyone to know it's us there."

A long sigh came through the receiver. "Jack, what the hell is going on?"

"I told you, it's complicated. You don't want to know much."

"Jesus, are you on one of your crazy scavenger hunts again?" Her jovial tone belied her words. She was game.

"The last one turned out pretty well, didn't it?"

She laughed. "Yes, it did. Especially since it got you out of my hair!"

She held me in suspense for a few moments.

"I'll reach out to the campaign to invite her in. We'll see what happens."

After we hung up, I made one more call. The haunting thought of George Vassos being held captive somewhere—or worse—was never far from my mind.

"Sergeant Murphy here."

"It's Jack Sharpe. Any sign of him?"

"None, sir. We've got a whole army on it, but not a thing."

"Damn. Well, keep me posted."

So frustrating that there was nothing I could do. *Work the story*, I told myself. If the cops couldn't find him, maybe we could.

CHAPTER 24

MELBOURNE, FLORIDA

"NO WAY AM I talking about that campaign. I've put it in the past."

Like a lot of former athletes—including me for a time—Chuck Groppe had blown up, now weighing at least 300 pounds. As he spoke, depending on his posture, he displayed either two or three chins, squeezed against his collar so tight I was surprised he could breathe.

Despite his initial protest, he would come around. Politicians couldn't say no to the press, especially television. Once out of office, most craved it even more than before.

"It's totally off the record," I said. "The story's not about you. I'm trying to learn something about campaigns generally. Why people run as longshots for higher office, even giving up a safe seat to do it."

Groppe had landed a government affairs gig at an insurance company back in Melbourne. We were meeting in his office, which overlooked a small wharf on the Atlantic.

"What inspired you to run against Senator Brewer?"

"Well, uh, I was just tired of career politicians like him. I still am. They need to be challenged."

"You sure achieved your goal. His career ended because of you."

"It sure did."

"Was it worth it?" I asked, leaning in.

"Worth what?"

"You gave up your state senate seat, tanked your own career, so someone else could beat him in the primary. And a Democrat ultimately beat her in the general election. Seems like a bad trade, for you especially."

"Brewer's gone," he shot back defensively. "I'll take it."

"What made you pick guns as your big issue? You had never really pushed hard on gun rights before."

"Well, we knew it was an issue that would hurt Brewer. He had some weakness on it."

A slight opening. "Who's 'we'?"

"What do you mean?"

"You said 'we' knew. Who does that include?"

"My team. My advisors."

"Right. Who was on your team?"

Two chins quickly folded into three as he jerked his head backward, stretching the already tight collar to its breaking point. "Sharpe, where's this going?"

"Your campaign budget seemed very small. Virtually no staff. Who were your advisors?"

"Friends and others who wanted me to win. My kitchen cabinet. We all knew that guns were a weak spot for him."

I kept expecting him to end the interview, but he didn't. Another mistake politicians made—they kept talking. So a good reporter kept pushing. "Polling too?" I asked.

"Huh, no, that was just our hunch. And guess what? We were right!"

Bullshit. Like a torpedo, the focus on guns was precisely targeted to take out Brewer, likely based on serious research. But Groppe's campaign reports showed no expenditures for polling or focus groups. Someone savvy had guided him to make it about guns, and it wasn't just "friends."

As we talked, I'd been scanning the room. His walls told me a lot more than his words. This guy had one passion, and it wasn't politics.

A dozen or so wrestling photos adorned his office. A few featured Groppe in his glory days, looking young and trim, a three-time state champion and a college star. But even more photos captured his coaching days, surrounded year after year by his winning Seaside High School wrestling squads. All smiles, especially Groppe himself. An impressive collection of plaques commemorating regional and state championships. But the display also felt a little intense for a guy in his late 50s.

Time to stroke his ego a bit. "Looks like you had some good teams, coach."

"You noticed?" he asked, leaning back in his chair, opening his arms widely as if to display all the photos and trophies. The gesture revealed the sweat-darkened armpits of his blue shirt.

"But you gave that up, too?"

"Yep. The Statehouse called and I had to stop coaching. I couldn't do both."

"But it looks like that's still your top priority. Nothing on your walls about insurance, or even politics. Why didn't you go back to that rather than insurance?"

The question soured him instantly. Back to three chins as he looked down grimly.

"I had to pay the bills, which this job does. Coaching wouldn't have."

"But still seems like your true passion."

"Oh, it is. Nothing better captures the human competitive spirit. You think politics is fierce? Try wrestling."

I had once. Sophomore year. I'd hated everything about it—the headlocks most of all—and quit a week after making the team.

"You keep up with a lot of your wrestlers?" I asked.

He looked down.

"Some of them. Many have gone on to do great things. I taught them well."

"Good for you . . . good for them."

But I wasn't going to take his word for it.

* * *

On the outside, it looked more like a resort than a school. But with banners touting school spirit and long hallways of painted student lockers, the inside of Seaside was as high school as it gets. The campus was on the way back to the airport, so I figured a short visit was worth a shot.

"How can I help you?" Seaside's athletic director asked as we shook hands past security. "We're excited that our baseball team is undefeated, but I wouldn't have expected a visit from Republic News about it."

Perfect. A guy like this was used to dealing with fawning local sports media, not the tough stuff.

"Congratulations, but I'm not here for baseball. We're trying to do some positive stories on politics."

"Positive about politics? It's about time. But why would that bring you here?"

"Oh, we're doing a profile of Chuck Groppe, his career in office, and as an inspiring coach here. We know he turned a generation of boys into men, and champions. And then he did the same in the Statehouse." On a fishing expedition, with little to lose, throw out oversized bait and see what happens.

The A.D. swallowed it all. "You're doing a story on Chuck Groppe?" he asked nervously, his smile disappearing.

"Absolutely! He made a difference as a public officeholder. But we also know how much of a difference he made here. We'd love to talk to you about it. Will be a great piece."

The poor guy looked sick. "Jack, if you want to cover our current success, that's great. But we can't be part of a story about—"

I swatted my hand, brushing away his hesitance. "Of course you can. Coach Groppe was an institution here. He *was* Seaside—"

"We can't be part of it." He shook his head forcefully, and started walking toward the school's exit.

I didn't budge. "I don't understand. He was a championship coach. A mentor. Why wouldn't you want to be part of a story on him?"

"It's just against our policy. I'm going to have to ask you—"

"Can I at least look around? Maybe get my camera crew to take footage, capture the team photos and the trophies? You certainly can't have policies against that."

"Jack, I'm trying to be nice here, and I'm a fan"—his tone of voice changed, becoming much more serious—"but we can't be part of any story on Coach Groppe. There are no pictures of his teams in the gym. I can't say any more than that."

I knew it—the school was definitely hiding something. One last push. "No pictures? High schools always post pictures, show their trophies, you know—"

There was a trophy case down the hallway.

"—There!" I said, pointing. "Looks like Seaside also won some basketball championships too. You must have the same thing for Coach Groppe's teams."

"We don't have those here. Not for his teams. That's all I can say."

He took two more steps towards the door, and I followed. "We'll just do the story without you guys, then."

"Jack, I may be overstepping my bounds here, but you should not do the story at all. Let me leave it at that. Have a nice day."

"Same to you. Good luck with that baseball team."

I walked out the main entrance and headed towards the car. Halfway there, I veered left and circled around to the gymnasium on the south end of the school. Classes were just getting out, so kids were scrambling into the entrance to change for practices. I slipped in as a flood of girls rushed in. After I passed through the door, a straggler walked in behind me.

"Excuse me," I said, "can you tell me where they train for wrestling?"

"Mister, that's a winter sport," the girl said, silver braces shining. "No one's wrestling right now."

"Oh, I know that. But where do the practices take place?"

"Over there." She pointed to her left. "The door is right next to the wrestling Hall of Fame wall. It may be locked."

Short on time, I walked down the hallway. The "Wall" was actually three cabinets of trophies. An impressive bounty. Seaside had won ten state championships and dozens of regional championships. Each championship was memorialized by not only a trophy, but a photo of the championship team, with Seaside's coach proudly positioned in the middle.

The earliest photos, from the 1950s and 1960s, were black and white. The same coach—Coach Hayes, short, stocky, crewcut—smiled proudly in all of them, along with teams of kids with nearly identical crew cuts. All the kids were white, wearing dark T-shirts and tight shorts. Coach Hayes' teams had won two state titles and a bunch of regionals. The photos went from black and white to color after 1968, and the 1970s and early 1980s kids looked exactly as you'd guess—long hair, long sideburns, lots of facial hair, and their outfits were far tighter and a gaudy green. They were more diverse, too, with several African-American and Hispanic boys in the group photos. A skinny, youthful Coach Carlson stood proudly with his squads, who'd won a state title and three regionals in his eleven years. In the far right of the cabinet, beginning in 2005, Coach Suarez also had some success. Several regional titles, if no states. But the diverse set of kids in his photos looked pleased enough.

But the true glory years for the Seaside wrestling team took place in between Coaches Carlson and Suarez. Took up the entire middle cabinet. A 22-year streak in the '80s, '90s and early 2000s like no other in the school's history. Trophy after trophy. Seven state titles and sixteen regional titles.

Despite the enormous success of Coach Chuck Groppe and his teams, one thing was missing. No pictures accompanied those trophies. Photos had clearly been taken, because they were proudly displayed in former Coach Groppe's insurance office. But they weren't on display here, at least not anymore. And among the plaques and trophies, not one mention of his name. Seaside High had wiped away any trace of the most successful coach in its history.

They were definitely hiding something.

* * *

WASHINGTON, D.C.

"So what's the breaking news you want to tell me about?"

After the quick trip to Florida, Alex and I were sipping stiff drinks at the outdoor bar at the top of the Fairfax. A full moon lit up the stately foreign embassies along Mass Ave., with the shadow of the three towers of the Washington Cathedral off to the right. All the ambiance of a date, which I found so comfortable. But we still held back, keeping our discussion all business.

"We've been assuming that Bravo was an active participant in the plan," I said. "But now I'm not so sure. They may be blackmailing him."

"What makes you say that?" she asked, still skeptical.

"A pattern. Brewer was right about his primary. Groppe crushed his chances, yet had no reason to run. Gave up a safe seat for nothing. His campaign served only one purpose—to take out Brewer—and he clearly got help to do so."

"And you think he was blackmailed?"

This was going to be a hard sell. Alex hated speculation.

"My guess is he got caught up in a scandal in his past. Had been a wrestling coach for decades at a local high school. It's clearly still his passion—still lives surrounded by wrestling photos in his office. But he didn't return to the school when he—"

"Jack, this seems a little on the iffy side."

"I actually stopped by the school, and the athletic director responded to the guy's name like he had leprosy. And they've gotten rid of all the photos from his years there. Best coach in their history, but no photos? No trace of him? What does that tell you?"

"They remodeled?" she asked sarcastically, flashing a disarming smile.

"My guess is we had a Dennis Hastert situation." Hastert, the former House Speaker and wrestling coach had kept his secret quiet for years, until one of his victims tracked him down.

"So you think DroneTech threatened to expose his secret?"

"I do. Plus they probably offered to help him run, and to make it go away. Think of it as opposition research, but used to blackmail as opposed to attack."

"But you can't prove this?"

"No, I can't. But I can read people. And it fits the exact pattern of the Nicholas-Bravo primary. A guy with a big secret plays the spoiler role."

"Did you ask for his personnel file from the school? Documenting his time there?"

"Of course. Called while I was driving back to the airport."

"And?"

"Gone. They didn't keep electronic records when he was there. And somehow, the paper file on him had gone missing. Reminded me of Bravo's mysteriously amended records at the Pentagon. Remember those?"

She flashed that stunning smile again. "Okay. You win. There's a pattern."

* * *

Cassie had struggled to sleep all week, but last night had been the worst. Being separated from Rachel wasn't helping. Neither was happy about it, and it was adding tension to their new marriage. Now they had argued before going to bed.

But Cassie was consumed with Kristina, who'd been tortured, then killed. And just like with Jimmy Cull, Cassie had contributed to her sad fate.

There had to be a way to do something. To find Dean Gamble, who clearly was behind it, and to bring him to justice. So after a restless night, she stumbled out of bed just after 8:00 a.m., downed a large cup of coffee, and called the one person who could help. Corporate associates only survive if they bill thousands of hours a year, so she guessed he'd already be there billing away.

And he was. "Ned Livingston here," he answered.

"Glad you're an early bird, Ned!" She fought through her lack of sleep to sound as peppy as possible.

"Thank you. Who is this?"

"We talked a while back. It's Cassie Knowles. From Republic News."

"Oh. Hi."

"Don't sound so excited to hear from me!"

"Mr. Gamble almost fired me for talking to you last time."

"I'm sure. And where is he now?"

"Um, he left the firm."

"It sounds like he wasn't the only one." When she'd tracked down the D.C. office a few days back, it had entirely cleared out. The security guard said they were there one day, gone the next.

Silence on the other end of the phone.

"Ned, you know what happened to Kristina, don't you?"

"Yes, she was abducted and killed. While jogging. We're all still in sho—"

"Ned, it's more complicated than that. This all goes back to Jimmy Cull, and the role Mr. Gamble played in that trial. Kristina starts asking questions, she gets killed, and Gamble disappears. Think about it."

"C'mon. You think Mr. Gamble killed Kristina?"

"Not directly, no. But he arranged it. But we know this is all part of something much bigger and very dangerous. And Mr. Gamble and your D.C. office played a role." She slowed down to let her next words sink in, appealing to this young lawyer's conscience. "I know you know there was something off about that trial. I could hear it in your voice when we talked. You're an honorable person. You know that trial was not honorable."

A long silence affirmed he was stewing over her suggestion.

"So why are you calling me?" he whispered.

"Because I need your help. Not to get too dramatic, but the country needs your help. The plot he's part of has major national implications. That's why they killed Kristina."

"What the heck can I do?"

"We need access to Gamble's files. Not just what he sent you, but what he might have sent others, going back as far as possible. It'll help us understand what's behind all this."

"I can't do that! I'm just an associate. Plus, it wouldn't be right, ethi—"

"Ned, Jimmy is dead. Kristina is dead. There's a higher level of ethics in play here. You don't have to do much but provide us a way into the Baker & Strauss system. We have people who can do the rest."

Cassie knew that Sharpe had some kind of hacking operation going on, so she might as well take advantage of it.

"Our system is really secure," Ned said timidly. "Plus, our old documents get archived and then deleted. I doubt they'll find anything"

"All we can do is try. You can help get us in. Once in, we'll see what we find."

"Okay. I'm going to lose my job over this. But tell me what I need to do."

* * *

The son left 30 minutes ago, Arthur texted at 10:00 the next morning. *And she is now on her walk.*

Still nothing? I wrote back.

Nothing.

Not good. Mrs. Kroon had had all day yesterday. Nothing. And another window this morning. Something was wrong. But five minutes later, the Russian wrote again.

Wait…the drive was just installed.

It was? Isn't she still walking?

She is. But someone just put it in.

I thought for a few seconds, confused. Then reached the only plausible conclusion.

Mr. Kroon.

Minutes later, the moment of good news ended with a thud. The call I'd been dreading finally came.

CHAPTER 25

Perhaps only second to the police ride-along, visiting the morgue was a rite of passage for local journalists. The details never left you—the chill in the air, the black and white body bags on gurneys and shelves, the smell and sting of ammonia. Never fun, but after several visits, you got used to it. Nevertheless, this visit had me on edge.

"Jack Sharpe?" asked the man in a gray suit who'd been waiting just inside the main doors.

"Yes. That's me," I said. "Sergeant Murphy?"

"You got it. Follow me."

"Where'd they find the body?"

"The Potomac, not far from Mt. Vernon. A boater spotted it along the shore, snagged on a tree branch in the water."

"You called his wife?"

"No. Because of the circumstances, we wanted to bring you down first to confirm it."

We walked in silence down a hallway and through a gray swinging door. A young woman in blue medical scrubs greeted us, handing us each small white plastic clips.

"I'm Dr. Ryan, deputy coroner. You're going to want these."

I fumbled around to get them placed in my nostrils. Sergeant Murphy expertly attached his.

"Ready?" she asked, a blast of cold air hitting us as she swung open a second door. "Over here." She walked over to one of six tables where a black plastic bag covered a body.

"Ready?" she asked again.

"Yes," I answered, taking a deep breath.

She unzipped the top of the bag, and the bloated, wrinkled face of George Vassos stared back at me. His pale skin looked like plastic, except for the beard that had grown back since the last time I'd seen him.

"Yes," I said, lowering my head, exhaling slowly, trying to stay calm. "That's him."

"We assumed so. He's very intact, not a lot of decomposition yet. Cold water will do that, but it also indicates he died quite recently. Perhaps two or three days ago."

"Have you determined a cause of death?"

"Oh, yes. Drowning."

"Nothing else?"

"Nope. A straight drowning. But he must've been gagging for air. Lots of tissue damage in his lungs."

Alarm bells went off in my head, and I struggled to keep my expression neutral. Cassie's contact in Texas had been waterboarded. Now Vassos had drowned too? What were the odds of these two deaths being so similar? Either way, I didn't want to bring this up in front of the cops.

"So can you tell if he drowned in the river, or somewhere else?"

"Not definitively. Would seem like the river. But—"

Ryan took a step around the table and unzipped the bag further, down to Vassos' left arm, revealing more puffy and wrinkled skin from his hand to his elbow. The pale hue was interrupted only by a deep purple ring around his wrist.

"—he had deep lacerations like this one on his wrists and ankles, which indicate he was bound. He also had some nasty scrapes on his knees. Who knows what they did to him?"

Awful. George Vassos had worked his way up from nothing only to die like this. My mind fielded a dozen questions at once, and I had a hard time focusing on Ryan and Sgt. Murphy. How was I going to tell Helen Vassos about this? Why did I feel like Cassie and Alex were going to blame me for this? More important: why did *I* feel like blaming me for this?

"Any other findings to speak of?" I asked.

"Not really. I'm surprised they let us find the body so quickly."

"*Let us*?" I repeated. "What do you mean?"

"If you abduct and kill someone, you'd want to make that body disappear. And there are many ways to do that, even in a river. You anchor it. You take it apart."

I winced.

"Sorry," Ryan said.

"No, it's true," I said. "I get what you're saying."

"In this case, they didn't do any of that. Whoever did this wanted us to find him. They wanted *you* to find him."

Sgt. Murphy looked at me. "Mr. Sharpe, what the hell is going on?"

* * *

The call came through as Alex sat at her desk. A strange number. The area code was 619. San Diego. She knew no one in San Diego.

"Ms. Fischer?"

"Yes. Who is this?"

"I can't say."

"Okay," Alex said, unfazed. This wasn't her first call to have started like this. "How can I help you?"

"I understand you're digging into DroneTech."

Her heartbeat picked up its pace, and she went silent for a few seconds. A trap? An opportunity? A fishing expedition? She wouldn't take the bait . . . yet.

"How did you get my cell phone? And what is DroneTech?"

"Ma'am, I don't have time to waste. You don't either. We both know what DroneTech is. And what they're up to."

The caller paused, but Alex didn't fill the silence.

"Are you there?" he asked.

"Yes. Who are you?"

"Someone who knows an awful lot about DroneTech. Things that would scare the hell out of you and the country, as I think you're already learning."

"Sir, I don't make it my business to affirm or deny anything I am covering."

"If you want to stop what we both know is happening, you're going to need to come up with something better than that."

His snide tone crossed the line. "Sir, if you have information you wish to share with me, I am happy to receive it. Otherwise this phone call's ov—"

"Well, I do. You and your team are asking the right questions. But as I see it, you need concrete proof or you don't have anything. I can provide it."

"I am happy to accept any information you want to prov—"

"I need you to come to San Diego."

"Excuse me?"

"If I were to get on a flight to Washington, or anywhere east, they would suspect something. So you'll have to come here. And you'll have to do it in a way that doesn't let them know your destination."

"I understand." Time to take control. "Before traveling to San Diego, I need to have some confirmation of your identity, and of the type of information you wish to provide."

"Ma'am, I work for DroneTech, in their digital security and support department. So I see everything. And I can show you everything."

A credible answer. No one knows more inside dirt on an organization than the folks in digital and tech support. They have unfiltered access to everyone's information, and know how to dig through it with no one noticing. So there was no reason not to turn this into an interview on the spot.

"How long have you worked there?"

"About a decade. I got there shortly after it started."

"And where were you before that?"

"Cal Tech."

"When did you—"

"—Ms. Fischer, this is going to have to happen in person or it's not going to happen."

So much for the interview. "Fair enough. I need proof confirming who you are, and that you have information worth pursuing."

"That is difficult to do without being detected."

"You're a digital guy—that's your expertise. I'm confident you'll find a way. I have to go." And with that, she hung up. Given the risks involved, he'd have to earn it.

* * *

"We are in!" Arthur said exuberantly after I opened my hotel door.

"You are?" I asked.

"Yes. Mr. Kroon arrived home at six, and logged on at 6:20 last night. We followed him all the way in."

"What now?"

"We have access to all the files on his computer. We will begin scrutinizing them immediately."

"What about data and systems beyond his computer? His institute?"

"The hope is that any systems that he accesses from that computer, we are able to access as well. Consider him the man with key. Every door he opens, we walk in with him. So our progress will depend on what he does, where he goes."

"Great. Let's hope he goes far and wide."

"Indeed." He reached into his jacket pocket and handed me a thick file folder. "Also, Mr. Holmberg wanted me to pass this information along to you."

After he left, I sat on the bed and opened the folder. Inside were a single sheet of white paper on top and a clipped set of papers beneath. The paper listed the four caucus organizations I had sent their way the day before.

Next to "Minnesota People Power" was a large X. "Secure."

"Rise Up Maine." Same X. "Secure."

"Kansas Can Do." X. "Secure."

"Colorado Rising." Next to it, a large check mark appeared. They must have penetrated the Colorado outfit.

I eagerly unclipped the attached papers and leafed through them. Hundreds of pages. Emails, memos, spreadsheets, maps. A few things stuck out right away.

A number of emails were to or from Steve Doherty. The first time we'd seen anything with his name on it. And the first concrete proof that Americans for a Brighter Future was behind these groups' "grassroots" activity.

The content of the emails and memos largely involved targeting counties for get-out-the-vote operations for the caucus—staff assignments, voter contact goals, and so on. I grabbed the file from my desk drawer with the maps I'd put together. Yep, the targeting of the counties described in these documents overlay precisely where Governor Nicholas performed so impressively. But these guys had been careful. Nowhere did the name Nicholas appear, or that of any candidate, which would make the whole operation illegal.

The paperwork also documented the wiring of money to Colorado to support organizing, mail, digital, and other efforts. Millions of dollars, bankrolling a cutting-edge campaign—far more than even a well-funded candidate would spend on any individual caucus.

With all this in hand, I sat down at my desk and made one other phone call. Area code 303.

It was an impulsive call, but it also made sense. Both because of these new documents and because of the long-term consequences of what we were finding.

The best way to get her was through her campaign manager, not the official side. And even though those duties had ended, that manager's number was still stored in my phone. It rang through to voicemail, so I left a message.

"This is Jack Sharpe of Republic News. I hope you're well. Could you please ask the governor to call me?"

A former prosecutor, Governor Moore would know just what to do.

* * *

Cassie eagerly inserted the Will Kroon zip file into her desktop minutes after Jack had handed it to her. But that initial excitement waned as she discovered this research assignment would be a bear.

There were two major folders. One marked PERSONAL, the other DPI. She double-clicked the DPI folder, which opened to a long list of new folders. They had standard titles you'd see with any organization: BUDGET / DEVELOPMENT, MEDIA / COMMUNICATIONS, PERSONNEL, REPORTS, and others. She started with BUDGET / DEVELOPMENT. It didn't take long to confirm that DroneTech was a major supporter of DPI. The company had given between one and two million dollars for eight years, and an additional three million dollars each of the last two years. This made it the second largest supporter of the think tank over that time.

But the largest, by far, was a private foundation. The Hansen Foundation had given two million dollars a year over those same eight years, then a whopping five million dollars the past two years. A quick search found that DroneTech's CEO was named Doug Hansen. No doubt he scored major tax breaks by funneling the support through a private foundation.

She next opened the REPORTS folder, which listed dozens of documents in chronological order, going back years. "DRONE EXPANSION SAVING LIVES," was the first report. Cassie double-clicked on it to find a long memorandum, co-authored by Will Kroon six years ago, providing facts and figures on how many U.S. combatant lives drones had saved in Afghanistan the year before.

The documents further down the list contained similar reports. Memos described cost savings, as well as reductions in both civilian casualties and U.S. military casualties for particular timeframes and military theaters. A few documents described theaters she didn't expect to see. Madagascar. Kazakhstan. Somalia. Albania. Turkey—not places where the U.S. military was thought to be in an offensive posture.

Amid this long list of documents, she opened a folder labelled SOURCES/OPS. And that's when the informational maze grew far more complex. Hundreds of folders appeared in alphabetical order, labelled with a strange set of names.

ALABAMA

ASPEN

BLOWHARD

BRUSHBACK

All the way at the bottom, the list ended with the folders VINCENT, WINGMAN, WORKHORSE, and ZEBRA.

She double-clicked on the ASPEN file. A quick scan made clear that ASPEN was a drone operation, and the file provided the details, including the date, the location ("Aspen" took place in western Somalia), the "pilots," the target, the result, estimated civilian casualties (22), and the cost.

Cassie jumped down to BLOWHARD, then BRUSHBACK, then COWPOKE. More operations, same details. This was clearly the source material for DPI's broader studies. Interesting stuff, potentially another story for Alex Fischer, but none of it was related to what Cassie needed now.

For hours, she pored through other folders and documents. Still no smoking guns.

* * *

Years back, Alex had shut down her Facebook account within months of creating it. Strange men and creepy fans had inundated her with friend invites and message requests, along with a few unwelcome photos. The annoyance had outweighed any benefit.

She had a Twitter account, but that was to keep up with the news. She never posted anything herself. Her twitter handle displayed no photo and gave no indication of who she was, and she had ten followers. No Snapchat either. Or Instagram. She kept up with her friends and colleagues the old fashioned way—text, phone, and email. But Alex did stay active on one phone app: Words with Friends.

Back in Kansas City, her family had spent countless Friday evenings huddled over a Scrabble board, fiercely competing to find seven-letter words and triple word scores. So Words with Friends was right up her alley. She enjoyed dueling with a stable roster of wordsmiths, waging a dozen or so games at once. She looked for strong opponents. It was no fun playing amateurs, so she rarely added new competitors. Nor did many request to play her.

Amid all the chaos, days had passed since her most recent moves. So as she downed a veggie sandwich at the Subway just down the street from Republic, Olga lingering outside, Alex raced through a number of games that had languished. Thirty points here. Forty-five points there. Seventy-two points on a seven-letter word. Bad letters in one game forced her to play only a twelve-pointer.

Just as she caught up on her overdue moves, a request for a new game popped up. As always, the first thing she noticed was the initial word her challenger played.

SECRET.

Such a waste of an S. A good player wouldn't make such an obvious mistake. Definitely a challenge to decline. But then she noticed the name of the player.

CALTECH2005

She dropped her sandwich onto her tray and immediately accepted the game.

Words with Friends had a message function on it, usually used to congratulate rivals for good moves or good games, or to talk a little trash. Now she used it to probe.

Where do you live?

San Diego.

Job?

Tech support.

It was the caller. She had challenged him to get to her, and here he was. Not bad.

I*s this secure?*

Wouldn't be here if it wasn't.

Need your proof.

Sean Riordan. Cal Tech. 2005.

How do I know?

You couldn't send images through the Words with Friends' message function, so Alex wasn't sure what would happen next. She chuckled at what arrived.

Above the Words with Friends game board, next to the player's name, each player could opt to display an image. Some players posted photos. Others posted cartoon emojis or avatars. Initially, CALTECH2005 had displayed a simple cartoon of a beaver, the CalTech mascot.

But then it switched. To a picture of a CalTech student ID card.

"Sean Riordan, Class of 2005" appeared on the left, the orange CalTech logo on the right. Below the name was an address. And below the logo was a photo. Thin face. High cheekbones. Longish brown hair, almost falling over his eyes. A boyish look overall, with a nose ring and leather jacket to boot.

That's you?

In college. Different now.

Seconds later, a new image popped up. A new ID.

"Sean Riordan, Tech Support" appeared on the left side. On the right, DroneTech. And a logo—a shadow figure of a drone—just below it. She had seen the logo before. He was right, the new photo was dramatically different. Same high cheekbones, but his hair was cropped short and his face had filled out. With a mild tan, he looked healthier, and had lost the nose ring. Small wire-rimmed glasses made him look more intelligent than his grungy grad school days.

You've grown up! she messaged him back.

I have.

The image switched back to the original image of the beaver.

And the information you have?

Hold on . . .

A few more seconds passed. The beaver disappeared again. Replaced by what looked to be an image of a formal memo. Alex clicked on the image, and it expanded to occupy about a quarter of her phone screen. At the top, above the MEMO line, was the DroneTech moniker and logo. This was clearly a company document.

She couldn't make out the tiny words in the body of the memo. But a grainy photo of Congressman Bravo was to the right of the first paragraph. His hair was a little longer than the close-cropped style he had sported throughout the campaign. The longer hair made sense, because the date on the memo was three years old. Fortunately, the subject line of the memo was large enough to read. Two words.

Operation Wingman.

What the hell is Operation Wingman? she messaged.

Before any answer appeared, the image switched back to the CalTech beaver. Then a new message came through. *Come to San Diego and find out.*

* * *

ARLINGTON, VIRGINIA

"You may be walking into a trap, Alex. I don't think you should go."

Vassos' waterlogged face flashed in my mind as Alex and I walked from short-term parking to the departure gate at Reagan National Airport. Alex had booked a ticket on an evening flight to San Diego without even checking with me first.

"Are you kidding?" she said. "That memo showed that this guy was serious. You don't show that much leg unless you mean business."

She was right about that.

Operation Wingman. It was a fitting title for a company that manufactures drones, but also a perfect description of the political scheme we were unraveling. In aerial combat, the wingman flies just to the right and behind the lead aircraft in formation. The wingman's job is to provide protective support to the lead aircraft, remaining there through all risks and costs, willing even to be shot out of the sky. That was the precise role Bravo had played. Tactically, in debates and other forums, Bravo had led attacks and undermined rivals while letting Nicholas take the high ground. And more generally, he had become the perfect foil for other primary contenders. He had drawn critical votes to undercut frontrunners like Lopez and Moore in the early states, crushed Moore's momentum in Nevada and South Carolina, then diverted votes in later states to allow Nicholas to run up the score.

"He definitely whetted our appetite," I said, wheeling her small travel bag behind me. "But maybe we can get these documents in other ways."

"How?" she asked.

I still hadn't told her about Kazarov's involvement. And couldn't now.

"I have my ways," I said, smiling.

We stepped onto an escalator to the ticketing and security level.

"Jack, this is the best lead we have," she said, looking back at me. "I have Olga, who is clearly a badass. This guy risked a lot to show me that document. I'm going."

Of course she was right. This might have been our only hope to break the story. But the image of Vassos' purple wrists still flashed in my mind. Someone brutal was on the other side of this scheme.

"I don't like it at all," I said as we stepped off the escalator.

"Jack, is that because I'm a reporter, or because it's me?" She smiled sweetly as she said it.

I had been wondering the same thing. "Both."

She leaned over, pecked my cheek, then took the baggage handle from my hand.

"See you when I get back."

She turned around and walked into the security line. I stared for a few seconds, then forced myself to turn around and head back to the car.

CHAPTER 26

WASHINGTON, D.C.

I WAS THE ONLY one who knew what the Denver press conference was about. But given who had called it, every national cable station broke in live as soon as it started.

I didn't have time to get out west in person, but Cassie and I watched it from my office. As always, Janet Moore performed perfectly.

"I am here to announce that my office has received information about potential illegal campaign activity during the recent Colorado primary," Moore said, cameras clicking. "Specifically, the documents we received suggest a grassroots organization in Colorado, a nonprofit charitable organization, was given millions of dollars to help one candidate win our primary. I take this very seriously, and am therefore passing this information along to the attorney general to fully investigate and report back."

She stepped away from the podium, and a much taller woman, Colorado's attorney general, took her place in the national spotlight. With thick glasses, red hair, and the grim face of a longtime criminal prosecutor, she did not look or feel like a politician, which, in these circumstances, was a good thing. In a short statement, she announced that her office would conduct a full investigation. When she was done, the reporters wanted more.

"Governor, Governor Nicholas won the caucus here, are you saying he cheated?" one reporter asked.

Governor Moore laughed and waved her right hand, making it clear she did not plan to answer.

"Do you think this happened anywhere else?" another reporter asked. A good question, but still no response from Moore.

Both women started to walk away from the podium. Then a third questioner jumped in.

"Governor, is this sour grapes because you lost? Don't you have a conflict of interest here?"

Governor Moore stopped, turned, and took four quick steps back to the podium.

"Joanne, you know me better than that. I received this information and passed it along immediately. The attorney general will now investigate it independently. I will not be involved and will anxiously await her assessment of the case."

It was the most pissed off I'd ever seen her. This was a woman who took questions of ethics seriously, her own ethics in particular.

Good.

* * *

LA JOLLA, CALIFORNIA

It was time.

Alex Fischer walked out of her hotel room at 10:20. She had texted Sean Riordan first thing in the morning, and he'd given her a rendezvous point for 10:30. She was dressed casually, the yellow sundress and Jackie O sunglasses blending in well with the Southern California scenery. The sneakers felt odd, a faux pas she would never voluntarily commit, but Olga had handed them to her, insisting she wear them in case she had to run.

She exited the front lobby into the bright sun, turned right, and walked along the touristy boulevard that hugged the curvy coastline.

Heading there now, she texted Olga.

I'm in position, Olga texted back.

She then sent Riordan a message over Words with Friends. *There in 10.*

I will be there, he replied. *Padres baseball cap. Blue golf shirt.*

She relayed those details back to Olga. Minutes later, she spotted the sign for the Conch Cafe, perched on the beach side of the street, where they'd agreed to meet. Her heartbeat accelerated as the big moment neared.

I'm in sight, she texted Olga.

Hold there. He's not here yet.

She was standing outside a bathing suit store, The Twig, so instead of visibly pacing on the sidewalk, she stepped inside the door.

"Can I help you, ma'am?"

Alex looked up to see a teenage girl behind the counter, jet-black hair, tattoos covering most of her neck.

"No, thank you. I'm just looking around."

Alex walked over to a rack of bikinis on the near wall, feigning interest in a set of brightly colored suits she wouldn't be caught dead wearing. Then she looked to her left and smiled, spotting a few kids' suits Molly might like.

He there yet? she texted.

Not yet.

Her phone indicated it was 10:33. "…" appeared, indicating Olga was typing a new message.

He's walking up now. Sitting down. Table closest to beach. Come now.

Alex turned away from the rack, back toward the door.

"Have a nice day, ma'am."

"You too," she replied, stepping back into the bright sun.

She closed the final 75 yards to The Conch. As her heart pounded even faster, she clenched her fists as tightly as possible. Push all your energy there, her track coach used to tell her. It had always calmed her nerves before a big race then, and had that same effect now.

She crossed the street at an intersection, and looked over to the patio area of the cafe. At a far table, a man with a baseball cap and a blue shirt was staring into his phone.

She double-checked with Olga one last time. *All good?*

Yes. You are clear.

I'm entering now.

She entered the patio area, walked among a few empty tables, and approached the table. He looked up.

"Sean?"

"That's me." He stood up and greeted her with a polite handshake. He'd graduated in 2005, putting him in his mid-30s, but he looked like a kid.

"You look just like your photo," she said as she sat down.

"So do you!" he joked. "But you look a lot thinner in person."

"Thanks, I think," she replied, laughing. She'd heard that every day for years—television really did add a few pounds. From his clammy hands to his goofy opening line, this guy seemed nervous, which was a good sign. But then again, his phone was lying face down on the table. He easily could be recording her.

Just listen. Don't say much. "I appreciate you meeting on short notice," she said.

"No problem," he said. "This is important."

"What did you want to share wi—"

"You guys just having coffee, or you gonna eat too?"

They both jumped as a waitress's raspy voice interrupted.

"I'll just have coffee," Alex said. "Large. Black. No sugar."

"Me too," Sean said. "I'll have a blueberry muffin as well."

"Thank you," Alex added dismissively, making clear they wanted privacy. She looked back at him. "So what did you want to share with me?"

"I know that you're looking into the DroneTech network and what they're doing in this election," he said, his striking blue eyes darting around. "You are onto something really big. Really sinister."

She nodded, saying nothing.

"You got that image I sent of that memo?"

"I did."

"I was doing routine firewall work a few months ago and stumbled across that memo. You saw the name at the top? And the photo?"

"Sure did."

He leaned in. "Everything described in that memo has happened."

"Here you go!" the waitress piped in loudly, putting the coffee mug down in front of Alex.

"And here's yours, with the muffin. Anything else?"

"No, thank you," Alex said curtly. "That's all we're going to need." She and Riordan both watched as the woman walked away. "The text was too small in the image you sent," she said quietly. "I couldn't read it."

"Right. But you saw the title? Operation Wingman?"

"Yes."

"Congressman Bravo was literally the wingman for Governor Nicholas. He was in there to block all the other candidates so Nicholas could win. From the very beginning. And it worked."

"That's certainly what the name suggests. Were you able to get any other documents that explained more?"

"Once I found the first one, I began to access them on a regular basis. I also dug through past files and documents. This has been in the works for years, since right after the president was reelected"—he glanced around again before completing his thought—"and they're willing to do anything to make it happen. Anything."

He was genuinely scared, and he was spooking Alex despite herself. Thank goodness Olga was watching.

"What do you mean?" Alex asked. "Do you have any details?"

"Congressman Bravo had some secret in his past. That was the key to everything. So they worked to clean it all up, including getting rid of the people who knew."

"As in killing people?" Alex asked, wanting to hear it from him.

"Absolutely. I'm certain they killed a bunch of veterans."

"That's terrible. And you have documents on—"

"You don't know how terrible. And yes, I do. Some are cryptic, but it's pretty obvious what they're doing. Evil stuff."

"Needless to say, I'd like to get my hands on whatever you have."

"I'm sure. What would you do with them?"

Alex eyed his phone. He could be recording. "We want to put together a story exposing all this. Real proof like your documents will be the key."

"I know. My biggest fear is whatever you do will expose me. I don't want to end up like—"

"Sean," she said, sympathetically but firmly. "You are going to have to get as far away from DroneTech as possible, as quickly as possible. Whether you give me one document or not."

He nodded. "I wanted to meet you first," he said. "There are so many documents, I couldn't just—"

"Hold on!"

She'd casually looked down at her phone for the first time in a few minutes. Something was wrong. The usually calm Olga had texted twice in a row, and one more was now coming through.

Something happening.

Someone here.

"…"

Run.

* * *

WASHINGTON, D.C.

I was eating a late lunch at my desk when Alex's text came through.

It was a trap!

I knew it. I was tempted to call right away, but there was a reason Alex was texting and not calling. I shouted for Arthur.

You ok?

Don't know, she texted back. *Hiding now. Doubt it.*

Where are you?

In a store. The Twig. In La Jolla.

Arthur rushed into my office, looking more alarmed than I'd ever seen him.

"Olga does not answer. That is a very bad sign."

"Still getting details," I told him. "Hold on."

Arthur grimaced, biting his lower lip. He attempted to hide his grief, but the news clearly shook him.

What can we do to help? I texted Alex.

Get police here right away. Worried they'll find me soon.

"Arthur, please call La Jolla police. Tell them there's an emergency at a store called The Twig."

Calling police now, I texted back. *What happened?*

Meeting was going fine. Then chaos.

So he was real? Wingman was real?

Yes. Definitely real. But someone figured out we were meeting.

Was the contact in on it?

I don't think so . . . I don't know. We ran.

Arthur interrupted. "Police are on their way."

Police coming. Hang tight.

Molly.

"Jack," Arthur interrupted again. "She is alive only because they want her to be."

I hadn't thought of that, but it made sense. Like with Vassos, they probably wanted to know what she knew.

Alex, they may want to take you alive.

No answer.

Alex?

Nothing back.

You there?

I stared at my phone.

* * *

"Alex was just kidnapped?" Cassie shouted. With Arthur standing next to me, I had just briefed her on the events of the past hour.

After searching the area, the La Jolla police had found no trace of Olga, Alex, or Alex's contact. A young saleswoman at a bathing suit store told them that three men had burst through the shop's front door, dragged a screaming blonde woman out of a changing room, and forced her into the back of a white van.

Now Cassie was pacing my office like a caged animal, waiting for me to calm her down, but I had no reason to think either of us should be calm.

"I shouldn't have let her go, but she insisted," I said. "They know we're onto them."

"How the hell are we supposed to do our jobs if we can't do anything?"

"We have to keep digging, and we have to expose this," I said. "We're still in more danger if—"

"What does that even mean?" Cassie asked angrily. "Alex followed your order to keep digging, and look where it got her, Jack."

"It *means*," I said, giving her a warning look, "do your work without exposing yourself physically. And when you move, two people will be with you."

Arthur stood next to me, nodding as I said this.

"But we have to keep digging. We are starting to crack into their systems. We've already triggered the Colorado investigation, which helps. As soon as we have solid documentation of this other stuff, we can get the whole story out there."

"But Jack, we have the story," Cassie said definitively. "The SuperPAC. The attack ads. The interference in the caucuses you had me look into. What I don't understand is what Congressman Bravo has to do with any of this? And why that matters now?"

It only dawned on me then that I hadn't filled her in on everything Alex and I had found.

"Because Bravo's presence in the primary was essential to Nicholas winning. He was Governor Nicholas's wingman, taking critical votes away from Moore and, later, Stevens. Even Lopez in Iowa. Nicholas would've never had a chance to rise over the course of the primary if it hadn't been for Bravo."

"Holy shit," Cassie said. "And that's why they worked so hard to bury his secret. They needed him in all the—"

She stopped talking.

"Wait. Wingman?" she said.

"Yep. Wingman." I said. "If Alex's contact was legit, that's literally what they called him. And the entire operation."

* * *

Cassie sprinted down the hallway and flipped on her desktop. The Kroon zip drive was still installed.

She double-clicked on the DPI folder, then the REPORTS folder. She scrolled down to the SOURCES/OPS folder, and opened it. The first time around, she'd only looked through a handful of the operations from the long list. But when Jack Sharpe mentioned the term at their meeting, one operation she'd seen near the bottom of the list came to mind.

WINGMAN.

Even as she scrolled down to it, the WINGMAN folder now stuck out. The other folders took up very little memory. WINGMAN took up far more. She scolded herself for not having noticed that the first time. She opened it.

The other operations folders listed three basic documents in the same format. The WINGMAN folder was entirely different, housing a long series of documents in chronological order.

She opened the first document, WNGRESEARCH1, and skimmed through it, her eyes widening.

"This is it!" she yelled out to herself.

* * *

"You find something?"

Ned Livingston called Cassie as she was printing out the last of the WINGMAN documents.

"Not a ton. But something."

"That was quick. I'm impressed."

"Don't be. Junior lawyers like me? All we do is go through documents all day. It's pretty boring, but we know our way around."

Cassie smiled, enjoying the corporate associate braggadocio.

"What is it?"

"It looks like Gamble deleted his own files and communications before he left, even from the archives. There's no way to get those."

"Bummer." But not a surprise.

"And I went through all his emails to me. Nothing there either. If the goal was to throw the case, he covered those tracks well."

"So what's the good news?" Cassie asked, tiring quickly of the slow buildup.

"A firm like this is a huge bureaucracy. There's all sorts of official paperwork that lawyers have to complete before initiating any new cases, and as they proceed with those cases. Gamble couldn't delete those. I tracked them all down."

"And?"

"They're very strange."

"How so?"

"First, he always said this was a pro bono case. But it wasn't filed as one."

"It wasn't?"

"No. It originated out of our D.C. office. And it was a paying case."

"Is that rare?"

"No, but it's odd. Think about it. Why would a murder case in the middle of nowhere come to us from our D.C. office? From a partner up there who deals with government contracts?"

His confidence was growing. "Good question!" Cassie said encouragingly.

"And all of our billings—our hours, travel, other costs—were sent to the D.C. office, back to that billing partner."

"What was that partner's name?" Cassie could guess, but wanted to confirm her hunch.

"George Lyall."

Yep. The lead partner of the D.C. office.

"Those bills also show that Lyall and others in D.C. put a lot of time into the case. Hours of billings, including numerous conversations they had with Gamble on it. He also flew up there three times to report—"

"That surprises you?"

"Kristina and I were doing most of the heavy lifting on the case. He didn't once connect us with anyone up there. If they wanted updates, it would have made sense for us to be part of them. But we had no idea they were even involved."

"It sounds like they cared about the case for a different reason than you did."

"Exactly. For the opposite reason, I'm afraid. And they didn't want us to know it . . . Oh, and one other weird thing popped up. They kept billing long after the trial was over."

"Really? Why would they do that?"

"I have no idea. We didn't appeal. The work was done. Gamble must have been keeping tabs on Jimmy even while he was in jail and kept billing for it."

Making sure Jimmy kept quiet, Cassie figured. Jimmy had said they'd had phone conversations. That's when Gamble had planted the idea to seek a presidential pardon.

"Ned, are you able to see who paid the bills? Who the client actually was?"

"Sort of. It was actually another D.C. law firm. A small outfit I'd never heard of. My guess is they had a big client behind them that paid for it all. But they're the ones who actually paid us."

"What's the firm called?" Cassie asked impatiently.

"They go by DGA, short for Doherty, Graham and Allison. It looks like Mr. Lyall and the DGA partners all used to work at the same firm. Called the Progress Group."

* * *

"I have good news for you, Mr. Sharpe," Arthur said, standing in my doorway. I looked at him warily from behind my desk. For someone who had good news, he looked pretty serious. "Olga placed her tracking device on Alex. And it is intact."

"What kind of tracking device?" I asked. This was news to me.

"Every member of my team carries a small tracking device. Olga's is still transmitting, and moving as we speak. My guess is she placed it on Alex."

I nodded as I absorbed what Arthur was telling me. This probably meant that Alex was alive, but that wasn't guaranteed. What if Alex's kidnappers had— I couldn't think about that.

"Where is Alex now?" I asked.

"It stayed in place for a while. She likely remained in a vehicle as it was parked by a building. But she is now being moved along a major highway. We will see where she goes."

"Then what?"

"Then we will get her back. And, God willing, we will eliminate whoever killed Olga. Mr. Kazarov is very upset that she is gone."

"You're sure she's dead?"

"Yes," Arthur said gravely. "We are not taken alive."

CHAPTER 27

"THERE'S A FILE called 'Wingman,'" Cassie said, bursting into my office an hour after our meeting. "I just printed it all out."

"Let me take a look," I said, lifted by Arthur's update but still worried sick about Alex. Only made it worse that I'd just spent ten minutes explaining to her ex-husband Mike what was going on. He clearly still cared about her.

Cassie laid five thick stacks of paper on my desk, two or three smiling headshots beaming from each page. No names accompanied the photos, just numbers, printed in the upper left-hand corner in bold black type.

I looked through the first stack, recognizing most of the faces as politicians from across the country. Number four was the governor of Illinois. A congresswoman from Cleveland was listed as 28. There were a couple governors and senators who'd been around a while. Others were less prominent. More women than men, and lots of diversity among the group. In fact, only a few white faces appeared on the whole list, all women. A couple square-jawed generals were numbers twelve and 32 on the list, along with several women and Hispanic business CEOs.

"Okay. I'm intrigued. What are these?"

"Basically, the Wingman folder included a series of research files on different candidates. It's some type of vetting process, narrowing the list down over time. Each stack represents a different file."

I looked closely at the papers in the first stack. Two columns accompanied each photo.

One listed "strengths," assessing unique political assets of each candidate.

"Performs well with African-Americans."

"Big numbers with women."

"Great cross-over appeal."

"Appeals to progressives."

"70% FAVs w Hispanics; will pull them away."

"Very low negatives."

All in all, pretty standard political stuff. Clearly looking for candidates who could draw progressive and minority votes, precisely what Nicholas needed to win.

It was the next column over, listing "vulnerabilities," that offered more juice.

"Known drunk. Several run-ins."

"Mistress on side. Tracking down details."

"Three-year gap in resume. Research more."

"In closet. Multiple partners."

"Four DUIs."

"Three foreclosures."

"False claims of military service."

"Wow. They really dug up the dirt on these guys." Even for a professional political operation, this was deep vetting. Disqualifying stuff.

But as I leafed through each successive stack, an odd pattern emerged. Candidates who had little or no vulnerabilities had not made it to the next round. Those with the biggest skeletons and scandals had advanced. It seemed like Will Kroon and DPI had been doing the opposite of vetting.

Cassie noticed it too. "It's strange that they kept people with some of the worst problems."

I shook my head. "They *selected* the people with problems. The people with the worst stayed in longer."

Will Kroon's reverse-vetting process mirrored that Florida primary, where Groppe had been pushed into the race as a spoiler *because* he had something to hide. To confirm my hunch, I grabbed the five pieces of paper from the fifth round of vetting. They contained tales of mistresses, call girls, drug use, and a major financial scandal. But now there were details. For candidate 22, what was previously listed as a "mistress" included the name of the woman and lurid details about their affair. Candidate 40's drug use now included the dates and locations of her stints in rehab.

"Amazing. They ran down every detail they could find. And all of these would've been career-ending scandals."

Then it dawned on me. One candidate was missing.

"Where's Bravo?" I asked.

"He was in a separate file." Cassie tossed a thin sheaf of paper in front me. A beaming Bravo from a few years back, fuller face and longer hair, stared out from the top of the page. I pulled the new pages close. In addition to his photo, the front page catalogued an impressive list of strengths.

"Very strong support among young voters. A next-generation candidate."

"Veteran status, heroic personal story, keeps more conservative voters locked in."

"Strong appeal to women and minority voters who dominate in many primaries."

"Knocks out Lopez early."

"Charismatic speaker and dynamic presence."

"Initial polling shows him cutting into lead of likely opponents. Will win Nevada, take votes on campuses and in urban areas."

I nodded as I read through the list. Whoever had written this had captured the strengths that later proved to be so helpful to Bravo. And Nicholas.

"It's easy to forget how unknown he was way back then," I said. "Pretty impressive analysis. They nailed it."

"They sure did. Now turn it over."

I flipped to the back page. The list of vulnerabilities. Not a lot written. Shorter than the other finalists. But the words jumped off the page.

"Congressman Bravo was dishonorably discharged from the Army for violating the military's Don't Ask, Don't Tell policy while serving in Iraq. Due to award of Silver Star, the specific reason for the discharge was covered up. Author has personal knowledge of subject, and confirmed through witnesses. Early discharge noted on DD-214."

There it was. The whole story, laid out well before the election. Apparently none of those finalists was making the grade, so Will Kroon must have thrown Bravo in at the end.

"Looks like he was a last-minute draft pick."

I leafed through the other documents in the Bravo pile. Even more details. Once Bravo was their guy, they had dug more deeply into all aspects of the discharge. Even included the original DD-214, noting a dishonorable discharge. It was dated May 2007.

At the bottom of the pile was a memo with the subject line "Witnesses," which presented a short list of names:

William Bray, Boston, MA
Michael Choo, New York City
James Cull, Temple, TX
Dontavius Jackson, Baltimore, MD
David Sesler, Lawrenceburg, IN
John Williams, Topeka, KS

I shook my head. After Bravo was selected as Nicholas's wingman, making this list had sealed their fates.

"See if you can find out who Bray and Williams are."

"Will do," Cassie said.

"My guess is they're dead too. This became DroneTech's hit list."

* * *

SAN DIEGO, CALIFORNIA

Alex came to just as a giant of a man was hobbling toward her down an airplane aisle. The last thing she could remember was two large men pulling her out of her feeble hiding spot—the dressing room of that bathing suit shop in La Jolla. Now here she was, belted tightly into the passenger seat of a large airplane. Except for the man coming her way, she was the only passenger. The jet engines were humming outside, but they were still on the ground.

Remembering how much danger she was in, and the bullets that had rung out by the beach as she'd sprinted away, her heart began to thud. But she was conscious enough to hide it, and remained completely still as she watched the man approach her. His mane of long gray hair, parted in the middle, wavy and wild, shook as he lurched forward. A goatee hung from his chin, slightly longer than you generally see in the professional world. Lines of large veins bulged from his thick neck. And he was a hulk of a man. Big shoulders, thick forearms, and a barrel chest, all on full display thanks to the tight gray golf shirt he was wearing.

And then Alex recognized him. She'd seen him twice before, in a very different setting—on Capitol Hill, testifying on behalf of his company's expansion. As panicked as she felt, this presented an opportunity to assert some control over an otherwise helpless circumstance.

"Mr. Hansen," she said, as confidently as she could.

Still a few rows away, the man stopped and looked at her, surprised. "You know me?" he asked, cocking his head to the side, letting the traces of a grin appear on his face.

"I do," Alex said, forcing a smile through her fear. She gripped her armrests tight to keep from shaking. "I covered a couple Senate and House hearings where you testified. You were a little bit more gussied up for those."

He laughed. "Damn right I was! You gotta look good when you kiss political ass, Ms. Fischer."

Alex's mind raced to get its bearings and remain focused on Hansen at the same time. She summoned her reporter's composure. "It seemed like they were already in your corner before you even showed up," she said. "In fact, I remember them mainly kissing *your* ass!"

He laughed. "Damn straight!"

He resumed his awkward approach toward her, but slowed his pace. Three details stuck out. He favored his left leg. The distinct aroma of marijuana preceded him. And he sported a large tattoo of an eagle on each forearm. Both eagles gripped a trident and an anchor.

"Still reliving your Navy SEAL days?" she asked. There was no better way to butter up a SEAL than bringing up his service.

"Not reliving," he corrected her, firmly. "Once a SEAL, always a SEAL. I'm getting a drink. Want anything?"

"I'll take a water. Thank you"

"That's it?"

"That's it." Even though she was famished, she doubted she'd be able to hold anything else down.

"Get our gorgeous guest some water, right away," he yelled to the front of the cabin.

He stopped, turned around and sat in the seat to her left, with the aisle separating them. As big as these seats were, he filled all of his, his right shoulder and husky arm spilling halfway across the aisle. As he sat down, his khaki pant leg rose to reveal a thin metal prosthesis emerging from the top of his shoe.

Alex's glance down lasted a second too long.

"Roadside bomb," he said, patting his right thigh. "But I've never let this thing hold me back."

"I read that somewhere. Thank you for your sacrifice."

The plane jolted, then tilted backward slowly.

"Hell, I consider myself lucky. Lots of guys would have done anything to have this little damage."

"What happened?"

"I was the passenger in a Humvee. You know, stuck in substandard armor conducting a useless chore of an assignment. We had no business being out there, in those conditions, doing something so menial."

As he talked, she noticed several thick scars lining his neck and the right side of his face, and a deep crevice running from his wrist to his elbow. He talked a big game, but this guy had gone through hell—both the injuries and the recovery.

He pointed to his right cheek. "I still have shards of glass in here, and small shrapnel in my neck. The docs thought taking them out was more risky than leaving them in."

"I remember you testifying about this."

"Then you heard me say it's why I started my company in the first place. No one should be permanently scarred, lose an arm or a leg, or lose their life, on bullshit assignments that any machine could do."

The plane started to taxi forward.

"My guess is your company's now doing a lot of those assignm—"

"Oh yes we are, saving lives every day. The more, the better."

He suddenly jumped up, turned around, and walked further down the aisle.

"I've gotta hit the head. I'll be back in a second. Sit tight."

A door slammed shut a few moments later, leaving her only minutes to figure out how to get through this nightmare.

* * *

Alex tried to relax on the long flight, but struggled to settle down. She drank a few more glasses of water, but that was it. Her stomach remained in knots.

Doug Hansen displayed different taste. He was on his fourth fireball on the rocks, showing no signs of slowing down. Then he removed a bong from beneath his seat and lit it. As he inhaled, his face turned a darker shade of red and the veins in his neck bulged even further.

He exhaled. "It helps with the pain," he said.

Between swigs and the occasional cough, Hansen shared graphic tales of gunning down Taliban militia while watching comrades fall. He'd been through it as bad as anyone, and spared no detail or profanity in describing it all. Alex reacted enough to be respectful, but she was more focused on preparing for the tougher conversation that was coming.

The moment came as they bounced through turbulent storms over western Colorado. After a third bathroom break, Hansen sat back in his seat and turned toward her. The jovial frat boy disappeared.

"Ms. Fischer, we need to talk."

"We've been talking since you got on board," she joked nervously.

He shook his head and frowned, signaling that the harmless banter was over. It made her feel small, like a school kid scolded for an inappropriate joke.

"Why would you want to stop us? Our mission is to save lives, reduce injuries, position America to be as strong as possible without having the burden fall entirely on working-class kids."

She changed her tone too. This guy wasn't going to tolerate bullshit or weakness. She'd rather have him take her seriously even if it made the flight less pleasant, so even though she was cornered, she came out swinging.

"Don't play dumb, Doug. No one says you can't expand your business. But what you're doing goes way further."

It worked. He stayed calm, but firm.

"Don't be naïve. We have a lot of enemies who want to stop what we're doing. We've faced resistance every step of the way, not just from peaceniks and professors, but from within the Pentagon and on Capit—"

Stay strong, Alex told herself. "Right, and you've worked to eliminate those enemies for years."

"You're damn right we have. You ever hear of the First Amendment? The Supreme Court made clear we have every right to advocate for our views, as individuals, and as a company. The same rights you have."

Alex hated the *Citizens United* decision, but this was no time to argue its merits.

"No one disputes that. But again, your role in the primary has gone way beyon—"

"It has? How?"

"The SuperPAC attacks on everyone else? Bravo's role? You're pulling every string to handpick the next president."

The huge stained teeth returned as he smiled in response to her accusation.

"I'm flattered you think we're so important. And yes, we've pushed hard for the candidates we prefer. But SuperPACs are perfectly legitimate. We know the laws and follow them to the tee."

Images flashed in her head. Olga bursting through the bushes and collapsing to the pavement only seconds after having texted her to run. Mrs. Jackson's lifeless eyes as she described her grandson. Jack's description of a needle sticking out of Dontavius's arm. Her nervousness was turning to anger. Someone had to speak up for them, and she had little to lose.

"You keep saying that, but we're not just talking about campaign finance laws, which we all know are a mess. How about the laws against blackmail or murder?"

The frat boy returned, red-faced and loud, banging his fist against the armrest.

"Excuse me? Who the fuck did I murder? Tell me you're fucking joking!"

He was losing it.

"No, I'm not joking! You just killed two people in cold blood." She actually didn't know what happened to Sean after they both had sprinted away.

"Alex, I don't think you understand what deep shit you're in. We received advanced Pentagon and FBI approval for that operation. That woman you've been working with? She's from Russian special forces, KGB-trained. Sean Riordan? No better than Edward Snowden, a traitor putting classified military intelligence into foreign hands. Imagine if Russians get their hands on our latest autonomous weapon technologies. And you were the unwitting intermediary to it all! You're only alive because you're famous, you're good lookin', and I've always liked you."

Alex's confidence cascaded. First, he didn't deny that the two were dead. Second, he'd just presented a wholly plausible justification for killing them. Total nonsense, but he'd sold it well. Olga's involvement made it so easy to mischaracterize.

Hansen, reading her face, smiled. "Get it now?"

Alex tried to recover. "What about the veterans?"

"Veterans? What veterans?"

"Bravo's platoonmates. The ones who knew that he was kicked out for violating Don't Ask, Don't Tell."

He laughed. "Don't Ask, Don't Tell? Who the fuck cares if someone broke that old rule? It's been gone for years!"

"Right, but you and I both know there's a stigma attached to having been discharged that way, even—"

"C'mon! That's crap. No one cares. So what if Bravo and a guy from his platoon got close before the guy died. Trust me, people in the shit I've been in could care less where you stick your man parts as long as you do your job . . . Now who are the veterans you're talking about?"

"So you did know. A bunch of Bravo's platoonmates who also knew died around the time he announced for president. Too many to be coincidental."

He glared at her, squinting his eyes, shaking his head in disapproval.

"Alex, do you know anything about the plight of returning service members?"

"I do, actually. I've covered that in depth."

"Well, then, you should know. Drug abuse. Alcoholism. Depression. PTSD. When a bunch of veterans die stateside it's *definitely* not coincidental. It's because they're facing huge issues, and our government has screwed them!"

Now the guy who'd offed veterans was their champion? Insane.

"So you don't think it's strange that Bravo's war buddies, the only ones who knew his secret, all died within months of one another? And right before he launched his campaign?"

"Lady, nothing about the plight of returning veterans surprises me. Twenty kill themselves every day, for God's sake! I started my company to better serve our vets. I've donated millions to support them. I'd never dishonor the country I gave so much to by targeting those same veterans."

He was good, with an answer for everything. And he was convinced by his own lies, making him even more scary.

Time for a different angle.

"So you think it's OK for a major government contractor to handpick the next president?"

"We know the rules of the system. We're following them. There's nothing wrong with that."

"Including planting stalking horses and wingmen into primaries?"

He scowled, twisting his head. Hearing the codename of his top secret operation caught him off guard.

"We support those who support us. If their candidacies have secondary consequences, so be it. Again, that's the First Amendment, ours and theirs. And in Bravo's case, we're thrilled that he ran a strong enough campaign to impress Nicholas. They will make a great team."

She fumed at his repeated reference to free speech.

"If this is such important speech, why are you working so hard to hide it? To keep me and others from reporting it? All that information should be out there. Why hide?"

"Anonymous speech is also protected. The source of it is not important. That can get in the way."

"Yes, but the public has every right to know that you guys were helping Bravo and Nicholas together in order to help yourselves. You know . . . First Amendment."

She grinned sarcastically as she said it.

He was not amused.

"I think we both know what would happen. The scandal police and corrupt media would be all over it as if we were doing something wrong. Sorry, but it's not getting out."

He said it with an intimidating finality, a decisiveness she could not leave unrebutted.

"It seems like a tough thing to stop."

"Oh, it definitely is," he said, standing up and walking toward the cockpit amid the rough jolts of more storms. "That's why we're thrilled to have you flying with us today."

CHAPTER 28

WASHINGTON, D.C.

W*E HAVE YOUR girlfriend.*

In addition to labeling her my girlfriend, the 6:00 a.m. text message startled me for a second reason: it came from Alex's number.

I sat up ramrod straight in the hotel bed. *Who is this?* I replied.

The person who holds your girlfriend.

A smart ass. Just what I needed. I didn't want to acknowledge any relationship with Alex beyond that we worked together. Not only did the term *girlfriend* not feel accurate, texts like these often end up being scrutinized by others, including investigators, media and the like. Didn't need the world reading my business.

Are you referring to Alex Fischer?

Your girlfriend. Yes.

Have you hurt her?

We have not. But we are happy to if you do not cooperate.

Where is she?

Tightly secured.

These cheap lines were meant to goad me. I didn't respond. I'd let them make their ask.

You can keep her out of danger.

Tell me more.

Kill the story.

???

Kill the story. Your girlfriend was looking into DroneTech and the election. So are your other team members. So are you. Stop.

I wasn't ready to be bullied. No way was I pulling another Abacus. *We don't kill stories.*

We do kill people.

The bluster didn't scare me. But I cringed at the next image that followed. The pale, puffy face of George Vassos took up the left half my phone screen. Livid at seeing him displayed like a trophy, I started to respond but stopped. I needed to keep the conversation going.

We have never made a deal in past. How can we trust you? I wrote.

You have no choice.

Not the right answer. I again refused to respond. After a minute, a new text came through.

Dozens know. Few talk. Those who don't, live without fear. We honor their silence.

Need proof.

Will provide.

But no message followed.

* * *

"The electronic tracker turned back on early in morning." Arthur was filling me in after knocking on my door at 8:00 a.m. We had lost the signal late the night before, presumably because Alex was in the air—the last ping had come from a private terminal at the San Diego airport.

"Great. You know where she landed?"

"They have brought her close to here. In state of Maryland."

"Good."

"Yes. We will identify the location and analyze its security."

"Her captors contacted me this morning. I have not told anyone but you. They want us to stop covering the story, and they will guarantee her safety."

"How did they contact you?

"They texted me from her cell number."

"And your reply?"

"I stalled. Said I needed proof. Still waiting."

"What will you do?"

"I don't know."

"Mr. Sharpe, you cannot negotiate with people like this. Once you do, it never ends. Mr. Kazarov would say same."

"I understand. I'm hoping your help will mean I don't have to."

"I know you are close to her. That is why they chose her. To make it difficult."

"Of course." I smiled weakly. "They've succeeded."

* * *

NEAR FREDERICK, MARYLAND

Even after Alex opened her eyes, everything stayed dark.

She was lying on her back on what felt like a cold, damp bench. Cement. Soft cotton material covered both her legs and arms. Sweats, she guessed. Her arms were numb, still pinned back, secured against the bench. Her sneakers were gone.

Someone else was in the room, breathing heavily, probably sleeping. A steady drip of water made the room feel cavernous, reminding her of her old track locker room.

An overwhelming stench of sweat and body odor. So strong, he or she must have been there a long time. Others had probably been there as well.

The person to her right suddenly grunted. "Is someone there?" he asked. The slight Southern accent sounded exhausted. Defeated.

"Yes," she answered. "I got here last night."

"Who are you?"

"I'm a reporter. On television."

"Oh no. Not more media."

"They had another reporter here?" she asked, thinking immediately of Vassos.

"Yes. For a few days, but they took him away a while ago. He seemed like a good guy."

"A great guy." They had started out distant, polar opposites, but over time, George had won her over. He'd risen from nothing, was a family man, and was strong and loyal in ways she'd always wanted a man of hers to be.

"Gone?"

"Yes."

That ended the conversation for a few minutes.

"Are you from Virginia, by chance?" Alex asked. "Virginia Beach?"

"I am."

Kroon's brother, she guessed. The one who had talked to Jack, then Rob Stone, then disappeared. His words were drawn out, his voice faint.

"So you've been here a while," she said.

"I have."

"Did you meet the girl as well?"

"I did. Is she gone too?"

"Yes. Why are you so special?"

He managed a faint laugh. "I don't feel special."

"You're alive, aren't you?"

"I figured it's because I've told them everything. Not that I know much."

"Maybe someone's looking out for you."

Jack had mentioned that Will Kroon worked at DPI. This had to be the reason his brother was still alive.

"It doesn't feel like it."

"They aren't showing much mercy. They are with you."

"What I've been through has not felt like mercy. Trust me."

Footsteps interrupted their conversation. Like the dripping water, they echoed around the room.

They stopped talking.

* * *

WASHINGTON, D.C.

I had set my phone to sound a loud chime if a message from Alex's phone came through. It rang just before noon.

It wasn't a message, but a photo. There she was. Blindfolded. Lying down. Gray sweats and socks. Arms behind her back. Couldn't see her hands, but likely bound.

I shuddered at the sight. In fear. Then anger. Long before I'd met her, Alex Fischer had struck me as a confident, cocksure, badass reporter. And that was before we'd become so close. Made my blood boil to see her put in this position, helpless and captive. A pawn, all to get to me.

Still, I held back.

I get it. You got her. I need proof as discussed.

A new photo came up. Not what I expected. It was the smiling face of Rob Stone, a professional shot, likely pulled from his website.

What about him?

He knows.

And?

Has he said anything?

The realization hit me hard, but then made sense. I'd waited for Stone to break the story of Bravo's discharge. But he'd reported nothing.

You threatened him? I asked.

He values his safety.

Pathetic. And Stone had talked such a big game about being embedded in war zones. I needed more examples.

Are there others like him? Media?

A few.

I know them?

Oh yes.

But they stay quiet?

Yes, because they stay safe.

Others? Beyond media?

A new photo appeared. An older man. In his seventies. I recognized him, but couldn't place him right away… Then I knew. It was Jim Little, the former senator. The rare politician that had taken on DroneTech, but then lost in his next primary.

Before I responded, another photo came through. Chuck Groppe. No surprise there.

A short pause, then one more photo. The stately mustache gave him away immediately. Brewer himself.

Stayed silent for years. Served him well.

A new photo: a harbor, tall masts at a dock and a boat under sail in the distance. In the center, two people greeting one another, an older man and a woman. Again, the white mustache. Senator Brewer, facing the camera as he reached out a hand. The woman was facing the other way, but her hair gave her away—strawberry blonde, falling to the small of her back, slight wave. I had admired it from up close for longer than I should admit.

Alex.

"…"

Then she called him . . . Oops.

* * *

"It is an old school," Arthur said urgently.

Desperately trying to track down Senator Brewer, I had just left a message for one of the senator's former staffers when Arthur barged into my office.

"What is?" I asked.

"Where they are keeping her. Where they took her."

"In Maryland?"

"Yes. It is near the city called Frederick. At first, we found no building on any current map. But we looked more closely and found that it was the location of a school, closed years ago."

"Okay. Is that good?"

"No. It is not good at all. They can protect an old school like a fortress. And the site is quite isolated, with long driveways and poor roads. It is well protected."

"And these guys make military drones for a living, so they're probably watching from every angle."

"Yes," Arthur said. "Also, even with access to Mr. Kroon's computer, we have failed to penetrate DroneTech's systems. They have built an impenetrable wall."

Damn. Every move felt like checkmate. Against us. I beckoned him over to my desk and scrolled through the series of text messages I had just received.

"These guys are ten steps ahead of us," I said. "They've quieted the press, silenced politicians, and eliminated every obstacle standing in their way. Now they have Alex."

"I agree. Very difficult."

"I'm not sure if we have any choice but to back off. We're getting nowhere and only getting people killed along the way."

His frown made clear that he was about to object. But before he could speak, my phone rang. It was the number I had called only minutes before, so I picked up immediately.

"Jack, thanks for checking in." I recognized the voice of Senator Brewer's former staffer, Amy something, who I'd known years ago. She sounded sympathetic. "How did you hear?"

"Hear what?"

"About the senator. I figured that's why you call—"

"What about him? What happened?"

"He suffered a massive stroke last night. We've kept it under wraps, but the doctors don't think he's going to make it."

Tried to play it off like I'd already heard. "I'm so sorry to hear it. I'll keep him in my prayers."

"God damn!" I yelled as I hung up, looking at a surprised Arthur.

That was it. Everyone who had talked about Operation Wingman—and now a former US senator—had died. Alex, trapped in a fortress of a school in the middle of nowhere, was next on the list. I texted her number back. There was no other path forward. No sane path, anyway. Even

Kazarov was failing. I'd spent a year trying to put my Abacus decision behind me, and I was about to do it again.

You win. We're done.

PART 4

CHAPTER 29

WASHINGTON, D.C.

"Jack, I haven't cancelled with the Youngstown forum yet."

"Why not?" I asked Cassie, piqued. We were both checking out of the hotel, feeling secure for the first time in weeks.

"I figured it was our last chance to get to the bottom of it all."

I shook my head. "Cassie, we're not doing it. Youngstown may, but you can't be there. Too risky."

Three days had passed since I'd shut our story down. Alex was still captive in Maryland, but they'd assured me she was being treated decently. Photo evidence backed it up. No more blindfold, no more bound arms. We'd talked twice, and I was angling to get her back soon.

Time was running out on my excuses for Alex not being at work. As with George, I couldn't divulge to my bosses or the authorities what was actually happening. That would lead to a full-fledged investigation, stopping the story in its tracks, exposing my odd Russia connection and ending my career. I'd have to get her back on my own.

On the campaign front, Governor Nicholas had racked up all the delegates from a bevy of weekend and Tuesday primaries. The Cleveland convention would lock them into place in a month. And he was hugely favored over Gene Austin, who had edged out Governor Wexler after a long and listless Republican primary.

Then the text came through. An international number.

You are making a mistake, Mr. Sharpe.

Holmberg?

This is Oleg Kazarov. I am in Washington. We must meet.

* * *

"A wonderful city your ancestors have built for you," Kazarov said as we rode east along the National Mall in his black Escalade. This, I knew, was a not-so-subtle lead-in to an imminent lecture.

Arthur drove, Stefan Holmberg sat in the front passenger seat, while Oleg Kazarov and I sat in the back. As he spoke, the Russian peered forward, out his window, so my view for much of the ride was of his long, pointed nose. It was a perfect May morning. The Lincoln Memorial grew smaller behind us, the Jefferson emerged to our right. He couldn't have picked a more scenic route to appeal to my patriotism.

"Beautiful indeed, Mr. Kazarov. Almost as stunning as your hometown."

"Yes. There is no more beautiful edifice in the world than St. Petersburg."

"Edifice?" I asked, knowing I'd have to take his bait sooner or later.

"Yes. Peter constructed it to be Russia's window to the West. And it remains beautiful to observe. But thanks to our broken Russian system, our false democracy, that is all it is. A symbol, yes, but hollow within."

"And you think that's what's happening here, in Washington?"

"Mr. Sharpe, it is what you are allowing to happen. And when it is over, you will not get it back. All of this will be a hollow symbol—"

He gestured out the window as we passed the Washington Monument and World War II Memorial. At that moment, a group of elderly tourists occupied most of the memorial grounds. Many in wheelchairs, even more with canes, looking closely at the bleached stone pillars of the memorial. Veterans converging on the site honoring their heroic service.

"—and those men will have fought for nothing."

"Mr. Kazarov, I worry about it deeply as well. Every day. That's why we all risked our lives to go as far as we did. But I am also a realist—"

He cut me off, twisting his head to look right at me. "I am nothing but a realist. Have you not learned that? And they equally so. They gambled that fear would stop you, and all others too. That is how they win, and how your country loses. I've seen this many times."

"Mr. Kazarov, they've killed several times. Tracked our every move. Now they've got Alex. And as you know, we've been unable to penetrate their systems. I see no path. What would you have us do?"

"You must take control. Stop reacting, and begin acting."

"But how?"

"That is why I am here."

"Excuse me?"

"We have come to suggest a different approach. Arthur, please explain."

An hour later, I walked briskly into Republic offices, a file folder in my left hand. Kazarov's plan made sense. I had just been too close to things to see it. And except for a few details, we likely had all the information we needed. So focused on Bravo, we hadn't been looking in the right place.

As I passed Cassie's cubicle, I told her, "Go ahead and keep your Youngstown plans."

* * *

An idea that Alex had thrown out long ago now made sense. The timing was perfect. So I stepped into Bridget Turner's cavernous office to propose it.

"Bridget, we've got a really good story to run," I said, knowing she wouldn't mind skipping the small talk.

"What is it?" she asked, swiveling around to look up at me from her desk.

I remained standing. She'd either like this or not, but either way I didn't need to get comfortable. "It's a human interest thing. Really compelling. We've been trying to track down Congressman Bravo's old war buddies. To capture his time in the war, including the incident he described."

"Right. We talked about doing something like that after the debate. What's taken so long?"

I placed my hands on the edge of her desk and leaned forward, trying to add some drama to my response. "We found no one to talk to."

"No one?"

"No one. They're all dead."

"You mean to tell me everyone who knew the congressman in Iraq died over there?"

"Even worse. They died over *here*. Recently, and in the saddest of ways. That's the story. Really puts a human face on the plight of returning veterans."

She thought for a moment. "I like it. That's a big issue, and sheds new light on Bravo. Is he game for an interview?"

"He's not. Doesn't want to talk about his service. That was another hold up."

She leaned back in her chair and crinkled one eye, the look of skepticism all of America recognized. "Jack, I don't think the story works if he doesn't do a big interview. He's the draw."

I'd come prepared for this roadblock. I held up a large print-out of the photo I'd taken of Bravo and his five platoonmates months ago.

"No, he's not." I laid it on her desk. "They're the story."

She stared at it for a few seconds, then pointed at the young Bravo. "There he is," she said. "Where's the guy who died in his arms?"

"That's him there." I pointed to a young, beaming Tommy Kroon.

"Wow. A sharp-looking young guy, but just a kid." I watched her look at each face. "They all were. They're all dead?"

"They are. This guy died of an overdose. That tall guy had a car accident. And the big guy here, he died in prison."

"What about him?"

"That's Michael Choo. Great soldier. Was shot working security in New York City."

"Oh my God. So tragic."

If she was nibbling on bait, might as well hook her. "And then there's Bravo, likely our next vice president."

She smiled, never averting her eyes from the photo. "You're right. That's an amazing story. We can start by showing this photo, then walk through what happened to each."

"Perfect. That's what we had in mind, too."

On the way back to my office, I stopped by Cassie's cubicle.

"We have to go back into Will Kroon's files," I said nonchalantly.

Her broad smile told me she welcomed the news. "Really? Now?"

"No need now. Kick ass in Youngstown. When you get back, we'll dive in."

* * *

YOUNGSTOWN, OHIO

"So this is where the great Jack Sharpe toiled away all those years!" Cassie declared as she strolled through the *Vindicator* newsroom, Mary Andres at her side. They sat down in a small conference room in the back.

"Don't be impressed by him," Andres said, laughing. "We never were!"

Over the next hour, they finalized the plan. Cassie wore a *Vindicator* press badge under the pretense that she was helping organize the forum. She would do a brief prep session with Mrs. Bravo in the makeshift green room, and if the opportunity to speak arose, she'd take it. The good news was they'd already overcome the biggest hurdle: Andres had submitted Cassie's name and vitals—birthdate, social security, city of birth—for the required Secret Service background check and she'd been cleared. No one had made the connection back to Republic News, or her confrontation with Bravo in Vegas.

The *Vindicator* staff had teamed with the local television station to broadcast the forum live across "the Valley," the counties that surround the Youngstown area. At 6:00 p.m., two dozen women from across Northeast Ohio filed into the studio. Mostly in their twenties and thirties, white, Black, a few Hispanic, it was exactly the crowd Mrs. Bravo's team had asked for. Moms. Working women. Poor and lower middle class.

Isabella Bravo, her communications aide, a makeup artist, and Cassie all walked into the green room at 6:20 p.m. In a chic red suit, Mrs. Bravo only came up to Cassie's nose, putting her at 5'3" even in her black heels. Cassie had rolled her eyes when she first saw the perfectly manicured political spouse. So phony, all smiles and primped and motherly. She'd long thought political wives gave strong, independent women a bad name. Still, Cassie executed her game plan—lay it on thick, build a connection—immediately.

"Welcome, Mrs. Bravo," she said, grinning as widely as possible. "I am such a fan of yours. Thank you for doing this. It means so much to the Valley, especially these women, working so hard to make it."

Mrs. Bravo broke into her signature dazzling smile. "Thank you, young lady," she said, reaching out to grasp both of Cassie's hands. "You're very sweet. I greatly enjoy doing these. They're such a welcome escape from being the plastic political wife."

Her communications director cringed at her candor, but Cassie laughed. Mrs. Bravo sounded just like her. "I can only imagine," Cassie said. "I don't know how you do it. I know I couldn't. Please have a seat here."

Mrs. Bravo sat down in a plastic office chair, and Cassie sat across from her. Without her own seat, the communications flack paced at her boss's side, as Cassie had planned. The makeup artist applied blush, lipstick, and eyeshadow, and brushed her jet-black hair. Watching the clock closely, Cassie spent a few minutes walking through the logistics of the forum. Mary Andres would ask an opening question, then a local TV anchor would ask one more. Then Mrs. Bravo would lead an open-ended discussion with the women.

"That sounds good, as long as I and those watching get to hear their stories. That's what matters most."

"Oh, yes," Cassie said. "That will be the heart of it."

She had spoken quickly to allow time for small talk, and to keep building the rapport. Now she had time to do what she was there for.

"Mrs. Bravo, if I can ask, what's it like to be married to a war hero? Your husband's story of holding his friend was just gripping. It gave me chills."

"Anthony is an incredible man. He's very brave, and a wonderful father."

She delivered every word sincerely, and clearly loved her husband. But she'd moved quickly off the topic of his war story.

Cassie went right back. "Had you heard that story before that night?"

"Yes. But only a few times."

Her smile faded as she confronted this less comfortable topic. Cassie, feeling cruel, went in for the kill.

"We have been trying to find his close friends from the platoon. We would love to interview them. Do you have any recommendations on who we might talk to?"

Mrs. Bravo, who'd been sitting casually in her chair, now sat up. She looked right into Cassie's eyes, trying to size her up.

"Please, Ms. Knowles," the communications aide said from Cassie's left, trying to shut it down. "This is a difficult—"

"No, I can answer it," Mrs. Bravo said softly, reaching out to Cassie, holding both her hands again. "Sadly, the men my husband was closest to are all gone. They either died over there or died over here."

She knew.

"Oh my gosh," Cassie said, gripping Mrs. Bravo's hand tightly. "That is so sad. I hope he's okay."

"It has been difficult for him, as you can imagine. Some died recently." Her eyes narrowed, a far more serious look than before. She spoke slowly. "Very difficult."

The comms flack paced, visibly uncomfortable. "I think it's time we wrap this—"

"Please!" Mrs. Bravo cast her a nasty look. "The young woman asked an important question, and I will answer it."

Wow, Cassie thought. "You would never know it was so difficult. You both are so charming on the campaign trail. So happy, with your beautiful children."

"Oh, yes. It's all about our children," she said. "We do this for them."

While her smile returned, her eyes moistened as she looked directly into Cassie's. This was an unhappy woman, and she was not afraid to show it. No plastic here.

"Okay, time to head out there!" the comms aide said. This time, she was right.

Cassie and Mrs. Bravo stood up, stepped out of the room, and walked down a hallway toward the studio. The moment was almost gone and Cassie still had work to do. Only feet from the studio entrance, Mrs. Bravo spoke up.

"Quick, where can I use a restroom?" Mrs. Bravo asked, looking purposefully at Cassie.

"Right down there. Let me show you."

Mrs. Bravo took Cassie's hand as they walked down the hallway. The relentless comms flack followed a few feet behind.

"I couldn't help but notice that tattoo you work so hard to keep hidden," Mrs. Bravo said. "So pretty. Why a moon?"

Cassie hesitated, caught off guard. "My—my parents died when I was a teenager," she said. "I struggled to sleep for a long time, and the moon became a source of comfort many of those nights."

Mrs. Bravo's stunning eyes widened as she heard the answer. Then she smiled again. "What a sweet way to remember them, and keep them close to your heart," she said, squeezing Cassie's hand. "They'd be so proud of you now."

Cassie smiled. She would've dismissed the line as political cheese from anyone else. But the way this woman spoke, and held her hand, felt nice. It all felt real. Mrs. Bravo entered the women's restroom, and Cassie and the comms aide waited outside. After a flush sounded from within, she exited the door.

"We need to go," the comms aide said impatiently, then led them back toward the studio.

Halfway back, Cassie spotted Mrs. Bravo's hand reaching out again. She lowered her right arm and opened her hand slightly, expecting to embrace the soft, small palm one last time. Instead, Mrs. Bravo slipped a piece of paper into her open fingers, squeezed them shut, and held her own fingers over Cassie's closed fist the rest of way.

"It was a pleasure to meet you," she said, letting go as she walked through the curtain.

As she heard the audience applaud Mrs. Bravo's entrance, Cassie turned around and walked briskly back to the bathroom. She entered a stall and sat down on the closed toilet lid. She unfurled the small piece of paper.

Must talk more. Please call this number at 10:00 tonight. A ten-digit number was scrawled below.

* * *

WASHINGTON, D.C.

I've got a deal for you, I texted to Alex's phone just after getting home. *A story you'll like.*

As usual, the person on the other end replied in seconds. *No funny business.*

Not funny at all. A profile of Bravo's platoon. Provides a window into the plight of returning veterans. It will help your cause. Will boost Bravo.

A long pause followed.

We want to see it first.

Of course. I'd hoped they would demand this. My plan depended on it. *I'll run it if we can get Alex back.*

Is this a joke?

It is not. We run this, we bury Operation Wingman for good. It'll put the story out exactly as you want it presented, going so far we can't take it back. No need for you to keep Alex after that.

Let us know when it's ready. We'll decide then.

Deal.

Good. If Cassie's exchange with Mrs. Bravo had been step one, this was step two.

* * *

YOUNGSTOWN, OHIO

Cassie didn't recognize the voice that picked up, but it was not Isabella Bravo.

"This is Cassie Knowles calling," she said uncertainly. "With whom am I speaking?"

Not recognizing the 408 area code, she had looked it up. San Jose and surrounding counties.

"Hi, Ms. Knowles. My name is Sonja. I am Isabella's sister. She wishes to speak to you."

Perfect. "How can we make that happen?"

"She's always surrounded by people, and believes her cell phone is tapped. I will call her hotel number with you on the line, she will say it is her sister calling, and then we will have a conversation that you will listen to."

Wow. Mrs. Bravo was more than just a charmer. "I can do that."

"One moment. I'll call her now."

She dialed ten numbers, and then the phone rang three times.

"Hello," a man's voice said. "This is Mrs. Bravo's room. May I help you?"

"Yes. This is her sister Sonja calling from San Jose. May I talk to her?"

"You only will have five minutes. Here she is."

A moment later, Mrs. Bravo's voice came through. "Sonja, thank you for checking in. We had a wonderful time here in Youngstown. Do you still have your guest there?"

Cassie assumed she was the guest.

"Yes, she's here for a few more days. She's having a wonderful time."

Mrs. Bravo now knew Cassie was on the line. Smooth.

"Please tell her I really appreciated her nice comments," Mrs. Bravo said.

"I will."

"Sonja, I am so sorry for your dilemma. I have been thinking about your situation. Where you feel so trapped in your current job."

"You have?" her sister asked.

Cassie took notes. This was all for her.

"It must be because you're worried. Worried for your family. For their security. For your kids. If you left the job or were to complain."

"You're right," Sonja said. "I do."

"It's unfortunate that your boss has made the environment so intimidating."

"Yes, it is."

"Sonja, I have to tell you, I think your boss is dangerous. Digging up all that stuff from your past could really hurt you and your career. But he knows that."

Before Sonja could answer, Mrs. Bravo spoke to someone else in the same feisty tone she'd used with her comms aide. "I'm almost done!" she said. "Can I at least talk to my sister about a bad situation at her work? My God!" The poor woman was being watched like a hawk.

Then she continued talking with Sonja.

"I mean, your boss has gotten rid of a lot good people," she said. "Of course you're worried you may be next."

Again, she knew.

"I know," Sonja said.

"Even if you can't be the one to do it, someone needs to say something. To do something. You don't want to stay at that job!"

"You're right," Sonja said.

Mrs. Bravo snapped again. "Okay! Sonja, I have to go now. I'll let you know when I'm coming back there."

"Love you, Isabella."

"I love you too."

One phone hung up, followed by a dial tone.

"Are you still there, Ms. Knowles?" Sonja asked over the tone.

"I am."

"Did that all make sense to you?"

"Yes it did. I wrote down every word."

"She hasn't said anything to me, but something is wrong. We've had a couple phone calls like this in recent months. If you can help her, please do."

"I'll do my best."

CHAPTER 30

WASHINGTON, D.C.

THE MORNING AFTER Cassie returned from Youngstown, she leaned over my shoulder as I reopened the OPS/SUPPORT file that Kazarov's team had hacked from Kroon's computer.

I scanned the list from top to bottom, but nothing stood out as an obvious starting point. Of the hundreds of operations on the list, only a couple files deviated from the norm in the way WINGMAN did. But nothing related to what we were looking for. Maybe Kazarov had been wrong. Or if he was right, maybe Will Kroon or DPI weren't involved. And even if they were, maybe the file was somewhere else. It felt like we were looking for a needle in the wrong haystack.

And then I spotted the name.

SUSQUEHANNA.

"I bet that's it," I said as I double-clicked on it.

There were several documents inside, none very long. A cover memo with a long list of names. Some photos. A criminal report.

"Oh my God," Cassie said as we started to comprehend what we'd found. "How did you know?"

"Start looking for other supporting materials," I said. She grabbed her laptop and, building off details provided in the SUSQUEHANNA documents, searched the internet and started printing articles she found in the *Inquirer*, the *Post-Gazette* and especially the *Patriot-News*.

I had an errand to run.

* * *

I was looking so closely at the photos of DroneTech products hanging in the lobby of DPI—taking in details I'd missed on my previous visit—that I didn't hear Will Kroon come off the elevator behind me.

"Jack," he said, surprise in his voice.

I turned around and did a double take, shocked at his appearance. So vibrant just months ago, Will Kroon now looked worn, gaunt, and pale. He'd chewed his fingernails to half-size. Endangering your parents and playing a role in your own brother's kidnapping must take a toll, and he deserved every ounce of his suffering.

"Will," I said. "How the hell are ya?"

"Um, I don't have time to talk right now."

I flashed as big a smile as I could. "I think you'll want to. I have some great news!" I clapped him on the shoulder as I said it, and he recoiled.

"Did someone find Logan?"

"No. Is he still missing?" I asked innocently.

He frowned, genuinely miserable. "Yes, he is."

"How are your mom and dad handling it?"

"They're rattled, but doing okay. They've learned to cope over the years." He suddenly looked me right in the eye. "Like those letters she imagined."

Imagined? What a scum.

"Yeah," I said, nodding. "Figured as much."

"So what's the good news?"

"We've decided to do a major feature on Tommy's and Congressman Bravo's platoon. What they went through. How they struggled when they got home. Really focus on the plight of our nation's veterans."

"That sounds great, Jack. Why are you telling me?"

"We want to interview you. You can talk about your brother, but you also met these guys. You can help us round it all out, especially with your experience here."

He stared straight at me. Knowing what he actually knew, what he'd actually done, I struggled not to smile at the absurdity of my request. I could only imagine what he was thinking—what a clown of an investigative reporter I must be. But including him in the story was key. It would telegraph to DroneTech that we knew very little. Featuring the researcher behind Operation Wingman in a positive light would whitewash it all. It would make their day.

I raised my eyebrows at Will, ostensibly asking him if he was game.

He nodded. "Great," he said flatly. "Really great, Jack. Count me in."

CHAPTER 31

WASHINGTON, D.C.

IT'S DONE, I texted to Alex's phone. *And it's damn good.*

Fortunately I wasn't bullshitting. It was one hell of a story. Bridget Turner had narrated the piece, and, of course, was pitch-perfect. It opened with Congressman Bravo's stirring debate moment. And it closed, powerfully, on the photo of all six of the young men together—our Iwo Jima shot.

But the true magic came in between. Cassie, a few producers, and I had scrambled across the country over the past week to gather the footage. Dontavius Jackson's grandmother had given an incredible interview, the contrasting photos of Dontavius to her side as she spoke. The Cull family, in their living room together reminiscing about Jimmy, brought a tear to every eye that watched it. Dave Sesler's sister and Michael Choo's mother rounded it out well.

Cassie and I had groaned at the footage of Will Kroon waxing on about the heroic members of his brother's team, when we both knew that his dirty work had led to their deaths.

If this wouldn't propel Bravo to the vice presidency, nothing would.

The text came back in just over a minute. *The boss wants to watch it.*

The boss? I thought I'd been dealing with the boss the entire time.

Yes. The boss. He wants to watch it with you there. We'll send instructions.

* * *

Blindfolded, stomach tingling, I gripped the back seat's armrest to stabilize myself as the van raced to its destination. Just like my Russia trip, I'd voluntarily placed myself in the hands of a cabal that had killed repeatedly. Worse, I'd decided an electronic tracker or a tail would be too risky. Even as we drove, I was second-guessing the plan. Had I just launched my own kamikaze mission? Maybe.

But as we sped along a highway—my guess, the D.C. Beltway—the left side of my brain argued back. There was no other way. I needed to get Alex back before we could execute our plan, and this high-risk rendezvous was the only way to secure her while also laying the trap. And Cassie was right. I had sent everyone else out for months—time to dirty my own hands. In the old days, sticking my neck out had always led to my best stories.

Even with my eyes covered, I tracked the route. For what felt like an hour, we drove along a major highway. Then came twenty stomach-churning minutes swaying back and forth on hilly, curvy roads, followed by ten painful minutes jostling up and down on dirt roads. Given the distance and topography, the destination had to be that abandoned school in Maryland. Remote and risky, but also a hopeful sign I'd see Alex soon.

"Step out, sir," the deep New Jersey accent who'd welcomed me into the van said after we stopped. A large hand grabbed me by the right tricep, nudging me forward.

"We're walking into a door. There's a slight step." Same Jersey accent, now from behind. We walked down a long hallway. "Stop here. Turn left. Take about five steps forward."

A door closed behind me.

"You can sit here. He'll be in in a second."

A person from behind me ripped off the blindfold. I squinted, blinded by the first light I'd seen in an hour. I was sitting in the center of a square classroom—a chalkboard on one wall, a large bulletin board on another, a row of small cubbyholes on the third wall. Windows to the outside took up most of the fourth wall, but they were covered with gray blinds. The classroom was barren of furniture except for my chair and an empty one next to it. The look of the old, empty room took me back to my high school days at Canton McKinley.

The sole modern feature was the large flat-screen monitor on the wall, next to the bulletin board and to the right of the door I had entered.

That door flew open, crashing loudly against the wall. A white-haired bear of a man barreled through the doorway, reminding me of a fullback ramming into a goal line. He was far less kempt than the photos in Alex's research file, sporting workout attire and far-longer hair pulled back into a ponytail, but I immediately recognized him: Doug Hansen, DroneTech's CEO.

"When they said the boss, they weren't kidding!" I said. As

uncomfortable as I was, I tried to exude confidence. Guys like this react better to strength than to cowardice. And flattery never fails.

"Sharpe, *you're* the boss!" he said, striding across the room, laughing heartily. "I'm a big fan. I hear you used to be a damn good quarterback."

"I wasn't bad. But one hit took care of my best weapon," I said, pointing to the long scar on my right forearm.

He lifted his right pant leg, revealing his metal prosthesis. "Tell me about it! I wasn't a bad nose tackle in my day but a bunch of flying nails took care of me for good."

"You got me there, Mr. Hansen. Thank you for your service. Still looks like you move prett—"

"Call me Doug!" he said, rapping me hard on my right shoulder. "And yes, I'm a survivor."

From everything my team had gathered on Doug Hansen, this was a lethal man. But he knew how to pour on the charm. I knew I needed to play along.

"Why's a guy like you holed up in an old school?" I asked. "You can afford better than this."

"Jack, it's not about what I can afford. It's about what I can hide while also being able to fly out here quickly."

The "hiding" was what concerned me—hiding people, no doubt, including Vassos and Kristina Jones.

"Airport nearby?" I asked.

"No, we just land the chopper on the old soccer field."

"Convenient."

"You got it." Again, big smile. Tapped his right index finger against his temple. That's when I noticed the scars all over his ruddy face.

The whole thing was surreal. Here we were, yukking it up, even when we both knew the truth: that he'd kidnapped two of my reporters. Killed one. And that I was here to buy the other one back by airing a story that whitewashed his deadly conspiracy. The same thought must've occurred to him, because his smile disappeared in an instant. Now he was all business.

"Jack, I understand you want Alex back."

"I do."

He coughed a few times, then laughed. "I respect that, dude. A man will sell his soul for a little pussy, won't he?"

The smirk on his face sickened me as much as the words. In any other context, I would have decked the guy.

"It's not that, she's one of my top—"

His smile disappeared and his face reddened. He was no longer playing. "Stop, Sharpe. Don't embarrass yourself. We had your other guy here for days. We dumped buckets of water—buckets!—down his fucking throat. I gotta give him credit. He took it like a man, didn't he, Frankie?"

He looked up at the guy who'd been standing behind me. "Yes, he did, sir. Impressive for a civilian."

Hansen looked back at me. "And we didn't hear a thing from you, or anyone. Not a damn thing. You left a man in the field to die, buddy, but you come running for your girlfriend. You're a fucking joke."

My face heated up with rage. He had just bragged about killing one of my people, then blamed me.

Hansen suddenly stood. "Sharpe, follow me."

Frankie approached the back of my chair, making clear that staying put was not an option.

We soon walked along two long hallways, Hansen talking the whole time. Every word he uttered had me second-guessing coming out here, especially alone.

"You know, I haven't touched Alex once. Isn't that right, Frankie?"

"Yes, sir."

"I somehow didn't have the heart to."

"That's good to hear," I said.

"I still could, man. I still could." Shaking his head, he sounded like he was reconsidering.

"Either way, I thought you should see the room where your buddy went down. Jack, you left a guy in the field. In my world, that's as bad as it gets. You should see what he saw. Feel what he felt."

This nightmare was getting worse by the second.

Hansen pushed through two swinging double doors, and I followed right behind.

"Don't you agree?" he asked.

"Doug, you really don't need—"

"You want Alex back, you want me to leave her alone, you need to do what I say. You can take it."

I breathed deeply, reining in my anger, trying to keep a cool head. We walked through a second set of swinging doors and entered what looked like an old workout room. But only one piece of equipment was still there—a wide wooden bench right in the center. A plastic bucket sat on the floor, next to one end of the bench.

"It looks like you spend a lot of time at the gym," Hansen said.

"When I can."

"I bet you've never done this!" he said.

I said nothing.

Hansen approached the bench.

"Sharpe, we're going to need you to lie down. This way. On your back."

I stopped walking. Time to raise one final protest. "You're not really going to do this, are you?"

"Why the hell do you think you're out here?"

"But I reached out to you guys!"

"Jack, did you really think it would be that fucking easy? We are this close to pulling off our project. I need to be sure you're serious, and know what you know. Plus, I'm not going to give you Alex unless you do what we say. You've gotta earn it. She's worth it, isn't she?"

Frankie eased up behind me, ready to push me toward the board if needed.

"So you're going to waterboard me?"

"Your man went through it for your big fucking story. Alex is shackled a few rooms over for your big fucking story. She could've been shot. The Russian girl is dead. The turncoat is dead. What are *you* willing to do?"

Frankie's hands now gripped the back of my shoulders, pushing me towards the board.

"You'll free Alex if I do this?" Not that I had much leverage to make a deal.

"Yes. But you need to go through what your guy went through. And tell us everything you know."

I raced through every option, but there was no way out. I shut my eyes, resigning myself. A memory flashed through my mind. Ten years ago, I had agreed to be tased by the Youngstown Police Department, just after they'd bought Tasers for every officer. I had dreaded the day for weeks. It was like knowing in advance the precise day you're going to die, a torture in and of itself. But in the end, I had shut my eyes, sucked it up, and "ridden the bull" for five seconds. It had stimulated a deep, unnerving pain, far worse than even the worst football hit. In writing about the tasing, the best description I had come up with was imagining a man stuck inside your body, trying to get out with a jackhammer. But after enduring five seconds of that pulsating jackhammer, I'd walked away unscathed.

This would be worse, but I had no choice.

I stepped forward, sat on the side of the board, swiveled my body around, and lay flat on my back. Frankie promptly tied my legs, then arms, tightly to the board.

"Here you go," Hansen said, casually, as the man he called Frankie laid a cold, wet rag over my face. Streams of ice-cold water ran down my chin and the sides of neck. Then two large hands squeezed both of my temples like a vise, holding my head in place.

I debated what to do once the water came. Try to drink it? Swallow it into my stomach? Or do my best to force it back out? Really had no idea.

Hansen read my mind.

"Your man sure knew how waterboarding works. More than you do." Hansen's voice came from just to the side of my left ear, his mouth only inches away.

I couldn't speak, but he kept going as if I had said something. "Oh yeah. Too well. He even knew when the last one was coming. Yeah, he thrashed around more than normal for that one—really bloodied up his arms and legs trying to get out."

I didn't respond.

"Do you know how he knew?"

I still said nothing.

He chuckled ominously before answering his own question. "We didn't lower his head before pouring," he said. "He knew that lying flat meant the water would flow to his lungs and drown him. And he absolutely freaked out."

Jesus. He was right. Vassos had known more than I did. The board I was lying on remained flat, too, and I hadn't even thought about it.

Water splashed in the bucket behind me.

I clenched my fists tight, and waited.

A second passed. Then several. Then maybe 30. At one point, I was so intensely preparing my throat for the deluge, I gagged. Over a minute went by.

That's when a large hand crashed down on my right shoulder, forcing me to grunt.

"Jack, I'm impressed!" Hansen said loudly.

Bracing for a flood of water, it took me a couple seconds to process what he'd said. I still wasn't sure what was coming next. Then the rag was ripped away. To my relief, the painful pressure around my ankles and wrists eased.

"Excuse me?" I said.

"You manned up. I'm impressed. You were ready to take one for your team. Most people don't have the guts you do. Hell, you didn't even squirm."

He pushed hard against the back of my shoulder, forcing me to sit up straight.

"Get up. I know you've got something you want to show me. Some type of television special."

I coughed up some saliva, then worked to regain my composure.

"Let's go check it out. Get up!"

As we walked back, Hansen continued to celebrate my composure, giving me time to regroup. I was still shaking from a mix of fear and fury, but I realized that I still had a chance of pulling this off. Back in the classroom, I took the small zip drive out of my pocket and inserted it into the flat-screen monitor. Hansen sat down in one of the two seats.

"I think you're going to like this."

"If it helps me achieve my goal, I sure will."

I pushed play and stayed standing. The title, "The Bravo Six," appeared first, followed by the congressman's inspiring debate moment, some patriotic music, and then Bridget Turner's taped stand-up introducing the story.

"Man, I'd love to get me some Bridget Turner," Hansen said as he watched her walk through Arlington National Cemetery before kicking off the interviews. Thankfully, it was the last thing he said for a while.

For the next ten minutes, he watched our handiwork. He laughed heartily when family members shared humorous moments. He shed his own tears as the Culls and Mrs. Jackson shed theirs. He cradled his chin in his hand and shook his head as Sesler's sister bemoaned the alcoholism that destroyed her brother, and as Mrs. Choo detailed her son's unsuccessful attempts to find better jobs. I eyed him closely but couldn't tell whether he had deluded himself into forgetting that he was responsible for these deaths or he was putting on a show.

He stiffened when Will Kroon, his own researcher, appeared. But he eased up, relieved once he realized Will was simply there to describe his older brother and his buddies—as surprised as Will had been that we hadn't put two and two together.

The piece closed with a shot panning in on the photo of the Bravo Six together. He reached up and wiped away a few more tears, then turned toward me.

"Jack, what the fuck are you doing?" he asked, running his hand through his hair, looking as serious as he'd been the entire meeting.

My heart skipped. "What do you mean?" I asked.

"What the fuck are you doing—" he asked again, but then his frown turned into a wide grin. "—putting me through that? That was incredible!"

"You think?"

"I know! Jack, you fucking get it. You absolutely get it."

"Get what?"

"Veterans. When they get home . . . Chewed up. Spit out. Treated like shit. That photo, their lives, those families, sum it all up. I have spent my life trying to make the case that that piece made in ten minutes. I've been trying to end the pain before it starts, and after they return. Amazing."

I sat silently, still not sure whether Hansen was testing me.

"Jack, that thing's *gotta* run before the convention. It will *make* the convention, and the whole fall campaign!"

"That's the plan. But as I hope they told you, I need two things from you."

"They told me one, not two!" he shot back angrily.

"One is for me, one is for the story." *Finally*, I thought, *some leverage*.

"What the fuck's that mean?"

"There's a final element needed in the story. Something's missing."

"Okay?"

"We want to interview his wife."

He shook his head furiously. "Bravo's wife? No. Fucking. Way."

"Trust me, you want us to. It'll round out his image well. And she'll get women votes in particular. She knows him best, can describe him best, and is good on TV. And it'll look strange if she's not in it."

Hansen rapped his chubby fingers against his knee, clearly uncomfortable with the idea. From what Cassie had told me, they had watched Mrs. Bravo like a hawk in Youngstown. Didn't trust her. But I was prepared to push hard because it was a critical part of our plan.

"We'd have to set it up just right," he said. "And you try any funny business with her, I'll have both you and your girlfriend underground by the end of that day."

"Good. And I'll need Alex Fischer back," I said. "If she's here, I'd like to do that today."

"Still not sure I trust you," Hansen replied, shaking his head. "How about I return her after your feature runs?"

He was egging me on, challenging me to beg a little. But I decided to deal instead, gesturing toward the monitor.

"When we run that, it will be the best story you ever could have hoped for, and it will close the door on Operation Wingman. Clean it up better than you could have. And we will not say another word about Bravo beyond basic election coverage." I paused. "But I'm not leaving here without Alex, and nothing airs if I'm not back. Plus, we both know you'll be keeping a close eye on us."

Narrowing his eyes, he looked right at me, studying my face. We both sat completely still. He started nodding. He smiled.

"You got yourself a deal, Sharpe. We'll do it! Hell, you earned it!"

He reached out to shake my hand. I looked at it for a moment, then reached out to do the same. When our hands came together, he squeezed tightly. I matched his grip with as tight a grip as I could return. He grinned at the strange competition, enjoying it, but I refused to give him the satisfaction of anything but a straight face.

"We have a deal," I said.

He pulled his hand from mine, turned, and walked out.

I was blindfolded again as two men led me out the way we had come in. Door, hallway, doorstep, then outside. As we walked along a driveway, the high-pitched sound of an engine kicked on close by, then morphed into the accelerating whir of a rotor, and finally into the loud, familiar chugging of a helicopter taking off. Wind buffeted my face.

We took a few more steps as the chopper faded into the distance. A large hand nudged my right shoulder, pushing me back into the van.

"I got it, I got it," I said impatiently as I scooted across the seat, the rolling van door slamming closed behind me.

From behind, a different hand touched my left shoulder. Smaller, softer. And to my relief, it squeezed tenderly.

"Jack, is that you?" she asked, voice faint. Exhausted.

"Alex, thank God," I whispered. "Are you hurt?" The van pulled forward as I asked the question.

"I'm okay physically. I'm not sure where I am mentally. For some reason they never roughed me up, although Hansen is an absolute psychopath. Hot and cold like nothing I've ever seen. When he was hot, I thought I might die any second."

"Saw a little bit of that myself just now. Freak show. But we're all good now."

"Are you sure?"

"I'm sure. You're not going to like what we had to do, but we're all good."

We held hands the entire ride home.

CHAPTER 32

WASHINGTON, D.C.

"HOLY SHIT," I said, shaking my head. "He couldn't help himself."

"He really couldn't," Cassie said, looking at me from across my desk. "Pathological. No wonder his wife always looks so down."

The thick file Cassie had handed me contained the rest of her research, filling in what we'd found in the SUSQUEHANNA file. I had leafed through the papers for an hour.

"Looks like this one is the worst," I said, pulling out one stapled packet of papers in particular.

"Yes. There are lots of bad ones, but that's game over. He lost control, then got desperate. It's amazing they were able to cover it up, but I guess power will do that for you."

"And *to* you," I added. "I need you to break this down into a memo that's easy to digest."

"Why? I can basically write and produce this from here, then do a two-day shoot. I've got everything I need."

"Cassie," I said slowly, "we can't be the ones to do this one."

Incredulousness flashed across her face. "What? What the hell?"

"We can't have our fingerprints on this. It's too hot. I'm going to hand it off to someone I know will do it right."

"What's the point of doing that? It's our story. My biggest story ever!"

"It's a story that has to be told. And it will be. But trust me, we can't be the ones telling it. It will have the same impact regardless, as long as it gets out."

"Is this because of Alex?" she asked angrily.

"Yes," I said, to Cassie's obvious surprise. "It's because of Alex. And it's because of you. And Rachel. Alex's daughter. My family. It's for all of us . . . I had to make a deal. If I break it now, we're all at risk. And if we can get what we need done without risking our loved ones and our own lives, we should do it."

She shook her head, still unconvinced. "We run a puff piece covering up a scandal, and we give away the good one? That's a bad deal, and not what I signed up for. This is a career story—let me worry about me and Rachel."

I was getting nowhere with her, and didn't expect to. If an editor had told me this back in the day, I would have reacted just as she was. Maybe worse. Imagine Bob Woodward handing Watergate to the *Times*. But I didn't need to win the argument. I'd already made the decision. We were going to hand the biggest story of our lives over to someone else. We had no choice. The whole story would still come out. Even if we didn't get the credit, that was what mattered. A far better compromise than the one I'd had to make a year ago.

After Cassie walked out of my office, as dejected as if I had just fired her, I dialed the old number where it had all started.

"Jesus, Jack?" Mary Andres said, though I could hear that she was joking. "What do you need now?"

"Are you sitting down?"

"Yes. Why?"

"You're going to have to clear out another wall. I'm about to give you the biggest scoop of your career."

* * *

It was a breathtaking 30 minutes.

Isabella Bravo delivered as compelling an interview as I'd ever seen. And Bridget Turner, the best in the business, masterfully coaxed every word and emotion out of her.

"Had Anthony ever told you about holding Tommy Kroon in his arms as he died?" Bridget asked, leaning forward.

"Not for years. One night we started talking about the war, I asked about his medal, and for the first time, he shared the details. We cried together the rest of the night. These men, men like my husband, carry these horrible memories with them for the remainder of their lives. As the nation saw in New Hampshire, they remain just below the surface."

"Did you ever meet the rest of the Bravo Six?" Bridget asked, holding up the photo.

"I never did, but I always felt like I knew them all," Mrs. Bravo said, pointing at each face as she spoke. "'Bus,' as Anthony called him, was a gentle giant. Michael Choo, such a professional. Sesler was a wild man, Anthony always said, but loyal and good-hearted and tough as nails. And as strong as Dontavius was, he was a big kid, fun-loving. Anthony was so saddened by his struggles once he got home. By all of their struggles."

"Do you ever ask yourself why Anthony has been so successful while they all struggled so much? And, tragically, why all have passed while he lives?"

"We do, every day. We talk about it. But we know the answer. It is the story of our country. These men, their struggles, are not unique. They are common. Anthony is the lucky one. These men faced what most face coming home—PTSD, physical disabilities, depression, addiction. Anthony believes we must do far more to help them. It's why he is working so hard to win this election."

I'd been around a lot of politicians and their spouses. She was as good as they came. After they finished, I approached Mrs. Bravo as she walked off the set.

"Thank you for doing this," I said. "You were incredible. It will make our story that much more special."

"Thank you for giving me the opportunity. This means a lot to us too."

Cassie had given me the heads up. "She will reach out for your hands," she'd said. "That's her style." And she was right. With her two aides just a few yards away, caught up in the aura of Bridget Turner, Isabella Bravo reached out to hold both my hands as we finished our conversation.

I was ready.

I slipped the piece of paper into her right hand. She looked up at me, studying my face closely. I looked back at her, smiled, and nodded in the most assuring way I could. I closed my hands over hers, forcing her to conceal my note.

About an hour before the interview, Cassie had given me the small piece of paper. On it, I had written in my best penmanship: *We know. Escape hatch coming. Once Vindicated, take it.*

Isabella Bravo was a smart woman. Her meeting and indirect phone call with Cassie had made that clear. She wanted out, and she'd understand the connection immediately. She'd understand because my note appeared directly beneath the two sentences she had written on the same piece of paper only weeks before: *Must talk more. Please call this number at 10:00 tonight.*

* * *

Governor Moore called me a few hours after I left her the message.

"Governor, I'm going to send you some more information if that's okay."

"Sure," she said. "Same stuff?"

"Related. We've got data from other states that show a very similar pattern to the one in Colorado. This might be a lot bigger than we first thought."

"Really?"

"Absolutely."

"Jack, I'm curious why you're not just reporting this stuff yourself."

"Governor, you saw it yourself, there are some nasty people out there. We're keeping our heads low but think it's important that this get out there. I also assume this doesn't need further public announcements."

"I don't think so. It will just go into the investigation we already announced. Although we'll likely reach out to the other states to get their attorneys general involved."

"Governor," I said, knowing it was now or never. "Some other big news may be coming out as well."

"What kind of news?"

"I can't tell you. You'll know it when you see it. You might want to free up your schedule."

CHAPTER 33

TWO WEEKS BEFORE the Cleveland convention, after a week of intense editing and nonstop promotions, we aired the Bravo Six special. Prime time on a Friday night.

With Mrs. Bravo's interview, we had actually expanded what was supposed to be a ten-minute segment into a full 30 minutes, peppering in more footage and interviews with the other family members. Some things are just meant for television.

In the second half-hour, Bridget Turner interviewed veterans' advocates and senators of both parties about the need for deeper support, more treatment, and more job opportunities for returning veterans. We even offered a switchboard for people to call to make donations, raising three million dollars for multiple charities.

Seconds after Turner signed off, I got a call from a San Diego phone number. When I picked up, there was no greeting. Just hearty laughing.

"Jack, that was an unbelievable story," Doug Hansen said happily. "You really did it. You kept your word, too. I love a guy that keeps his word."

"Glad you liked it. The response has been powerful. Millions already raised." I did all I could to sound sincere.

"You did good. And the Mrs. was a home run. You were right! Wow. You guys know what you're doing."

"We do. We have a good team."

"Say hi to Alex for me. Hope you're enjoying her . . . I mean, having her back." He chuckled at his intentional slip.

Hearing him say her name sickened me, but I kept my composure. "Again, glad you liked it."

"Congrats again. You need to lighten up, buddy. And Sharpe, I'll probably see you at the convention!" he barked, before hanging up.

I doubted it.

I called Mary Andres once more.

"You guys track everything down?" I asked.

"Sure did. Cassie's memo was perfect. We just followed her roadmap.

We're putting it to bed tomorrow, then out Sunday. Thanks again, Jack. We owe you."

"Thank you! This is becoming an annual tradition."

"Jack, how the hell did you get this story? How did you find it?"

"Mary, you know I can't reveal my sources!" I said, laughing. "Talk to you Sunday." We hung up.

Of course I couldn't reveal my source. Actually, he wasn't exactly a source, just a person who had guessed right. Even if I did reveal him, she wouldn't have believed me anyway.

"Think, Mr. Sharpe," Kazarov had said in the Escalade as we drove up Constitution Ave. "If they dug so deeply to attain leverage over their choice for vice president, they must also have done so for their choice for president."

I had looked at him skeptically.

"Why would you compromise one and not the other?" he'd asked. "Winning is only the first step. Control is the final objective."

It had been clear he was speaking from experience.

"You're right," I had said. "That wouldn't make sense. We'll take a look."

"Good. Remember what their ultimate goal is. That is what you must stop."

CHAPTER 34

THERE'S NOTHING LIKE a front page, above the fold, banner newspaper headline screaming out national breaking news.

Just like a year ago, my old paper, the *Youngstown Vindicator*, had done it again.

"Governor Nicholas Snagged in Multiple Affairs; One Top Aide Drowned in Harrisburg"

The headline summed up the brutal, multi-page story that followed, walking through Governor Peter Nicholas's decade-long habit of sleeping with those who worked for him. But that wasn't the part that sunk him.

According to the dozen women interviewed, seven of them on the record, the affairs had all started out consensually—at least as consensually as an affair with a pushy and overbearing boss could be. Initially, Nicholas was quite the charmer. But then the governor would morph into obsessive. Controlling. And when the women got scared and tried to break it off, he'd boil over. Lash out. Punish. Most of the women had soon left both their job and the state, deciding that keeping their sanity was worth losing their livelihood.

But not Andrea McMillan. She'd been the unlucky one. She hadn't had a chance to make that choice.

A few years out of college, McMillan had been Nicholas's scheduler for ten months as his first term wound down, until the morning her lifeless body was found caught in one of the dams of the Susquehanna River, not a mile downstream from the State Capitol in Harrisburg. It was immediately clear that this was not a simple drowning. She was badly bruised, her face especially, but also her arms and several ribs. Four of her fingernails were broken; two fingers were badly fractured. The coroner speculated that there'd been a struggle, she'd been knocked unconscious, and then tossed into the river.

In the *Vindicator* story, McMillan's roommate described McMillan's late nights alone with the governor, her anguish after his dark side emerged, her efforts to break it off, her fear when he objected, and then her sudden disappearance. After her body was found in the dam, according to the roommate, the police department had opened a half-hearted investigation, and quickly sidelined it as an unsolved cold case.

"It was the governor," the roommate said to the paper. "Of course it was the governor."

A retired officer acknowledged that pressure had been applied on the department from the highest level to "make it go away." Some blood had been found under McMillan's fingernails, but somehow it hadn't been tested, and then it had disappeared. Now it added up. The same controlling behavior the other women had vividly described had exploded into a tantrum, causing Andrea McMillan's death.

And now, there it all was on the front page of the *Vindicator*. The picture of the young, bespectacled Andrea McMillan appeared on one side; on the other, a photo of Nicholas and his always somber wife.

"Oh my God!" Cassie yelled over the phone at 8:00 a.m. "They put it all in and then some."

"They sure did. But your memo and initial research were the key."

"Hell, I wish I could take more credit for it. But Will Kroon deserves most of it. He had every woman listed. The roommate listed. He even had the name of that retired police investigator who swore there was interference from the governor's mansion."

"I know," I said. "They should've given Kroon a byline."

"Jack, I've been thinking about this. Why didn't they get rid of everyone on Nicholas's list, like they did the Bravo witnesses?"

I'd pondered the same question.

"Would have been too obvious," I said. "Returning veterans die every day, so getting rid of them was easy. But a bunch of healthy women in their twenties and thirties? Too obvious. My guess is they paid them off or were convinced they had moved on, but once we and the *Vindicator* called, the women couldn't hold back. Either way, this should take care of the Nicholas presidency."

"You think he'll even be the nominee?" Cassie asked.

"Not a chance."

By Tuesday, most of the women in the story had appeared on national cable shows describing the monster that Governor Nicholas would become over the course of their time with him. The retired Harrisburg officer did an exclusive with Bridget Turner on Wednesday night. And every step Nicholas took, he was surrounded by media, hounding him with questions and flashing bulbs. Mrs. Nicholas stopped appearing with him.

By Thursday, dozens of Nicholas's delegates began demanding he step aside. And once that snowball started rolling, it grew quickly. Dozens became a hundred, which then became multiple hundreds.

And then America learned the reason that whenever a savvy candidate ended a failed primary run, she was careful to announce that she was "suspending" her campaign, not ending it.

* * *

DENVER, COLORADO

The Colorado press broke the news Thursday afternoon.

Governor Janet Moore had scheduled an announcement for 10:00 a.m. Friday, at the same location where she'd suspended her campaign months back.

Within an hour, Michigan newspapers also went nuts. Senator Wendell Stevens's press secretary had informed the *Detroit Free Press* that the senator was canceling all his public events on Friday for a major announcement. And that announcement would take place in Colorado.

I jumped on an evening plane to Denver, along with every major reporter from Washington. Unlike on most flights, we huddled with each other the whole way, speculating, comparing notes. Even Rob Stone was chatty. The fact that we were flying to Denver and not Detroit gave away most of the drama.

It unfolded as we predicted, with the white-tipped Rockies and gold dome of Colorado's statehouse as the scenic backdrop.

"Today, in this moment of great crisis for our party, and for our country, we are announcing a historic coming together," Governor Moore said, Wendell Stevens standing next to her. Despite the ebullient applause of the large crowd, neither smiled, appreciating the seriousness of the moment.

Stevens took his turn. "We are each ending the suspension of our campaigns. The governor and I have talked at length. And I pledge all my delegates to support her as the Democratic nominee for president of the United States."

"And I," Moore continued, "will nominate Senator Stevens to be the Democratic nominee for vice president of the United States."

Another round of applause, which Moore spoke over to continue.

"We have talked to many delegates and party leaders across the country, even those who supported Governor Nicholas and Congressman Bravo, and we can say that they almost unanimously agree that this is the best course for our party and our country. We will have more to say in the coming weeks, and in Cleveland, but we commit that we will come together as a team, as a party, and as a country, to build a better future."

They stopped talking and began to walk off stage together, making clear they did not intend to answer questions. The right call. But the press wanted more.

"Are you calling on Nicholas and Bravo to drop out?"

"Are those delegates legally allowed to switch?"

"Are you calling for a full investigation into Nicholas?"

"Senator Stevens, why aren't you seeking the presidency? You stayed in the primary far longer than Governor Moore did."

This froze the old boxer in his tracks. He about-faced and returned to the podium. The press quieted, sensing that some kind of line had been crossed.

"I will answer that," Stevens said into the mic. "First, I believe some ugly things took place in the primary. Things we do not all understand yet, that I know the attorney general here is already investigating. Governor Moore was ahead when those ugly things started, so she took the brunt of them. Once they took care of her, I came next, and got hit hard too."

He stopped again, gathering his thoughts. This was a big moment, and he knew it.

"Given all of that, and out of respect for our democratic process, my commitment to clean up the ugliness in our campaigns, and my deep confidence in Governor Moore, I believe it is only right that she be our nominee for the highest office in the land."

The crowd began to applaud again at this historic statement, but the reporter persisted.

"So you're okay being veep even though you have more delegates?"

"Young man, Governor Moore will be one of the great presidents our country will ever see. I am sure of that." Wanting to end the questioning, and knowing this was the moment, he reached for her hand and raised it, with his, above their heads. "I am honored to be her wingman!"

Both candidates smiled as the crowd exploded in cheers and cameras flashed. Every newspaper now had its morning cover.

An hour later, another campaign issued a one-sentence press release: *"The Nicholas-Bravo campaign is suspended indefinitely."*

CHAPTER 35

CLEVELAND, OHIO

It was the fourth day of the Cleveland convention, three hours before Governor Moore was scheduled to give her speech accepting her party's nomination. Bridget Turner and I had just wrapped up an exclusive interview with Moore that would air over the next two nights. Bridget thanked her profusely for what would no doubt be a ratings bonanza.

"Thanks to you guys," Moore said. "I just can't say no to Jack Sharpe." We each laughed, and she winked my way.

But I was distracted, clinging tightly to a stuffed legal-size manila envelope. One job remained, and there were only a few minutes in which to do it. My team had spent a week gathering all the information.

Alex had pulled together the DroneTech files she had compiled, along with the articles revealing the "test run" elections in Florida and in North Carolina. She'd also written a detailed, sworn description of everything Doug Hansen had said his team did—torturing and killing both George Vassos and Kristina Jones, waterboarding Logan Kroon, and other awful acts.

Cassie had printed out every document from the WINGMAN file, highlighting the witness list that had become the hit list, along with the dirt-digging reports on all the potential vice presidents. She also had compiled a twelve-page memo summarizing the framing and ultimate death of Jimmy Cull, detailing the appalling actions of Dean Gamble and the D.C.-based Baker & Strauss lawyers.

We'd written a long memo dissecting the deaths of each member of the Bravo Six. And I'd printed out my spreadsheets on the SuperPAC and the interlocking relationships between the network of law firms, lobbying firms, and contractors who were behind it. So we'd included those, along with dossiers on Steve Doherty, his former law partners, and other alumni of the Progress Group that we knew were involved.

And I'd submitted a sworn statement repeating what Doug Hansen had admitted to me in our short time together. On top of this thick pile of documents, I'd placed a one-page cover memo summarizing what followed, with the subject line: "*Operation Wingman.*"

If Nicholas had been the nominee, all of this information would have been useless. Turning it over would've created our own death warrant. But with Moore as president, she would fully investigate it all. My and Bridget's interview with her presented the best chance for a secure handoff. Maybe my only chance. An email or a mailed package could end up in the hands of an aide, or worse. To be completely safe, Moore needed this information directly, with no third parties involved. Not even close aides. So this was it. My final task of our investigation of Operation Wingman was to get the package in her hands.

"Seriously, Governor, thank you for this," I said. "Let me walk you out."

We exited into a small hallway, where a Republic assistant handed her the light jacket and handbag she had carried in with her. This was the moment.

"Governor, I've got a package you'll want to review," I said, holding up the envelope and handing it to her.

She was still smiling from her banter with me and Bridget, but my look told her this was serious. Her prosecutor's face reappeared. "What is it?"

"You need to focus on your speech, so don't worry about it now. My advice to you is to win this election, and then open it. Just you. You're a prosecutor—you'll know what to do after that."

She took the envelope and placed it into her handbag.

"I'll do what you say, Jack."

I opened the door and she walked through it. A secret service agent stood to her left and right, ready to guide her to her suite. They started to lead her away, but she turned back one last time. "Jack, you're one of the good guys," she said.

I nodded in appreciation.

It finally felt like she was right. There were no loose ends this time, like there had been a year ago. This time my hands were clean.

CHAPTER 36

GEORGETOWN

"YOUR WIFE IS an incredible woman," I said to Anthony Bravo.

"Oh, I know it, Jack. I'm a lucky man. The best day of my life was when we met in San Jose." Bravo paused and looked to my right, at Alex. "I hear you two are quite the item. I've always been a big fan of yours."

I cupped my right hand over Alex's, then squeezed softly. "We'll see what happens. Lucky she and Molly give a washout like me the time of day."

"Yes you are!" Alex said, looking back at me, her blue eyes sparkling.

Coffee in hand, Isabella Bravo sat back down next to her husband. Alex and I sat across from them. It was close to noon at the small deli in Georgetown, all four of us dressed casually, the congressman and I both in ball caps so that we wouldn't be recognized. We chatted for three hours. About everything.

It was a muggy June day in D.C., five months after President Moore's inauguration, and three months after the FBI had escorted DroneTech's top leadership out of their headquarters in handcuffs. The investigation had generated a nonstop perp walk out of the Pentagon and Capitol Hill, for everything from corruption to bribery. And the vast lobbyist and lawyer network that had supported the conspiracy also had been taken down, with the nondescript and mousy Steve Doherty serving as the poster child of the group. DPI had gone under as well—Will Kroon included—for illegal campaign activity.

The one man who'd been spared a prison sentence was Doug Hansen. In August, two months after the convention, his helicopter had seized up and crashed into the Pacific just east of Catalina Island as it returned to San Diego. No doubt revenge, Kazarov-style, for Olga's murder. Hansen's passing had been mourned by politicians of all stripes, including a posthumous Medal of Freedom by President Banfield, which was later rescinded by President Moore.

Two weeks after Hansen's fiery death, Logan Kroon had knocked on his parents' door in Virginia Beach, shaken and bruised. Worried about his safety and following long, difficult talks with his parents, he never spoke a word to the public about Bravo, his brother, or his months in captivity.

The Bravos, Alex, and I talked about all these developments, but I didn't care much about them. Old news. I had more pressing questions that I'd been dying to ask for a year. Alex did, too.

"So you really did get kicked out for violating Don't Ask, Don't Tell?" I asked.

He nodded. "I really did."

"And you and Tommy were together?" Alex asked. "A couple?"

"Not at first. We hit it off early, became close friends, then as the surge heated up, as we feared for our lives more and more, it blossomed into more than friendship. Tommy had known he was gay for years. I had never been attracted to a man before. But for several months prior to his death, we loved and loved deeply. We only could act on it a few times physically, including when we visited his family, but the flame between us was strong and real."

He paused, looking past us for a moment. Reminiscing. Isabella reached out to hold his hand, looking up at her husband.

"I look back and admire the beauty of what we had," he went on. "So brief, but our love sustained us at the scariest time of our lives. And it allowed him to feel wholly loved—not from a distance, but embraced in his loved one's arms—even as he took his last breath."

Bravo didn't cry, but the lost look on his face made it clear that he had many times in the past. He looked over at his wife. "I never truly loved again until we met. Isabella filled the hole in my heart."

Bolder than I would've been, Alex followed up. "That's such a compelling story. So human. But you felt like you had to hide it all later?"

"Sadly, I did. At first I was just a kid. And at the time and for years that followed, getting booted carried such a stigma. Those of us kicked out were told we had let our passions overwhelm our duty for country. That our brothers died in Iraq, or came home badly damaged, while we waltzed home scot-free. It was a terrible feeling, like we were traitors. And more practically, it was a career killer in many fields, but especially politics. And you guys know how it works . . . once you're in politics, you're obsessed with not getting taken out by anything in your past. I don't regret for a moment what I had with Tommy. I so regret hiding it later at all costs."

He went quiet. All four of us knew his secret had cost his four comrades their lives.

"And once I knew better, once we were in the presidential race, they had me. When we later learned about Cull's murder trial and the other deaths, it became clear that they were playing for keeps."

"Did you know who 'they' were?" Alex asked.

"I did. That whole network that President Moore took down? They were a powerful group of lobbyists in the Beltway. A few years back, they approached me, sold me on running—convinced me that I had a great shot in a crowded race, and promised to support me with money, top staff, you name it. And for a while, it all was going smoothly. Then they got too close for comfort, too controlling, we started to learn about the deaths, and then came the outright blackmail and threats."

Isabella shook her head. "It was like a vise, tightening every day. Tony and I talked about it all the time, but for the safety of our kids, we couldn't find any way out."

"And then you told the story," I said to Bravo. "At the debate, with everyone watching. That's when I decided to look into it. When it all unraveled."

"That's right. That was the first domino. You really did save us."

"New Hampshire. It was your big moment. Your Reagan-style breakthrough. And your opponents basically conceded the victory. But I'll never forget, you still looked so uncomfortable. Almost immediately."

"Did I?" He smiled, then looked over to his wife, who grinned back.

"I've always wondered. Why? Was it because you didn't want your relationship with Tommy to be examined, or because you thought DroneTech would be upset after all they'd done to conceal it?"

He gently shook his head. "Neither, actually."

"Really? What was it then?"

"Jack, I have to confess something to you."

"What's that?"

"I wasn't uncomfortable."

I narrowed my eyes. Surprised he'd try to deny it now. "Congressman, I was there. You clearly regretted having gone as far as you did. You wanted me to move on to something else. I saw it."

"Jack, I was there too. When I heard you'd be the moderator, I already knew you were a good reporter. The noose around us was tightening. We had to get out. On that debate stage, at that moment, I knew only you would really see my face. And my goal was to inspire you to dig deeper."

I jerked my head back. *Bullshit!* "Are you saying that you *intended* to look uncomfortable? To get me to look into your story?"

He flashed a confident smile. Nodded. Didn't say a word. Didn't need to.

"You're kidding!" I cried, feeling embarrassed and over-defensive, already dreading the teasing I'd take from Alex if what he was saying was true. "But you couldn't have known what questions were coming, or to whom."

"True, but if you remember, you didn't ask me the question. I interrupted to get myself in."

He was right. I had asked Stevens the question, then he'd barged his way in. I glanced at Isabella, then back at him.

"But—" I began to object again.

"Jack," Bravo said, "did you ever look into my claim to fame before I became a war hero?"

I shook my head. "Can't say that I ever did."

He smiled.

"Football. I played cornerback. I nabbed twelve interceptions my senior year, and was named all-state. Would've gone to Berkeley on a football scholarship if I hadn't joined the Army."

"Okay?" I said, lost.

"You were a quarterback, correct?"

"I was. All-state as well. College, too."

"I knew that. Almost no interceptions after your first year. Well done."

I smiled, proud of my glory days. Impressed he had looked them up.

"That's not easy to do," he continued. "So I knew you would know something that, as a good cornerback, I've known ever since my days of reading routes and picking off passes."

"Wait." I paused, the memory of that long-ago locker room speech ringing in my ear. "Don't tell me. It's all about the eyes?"

"Exactly."

EPILOGUE

LONDON

THREE JARS TRAVEL the same route every week.

The journey begins 35 miles east of Tunisia, in the hills of Pantelleria, a small island thrust out of the Mediterranean by a volcanic eruption more than 100,000 years ago. From high on the island, a three-wheeled mini-truck drives the jars down a small winding road to the island's sole port. They are loaded onto the Monday morning ferry, then transported for miles to the bustling port of Sicily. Shortly thereafter, they sit in the cargo hold for the three-hour Alitalia flight to London. An hour after landing, they arrive at their destination, and their contents are carefully portioned for the following week.

When Oleg Kazarov eats the world's finest capers—always picked wild, not farmed, then delivered in those jars every Monday evening—he never rushes. Having arranged for their long journey, he carefully selects them one at a time from amid the thin slices of salmon that accompany them. Then he dedicates at least a minute to savor each in his mouth before selecting another. Even on an important day, his pace doesn't change. The morning conversation starts and stops according to each Kazarov bite. As momentous as it was, the morning after the Cleveland convention was no different. He bit into a caper, enjoying it for a good minute, before initiating the briefing. The first item on his agenda was not about American politics, but business. His newest expansion.

"What is the status of accessing the drone and robotics technology?" Kazarov asked his longtime confidant, Liam Andersson, who went by the alias Holmberg when in America.

"All is going as planned. From his home, Mr. Kroon unwittingly walked us right into the central DroneTech database. We have now acquired the specifications of all their latest prototypes. This will be a very profitable enterprise for us."

"Excellent. Please move quickly. There are so many potential buyers across the world." Kazarov maneuvered the small fork to select another caper from the group. "And the American election?"

"Governor Moore has now officially accepted the nomination as the Democratic candidate for president," Andersson said.

"And Mr. Stevens?" Kazarov asked, lifting the next caper to his mouth.

"The senator accepted the nomination for vice president the evening before."

Kazarov nibbled, then sat quietly again. Andersson waited patiently.

"They will be a strong team," said Kazarov. "You are certain they will win?"

"Oh yes. The Republican Party remains deeply unpopular due to the scandal of last year. They have no chance. Governor Moore will be president, and Senator Stevens will be vice president."

"And what of Mr. Nicholas?"

"The information in his file has destroyed him. He will likely be sent to prison in the next few months, and remain there the rest of his life."

"Good for Mr. Sharpe, identifying his file."

"How could he not? You led him right to it. And like the file on Congressman Bravo, we made it impossible to miss."

Kazarov allowed a smile. "Yes, we did. And he never noticed the absence of the others?"

"I believe not. If he did, he has not asked, and he gave no indication to Arthur."

Kazarov shook his head, wincing. He respected Jack Sharpe's persistence. His courage. His dedication to his country. He represented everything the Russian liked about America, and Americans. But for a famous investigator, he could be sloppy. Short-sighted.

"How could he be so blind?" Kazarov asked.

"We left no trace. The files were removed, and we eliminated any evidence that they had been there."

"True. But such a glaring absence. Illogical."

As he had explained to Sharpe on their drive up Capitol Hill, any mission to dredge up information to compromise one candidate would not end with only that candidate. That observation had inspired Sharpe to search for and find the documents detailing Nicholas's past misdeeds.

But of course the implications of Kazarov's wisdom reached beyond Nicholas. Any such research operation would have examined the other viable candidates as well, and especially those most likely to win. The research Kazarov's team had discovered on Will Kroon's computer had done exactly that, digging into *all* the major candidates. After finding them, they'd removed those files, leaving only the Bravo and Nicholas research in the zip drive they handed to Jack Sharpe.

"Have you explored all the information from the Moore and Stevens files?" Kazarov asked.

"We have," Andersson said. "The original files touched on the problems, but did not analyze them deeply. Our additional research has found far more. Very damaging for both."

"As much as we had hoped?"

"Much more. This information would deeply embarrass them."

Kazarov bit into a new caper, then savored it, all while nodding his head in approval. "Good. And when do we let them know?"

"We must be patient," Andersson said. "Let them get elected first, then sworn in. Once they are locked into place, and when we need something, we will inform them of what we know."

"And then we will have them."

"Yes."

Kazarov reached for the last caper, enjoying it for longer than the others. "And we have Jack Sharpe to thank for our good fortune." He smiled. "Again."